THE GIR WHO WA
GOI

C Maxwell has written
partic arly celebrated as a
He has won a number of pr
including the Somerset Maug Aw
the Geoffrey Faber Memorial Prize.

BY THE SAME AUTHOR

Poetry

Tale of the Mayor's Son
Out of the Rain
Rest for the Wicked
The Breakage
Time's Fool
The Boys at Twilight (Poems 1990–95)
The Nerve
The Sugar Mile

Travel

Moon Country (with Simon Armitage)

Plays

Plays One: The Lifeblood, Wolfpit, The Only Girl in the World
Plays Two: Broken Journey, Best Man Speech, The Last Valentine

Fiction

Blue Burneau

THE GIRL WHO WAS GOING TO DIE

GLYN MAXWELL

JONATHAN CAPE
LONDON

Published by Jonathan Cape 2008

2 4 6 8 10 9 7 5 3

This book is a work of fiction

First published in Great Britain in 2008 by
Jonathan Cape
Random House, 20 Vauxhall Bridge Road,
London SW1V 2SA

Addresses for companies within
The Random House Group Limited can be found at:
www.rbooks.co.uk/offices.htm

The Random House Group Limited Reg. No. 954009

A CIP catalogue record for this book is available from the British Library

ISBN 9780224081726

The Random House Group Limited makes every effort to ensure that the papers used in its books are made from trees that have been legally sourced from well-managed and credibly certified forests. Our paper procurement policy can be found at:
www.randomhouse.co.uk/paper.htm

Typeset by Palimpsest Book Production Limited, Grangemouth, Stirlingshire
Printed and bound in Great Britain by
Mackays of Chatham PLC

You are going to be famous

You're beautiful but crying.

Aren't you? Beautiful but crying.

Just sittin here of all places, beautiful but crying.

I'm sorry I don't understand what you're saying, I keep thinking you mean someone else.

No no one else sweetheart just you. Just sittin here with ya margarita. It's been a long day for you I reckon. Fancy another?

You know I am allowed to ask you that, cos you're looking at me like I'm what, I work here, right? Got a cash till, got a towel, I can stand you a drink.

Beautiful. But crying. Look at you, just sitting here of all places. I understand you, beautiful-but-crying, I seen you. Quite a day, quite a day. You want to be alone and yet you don't want to be alone.

You know what you're half right.

I reckon. You come to where it's happening. Moth to a flame. Butterfly I should say.

Butterflies don't do that.

You're no moth, beautiful-but-crying. You know something?

I said you know something?

No.

You don't? What we learned today is that the world is a frightening place, but it can be beautiful too, and miracles can happen.

I'm sorry when did we learn that.

The whole world's beautiful but crying, the whole spinning planet is, for a little while longer. And you're beautiful but crying.

I'm not beautiful but crying. I'm not beautiful or crying.

*

Why does he keep saying you are? Where are you?

I'm in Arroyo's in Covent Garden.

Which one is it?

It's in the, you know, right by the, where the awful acts are and the crowds. I'm having a margarita.

Not which place is it, which guy is it who keeps saying.

I don't know, Minni, I don't come here. Maybe it's Arroyo himself taking an interest.

Arroyo said? The owner of the place said you were crying? Does he want you to leave?

Beautiful but crying. One of the barmen. He said the world's a miracle or something. He said we know that now and I told him,

You're not crying, are you?

No.

I mean,

I'm beautiful though. Oh that was a bit loud. Joke everyone.

Did you really just say that? Suse!

It's filling up in here Min I can't keep this seat much longer. Hang on he's passing by again, I could ask him he's gone now.

Is it Calum?

How do I know if it's Calum?

Ask him, he's the barman, is he Calum.

It doesn't matter who, I didn't think he meant me but he kept saying it, he kept throwing his stupid cocktail stuff in the air and round behind his back and I wish it would go wrong but even with it spinning in mid-air he kept going 'You're her, you know you are!' and I'd just shrug and he'd go 'It's over now, it's okay . . .'

He was right about that.

What do you mean he was right about that? About what?

Right about how it's over. That thing we believed. Our terrible . . . belief.

What? Are you far away, Min, I can't sit here too much

longer on my own you know I've had a terrible day. This is my second margarita I'm having. Also, plus, look there's something in it. (Excuse me there's look, what's that. It didn't come with it last time, can I have one without it? Thanks Calum. Assuming you're Calum.)

We all had a terrible day Suse.

Did we? I wasn't really monitoring anyone else. Where are you you sound weird.

I'm walking straight towards you and that's not Calum it's Liam. I mean hello? name tag? look at you with your drink! What's that, a margarita?

No a lucozade.

What's all that round the edges is it salt?

It is salt. Hi then.

I've never had one it's bad for you all that salt, are you supposed to, there's no TV in here, Liam could I have a margarita but without any salt? And why did you call my friend Suse beautiful but crying?

Look Min I suddenly sort of don't think it was him.

It wasn't him? You didn't say that, Liam? You don't think she's beautiful? You do? He does!

It wasn't him or Calum, the one who said it was taller. We're sorry, it wasn't you, thank you, go away, get taller.

No I'm still ordering my drink! I'll have this one this Blue Russian in the picture. Number Eleven. It's good having pictures.

Yay pictures.

It wasn't him, how embarrassing for you, Suse.

Well they all wear black, they all belong on a beach, they all do that trick stuff with the drinks, nothing ever smashes what's the difference.

Though that is two different barmen both said you were beautiful. Good start to the night!

Downhill from here.

I mean on a day of loss.

What?

Beautiful but crying!

The first one said I was crying. And now he's gone forever.

You and your men.

What men.

What men, listen to her!

Yes, listen to me. Listen to me. Because I may be, in fact, dead soon.

Right!

Pardon?

Dead soon. Me. May be.

Yeah Suse.

Someone told me.

Right, I think that's too salty, how can you drink that?

Look what he's putting in yours.

Those are what goes in it, Suse, it has to be blue cos of the name so it needs something blue. It must be some kind of blueberry flavouring. It's what they use. Not forgetting the vodka! Or you can't call it a Russian as vodka's a Russian look how he pours it in from way up high a Russian drink like a clear, clear stream of pure, blue

Russian

Russian – I wonder what that's for. He never spills a drop. Part of his act, that is, he takes our mind off things.

Actually he doesn't.

I can't believe today. Can you believe they did that?

Believe who did what?

You know! What they did! Where's there a why's there, there's no TV in here you'd think there'd be coverage.

Oh. The thing that happened. I had my own thing happen.

Twenty-four-hour coverage. People may have loved ones. God forbid but they may. They need to know even if we don't, and we do on a day of loss. I haven't seen <u>*any*</u> *coverage. Here comes my Blue . . . look at that! I have seen the making of it! 'Just how I like it!' I go and I've never had one! It's incredible the news.*

Charming sound you're making.

Mmm it's a cocktail actually Suse, you drink it through a straw? I'm drinking my usual at my local. Hardly! See that guy standing between the tables that's, you know who I mean

From

Yeah, Shane something from that

TV I know who you mean and it's not

It looks like him. No. From the side it did. Shane thing but it's not at all. God I can't believe today.

Min, can I just say,

They say it was ninety-nine minutes!

What was ninety-nine minutes? Who's they?

God did you even <u>*have*</u> *the same day the whole of the entire Western world just had?*

No I had my own little day. Can I

Ninety-nine minutes exactly, when the Western world believed he was . . . passed away.

What are we talking about here.

You're giving me that look like you're going to ask me <u>*who*</u> *was!* <u>*Who*</u> *passed away!* <u>*Who*</u> *died and was reborn!*

Look at you!

I'm not.

You are though look at you!

I'm me, I can't see.

Who then. Who do I mean.

You mean him, the star, the star chap, Tom Bayne.

As if you didn't know, when it was breaking news all day and now it's it's now it's

Broken

And it's Thomas Bayne, never Tom, apparently he insists

I'll try and remember that

Yeah, we were broken too. For ninety-nine minutes.

Ninety-nine minutes.

No one doesn't know!

I heard someone say he wasn't dead. But I didn't know he was dead.

He was never at <u>*all*</u>*! that thing. It was never true! Except in the eyes of the world . . . It's like some people almost* <u>*wanted*</u> *him to be, you know, that thing. 'Departed' he's said that in interviews, that you* *can rise too high, you can be shining too brightly, people turn against you, dazzled by your like, shining? There's dark forces out there, unknown terrors, that was in Hello!*

Some are dead, though.

Or OK! They are. Between eighty and a hundred are, in that status. They were working on the set.

Set, what do you mean?

Suse this is embarrassing I'm having to be like you know the News myself, like what's her name Natasha Klabinski? 'and today, in other news . . .' or I'm like shuffling papers and agreeing with the man and waiting for the music to end.

This is so yummy.

What was I saying?

What set with a hundred people?

What set? Unbelievable. People in this bar have no idea you know nothing.

I had no idea they knew everything.

They only,

They bombed The Book of Revelation.

I'm sorry say that again.

They bombed The Book of Revelation. They only went and bombed it.

You mean, like an original copy?

Original copy of what?

The Book of Revelation. It's a book, Minni. Of revelation.

Well maybe in some museum it is, you're the reader, but not to the general public. No they bombed the set. They bombed the set of the film The Book of Revelation starring Thomas Bayne which is due out in autumn 2008 though that may probably change and between eighty and a hundred people were you know, fatal casualties, and about a hundred and five more were you know not fatal but things like critical and stable, like they're on those lists, they're still counting but there's no TV in here weirdly of all things. There must be a way to give blood, or, sign a book of, you know, when you queue up with candles. Imagine what they did. They bombed innocent people. Just innocent film people, going about their, their,

Their film.

In an act of total, you know, like pure evil.

Okay. I didn't know they did that.

It was in the deserts of Libya. It was just a location.

And Thomas Bayne isn't dead.

Some of the stars are! It wasn't just, you know, people you get in the credits, like, assistant this or third cameraman.

Thomas Bayne's okay.

He was completely apparently not, you know, wounded in any way. He had a day off filming, he was in a whole nother country.

But supporting actors are dead. Famous people are down.

I can't even say their names. I refuse to. And you know this is probably bad taste Suse, but it was a thought I had, I need another sip of this . . . there's a blue flavour. It's just a question in the end. Some of those supporting actors, like, I don't know, those who were fatal victims of this atrocity, would they still do you think, I don't know, could they still be nominated?

What?

It's possibly not the time to think about it, but it may come up as a question. If they'd put in great supporting performances you know like selflessly, and the nominations are, if they'd put in great performances before, you know, the actual incident, with the, you know, the loss it's weird to be drinking a blue drink you only see that in films from the future.

(Can I have some crisps please really like now.)

Thomas will make a statement, he's bound to, about all this. Then maybe we can kind of talk openly, say our feelings, he'd want that. It's hard to imagine it happened to him, or nearly did, but he's going to have to rise above it, for the sake of, just, us who survived.

(No I want ready salted, I hate these.)

But he's been among the, among the. Departed I mean at least, in a way. For ninety-nine whole minutes, Thomas Bayne was among the, the departed even saying it's, just . . . For the sake of his fans . . . Can we have two menus Liam I'm like I'm shivering.

Specials.

It's just so different from yesterday. That's what gets to me, Suse, it's just too different from yesterday, today, it's like today never even heard of yesterday if that's not too weird, you're the reader!

You used to say that at school.

Mm, you were the reader then. You're the reader now.

Actually you were a reader then too.

No but there was time then. Plus it was part of homework. Everything's different now. I mean even before now, I mean today everything's different. Now this, event, has come to pass. It's not a time to be reading in a way. You have to more keep your eyes open, like for packages? Not hide them in some book. Your eyes.

That's my whole opinion on a day of loss.

Are you okay Suse? Are you crying? I can't tell. It's all right if you are but I'm not saying you are.

You never used to.

★

Good morning everyone. I'm your guide today. My name is Susan Mantle and I'm from Outer London. You're in Inner London. You're very welcome to Inner London and to this tour bus which, if you look closely, is red and two storeys in height. The upper deck was added to accommodate the increasingly taller people coming to these shores in recent centuries. You might have noticed it doesn't have a roof and you'd be right there. See? Look! Don't be afraid. We're aware of that situation so don't be if at all possible. It's a nice October day if you notice. It's a Monday morning, so all these people you see down there to your right and left, these are working people of Inner London, that's right, get some snaps of them while they're there, whereas, whereas, you're all holidaymakers from, let me think, from the United States of America? Yes! Holidaymakers, makers of holiday! America! Beg your pardon? Kansas? The state of Kansas. The what? The Sunflower state. That's perfect. Tall big sunny flowers of America. Excellent. And tornadoes, right, yes, and witches and dwarves obviously, no? Monkeys with wings oh no I suppose not, that ain't Kansas is it, as she, well, specifically says. Ha ha ha, superb, ha. Ha can I not say what? I can't say dwarves any more. O-kay. I'll; try hard, not to.

But you two come from Nebraska, where, where they, well, where you two, are. From, good, you'll be able to, see the sights also. And then, remember them, there.

Here we go, we've started and the street we're on is called Oxford Street, that's right, Oxford, just like the university which shares its name. There's an interesting story (dwarves) about that. In the seventeenth or eighteenth century, you decide, a lot of people who wanted to attend Oxford University but couldn't really be bothered to make the journey would come to this street of a Sunday and all these buildings, which are now department stores, or as we say department shops, see, to the left, to the right, other way round, would transform themselves into Seats of Learning just for that single day. This one Marks and Spencers just coming up, this was called Christus Jesus College, and high learning went on in the seats and then, hey presto, the next day being Monday, it just looked like that again, with people walking past or going in and getting things they needed like trousers or soup. Strange but true. What's that? Yes, *Christus*, like *Christ* with *us*, then Jesus, like the gentleman who, you know. I'm sorry? Yes, died to save us all, ma'am, thank you. Died to save us from, obviously, further, further dying.

(dwarves) this is Selfridges, or, Balliol. Are there any what? Ghost stories about that? I believe I, what's that? Ghost stories about anything? Well yes I was just coming to that, in regard to this very building. On every I think it's every alternate Friday in, in, June, Lord Selfridge of Balliol is said to, what is it, walk the floor. I mean on the floor, across it in a stately way. How did he die? No one knows. Just like that. One day he was there, being a Lord, lording it around, ringing the bell for service, muffins Jeeves, riding his high horse over the moors, the next day no one's ringing the bell, Jeeves sitting there, horse just saying now what, muffins in a foil pack and so on. That's how it happened. But he does this sort of, you know, moaning.

It's . . . horrible, people have heard it. What's that, sir? And lived to tell the tale? No. No, sir, they didn't, sorry. This is Piccadilly Circus. It's not a real circus, but there's an interesting story about that because every last Tuesday in December

*

It was a normal day Min, I was doing the West End morning shift and all the time I'm not talking my old rubbish I'm thinking about him.

The new guy! Him! Suse and her New Guy!

Right who I've met twice.

Yeah but who you were thinking about.

I didn't think I would be, I didn't think I felt anything. But the more I thought that, the more he just sort of came to mind, Nigel,

Nigel . . .

Nigel Pilman horrid name and I was thinking why bother, I'd been thinking that all weekend, why bother, why bother again, then all of a sudden I started thinking why <u>not</u> bother?

You have to! Then you can forget about that John.

Well thanks for that, Min.

Put him behind you.

He's very far behind me. Who's there? No one.

I know, cos Nigel's the One!

Maybe he was. Maybe he is. I'm not sure he can be now. He's a tall dark stranger.

Yes and fanfare isn't that what we want?

Is it?

Hello! Yes!

Well it was.

What do you mean it was, that's like saying it isn't now.

It's what I wanted this morning. I thought the day would be all about him. Only now he's, he's like at the other end of some, forest.

Like in that film.

What film.

You know. With the forest. She was trying to reach him but he was like in flashback? It was to do with Time, and how you can never . . . or though I think they did in the end. They proved you can. I think Love means you can if it's, you know, kind of. I like these coasters. I'm going to ask them where they got them.

Well I was on the tube all the way he was on my mind, it was, that I might bother with Nigel Pilman, 'Nigel Pilman' can't be helped, he was okay, it could be him I was even saying my name and this is deeply sick with his horrible surname attached –

God Suse!

Susan Pilman and I don't even intend to change my name ever but

God

I couldn't stop myself.

I can't believe you sometimes.

I sat there like a fool. Like someone at the start of a joke: 'There's this girl, right, and she's sitting on the tube . . .'

What girl?

Doesn't matter.

Here come our starters!

*

This just passing by with lots of policemen is of course the famous Westminster Abbey, where quite a few things have been filmed, you may remember the funeral of the former Princess of Wales with the Sir Elton John recital about Marilyn Monroe that was widely requested, that was here, yes, Charles and Di, yes, they were in love remember, whatever love is, right here ma'am, inside though, through that vast big door probably the many people went in to hear it in their solemn trappings, and also people being crowned, that often happens in England as you know and well, here's where. What's that? Yes, he did. And all of his Six Wives, one after another, through that vast big door, not together of course, one by one, over the years, in a stately fashion, knowing not what was to come. And we all know what was to come. That's right, you know the rhyme. 'Divorced, beheaded, separated. Poisoned, garrotted, fell in a hole.' There's some more policemen coming up on the right.

*

SUSAN PILMAN . . . I can see it printed up, SUSAN JANE PILMAN. SUSAN J PILMAN. MR AND MRS then you'd have your mum and dad's names I don't know them, CORDIALLY INVITE YOU

Don't don't it won't happen

SUSAN JANE PILMAN née MANTLE you wouldn't put that on a wedding invitation I just like saying it! I'd be MIRANDA ALISON something, say JONES, née KAYE. Née-Kaye! It rhymes but it can't be helped, you have to say née. It means 'no longer known as'.

It means born.

It's getting quite crowded in here, isn't it? Lucky we got these stools! Comfy or what! Susan Jane . . . what-was-it?

Mantle. I'm not getting married. Not to him, not to anyone.

You would have married that John, you said!

Again, thanks for the memo. Could you cc the world in?

This Nigel's the way to go, you have to get started!

You're right. I have to. It's the law.

No it's not but you know Suse.

It's never going to happen.

How can you suddenly know that?

Because I

Because I went to see a fortune teller and she told me I'm going to die.

You did what? No you didn't.

I went to a fortune teller. And she told me I was going to die.

You're not though.

I mean, you are but,

God. When?

On my break, today, at lunchtime.

You can't die then it's been!

When I went.

Oh.

She has an upstairs flat and I'm always passing her little sad sign and she has these curtains with optical illusions like spirals and I always say under my breath what a scam but today I thought okay. Turn the corner. I'd like to know. I'd like to know if he's the one.

God I want to do that!

You don't.

And was he? Is Nigel the one?

May have been. He's not now.

What, because of a, one of them? One minute there's a wedding, next minute there's, what, nothing? That's like against the rules of

Rules of what

I don't know. Kind of, endings, happy endings you're the reader, there's always something, you know like a twist or a catch. There can't be love, or something, and then just forget it, just because you went to some weird – can there? There can't be look he's leaving, that guy.

But it's not him from TV, Min, so it doesn't really matter, does it.

I'd forgotten it wasn't him. It doesn't matter at all! Goodbye stranger, have a nice life without us! He's gone. What a day!

*

Hello, is that Mrs Sage?

Yes it is. Speaking.

I saw your sign, I usually pass it, but this time I'm, never mind, I'm right outside. I wanted to check if it was okay to visit for a session of, you know, what you've, what you do in there.

Of course it is! Don't be afraid!

Um. Okay.

I'm looking down out of the window, the one with the images on the curtains. Hello! You see that's me waving.

No.

I'm right here!

I'll ring the bell.

I'll buzz you in, Jane.

My name's Susan, Mrs Sage.

Not Jane?

My name's Susan.

My eyes aren't what they were. But I can't see you now, so you must have gone to the door.

I have gone to the door. I'm not where I was at all.

It's fifty pounds the hour.

*

So I go in. Her name is Dawn Sage and she's this little dumpy woman dressed in black and all these shades of purple, and her place is what you'd expect. It's dark, there's curtains everywhere, there's joss sticks burning, there's cats, I mean, not a nice fat cat like Bonner but sly green-eyed creatures there's these weird charts and globes and sort of articles of divination I mean it's this whole big nonsense. And she's coming on like she's my gran or something, like she was expecting me, which I hate, she doesn't know me, I'm like Little Red Riding Hood in there and I sit down in a deep black armchair which sort of, digests me.

I think she was a fake.

Gosh do you reckon.

Sounds like it. Sounds like you've been had, Suse. The real ones who can do that probably don't look as if they can at all, they just can, they're gifted, they do it walking along or at a desk or something, they don't need cats or magic spells. They're naturals, they're probably in this bar right now. It's like, you know, visible to them. Like plasma.

If they're so good at seeing the future they'd know this place would be crowded as hell tonight and they wouldn't bother coming. (This guy keeps elbowing me.)

It's dangerous to use their gift. I may even have that gift, but I know it's dangerous to use it, and I keep quiet about it, or would do, if I did. This woman didn't know that. That's all I'm saying. I think we should go to Brasserie Louis.

O-kay . . .

For desserts.

Of course she was a fake. What do you take me for? And you don't have that gift or you'd be able to look in my eyes and tell me what happened next. Look into my eyes Miranda, go on then.

I choose not to use it.

*

This is a very comfortable chair.

So people say.

It's good to know people ever got out of it and lived to tell the tale, I mean that they're not still down here in the depths of it it's so deep! Little people wailing softly for help, sort of thing.

No. No one's there.

Good. I was, yep.

Now, most important question of all . . .

Oh let me get you the fifty quid,

Oh I didn't mean the money! That dirty business! Though also of course, sadly, yes, one has to make a living alas that's forty, forty-five, fifty for the hour . . . would you like a glass of water?

Has the hour started?

A glass of water, for clarity.

Okay so it's started?

I will be less than a second.

Okay.

Great. So. Well. Meanwhile . . . You know I had a pack of um, tarot cards? once when I was a child. I got it for my birthday from my mum, who knew this man who was into the occult, I think she just fancied him, is that dangerous do you think, letting children play with tarot cards? Do you think? I used to know what they meant. Some of them. The Hanged Man isn't Death. You'd think it would be. I mean I don't know what it is, I don't think it's a good one. I don't think if you turn it over you sort of punch the air and go yesss. That's how you'd react if you turned over the, Angel of Delight, or the Foaming Tankard, or the, Cake in the Clouds. You can tell I skipped lunch for this. I think Death is the Tower of Bricks. Isn't it?

You can't hear me, can you. You said you wouldn't be a second, but you've obviously travelled into some other realm. With your secret stash of, whatever, Volvic.

I have a cat too, you know. He's called Bonner. He wouldn't fit in here. Not because he's fat, which he is, but because he, I don't know, is of the realm of daylight. What am I doing here. Help. I'm leaving now. Susan has left the building. Not really. The Tower Struck By Lightning. It never came up for me. It came up for my best friend Emily and she started sobbing, she was fourteen. She didn't know what it was. I said all it meant was your house would need retiling. She said her mum couldn't afford that. She's still alive somewhere oh hello.

Soooooooooooooo here we are, in position, and I thought we might just have a biscuit before we begin . . .

Well thank you I may well avail my, you know, and so on. Bourbon, crunch, yummy, chocolate filling, twelve-fifteen, wow, working girl.

And . . . Something Is Missing – we can't go far without that, can we, here. I keep it safe in here. At a certain temperature . . . at a certain height . . . at a certain angle . . . and . . . whoops . . . et voilà!

It's. A crystal ball.

Exactly, a crystal glass.

You use, a crystal ball.

Glass, you seem surprised.

Er, no, not at all. It says on your sign that you're a *CLAIRVOYANTE*

A clairvoyante, so obviously a crystal glass and/or ball would be one of the things you might choose to, allow you to, properly, see things, out there. Very traditional. Very much, of a piece.

It is my window of choice.

Your window of, well. It's very, yes, I'm on my second biscuit. And you've started looking at me, I notice. Do you need to know anything?

One of my names is actually Jane, after all, it's the middle one, so, you know, bull's-eye, nearly.

What's the name you go by?

Susan.

Susan Jane . . .

Mantle. Like the coat. Or in Shakespeare the scum of a pond.

Do I talk while you're doing this?

Does it matter either way?

No it doesn't matter either way.

That's quite like my job. I have to be back at one. I'm going up the Thames with some Texan ladies. I'm looking forward to that.

This next bridge is called the Capsize Bridge. Not because

it's the size of a cap, or resembles a cap in any way. No. But because a party of rich Texans once chartered a boat that capsized right here, because they all stood up at the same time to take pictures of it, because they'd just heard that a party of rich Texans once chartered a boat that capsized right here, because, and so on. It's sometimes called the Ironic Bridge, or the Loop Bridge. Or Vauxhall.

You probably wish you'd said it did matter if I talked. I find the silence a bit, I find the silence a bit hard. I find if I don't say anything no one will know where I am. You know in case there's someone out there who needs to know. Guardian Angel, God, Stalker, Murderer. It's just a feeling I sometimes get. Well always get. I'm a tour guide.

I know you are.

Okay. Only in the summer, mind. Well, also now I suppose. In the Indian summer. It's my parents' fault. They suddenly realised they were sixty and just sitting there while it rained, so they moved to the south of France to be soixante and just sit there while il fait beau and they sold their house to me somehow and I think they sort of miscalculated, because now I've no rent to pay, and I've lost any incentive I had to do anything with my limp useless English degree. So I just hang around at Silverlines, and when someone says there's a party of German students want to see the Changing of the Guard I just sign my name up with a felt tip and say leave it to Susie.

You're a creative person, I can see that. You like to laugh, and I see laughter in you.

See those big tall beehive hats they wear? There's an interesting story about them. They are all connected by subterranean fibre-optics to one single huge big tall beehive hat housed in the Admiralty. And it glows and pulsates like this great knowing insect. You're frowning.

Someone wanted to make you happy. You didn't want that.

Well. Okay. That's, more in the past kind of thing.

You wanted to make someone happy. He didn't want that.

Oh he's in there, is he. Okay. But again: been there done it.

The roots of the future are in the past.

Right. I suppose.

There is . . . something coming, something fluttering by.

You see that through the mist?

The mist is partial it's very clear. All eyes are turned one way.

All eyes are turned one way?

All eyes are upon you.

Fine. I am paying.

All eyes are turned upon you.

Okay.

You are the focus of all.

What did I do?

Nothing. You did nothing. You are going to be famous.

Right. Everyone's famous.

You are going to be famous.

What . . . really?

You must say it.

Why?

To receive the gift. This is the First Light. You must say it. You are going to be famous.

You mean like I sign for it?

Do you wish to receive it?

'I am going to be famous.'

It means nothing if you don't believe it.

It's not easy to, I'm not seen anywhere. I just read books.

Then it means nothing.

Should I try harder to believe it?

You paid fifty pounds.

Hm. Famous in what field?

I can't tell you.

Why not?

It's clouding over, it's gone.

That was it?

That was it?

Something else is coming.

What's coming?

There is many of something.

Many of what?

It is coming towards you.

It is? Is it many of money?

Yes.

Is it? Really?

Yes. It is much money, it comes like a great cloud.

It's okay if it comes as a cloud, cloud-form is no problem.

You won't see it.

I won't see it?

So much money, moving towards you.

What do you mean I won't see it?

I don't know, I only see.

You don't know, you only see . . . Does it cost more for you to also know because I can go to the cashpoint.

You will be rich.

Mind you there's nothing in it. So you're saying I will see it?

You will be rich. It is the Second Light.

O-kay.

Say it.

'I will be rich. It is the Second –'

You don't have to say that bit.

Sorry. Do I have to believe I'll be rich?

It means nothing if you don't.

Right. Here goes.

It's the truth, after all.

I think it's working. 'I am going to be rich.'

You won't see it.

I . . . I'm going to be rich but I won't see it, why is that, why is that . . .

The picture has clouded over.

Why won't I see it?

You are helpless.

I'm what?

I see you walking.

You do? Am I alone? Why am I helpless? I'm rich and famous, why am I helpless?

You are alone.

I'm alone?

Yes.

That's a formidable detail. Forever?

Yes and no.

That's cleared that up.

You are here, you are not. It's a journey.

A journey? Mrs Sage I'm a tour guide, I'm always on journeys.

As soon as you say it, you see it clouds over, it hears you, it knows you know, so it rubs out the picture and starts on another. It's like a child, it needs to know you understand.

I understand. A journey. Is it a long journey?

You will journey over earth and water. This is the Third Light.

'I will journey over earth and water.' A lot of earth? A sea? An ocean? We're journeying all the time, I mean I could journey over this carpet it's the earth, and there are these hidden rivers of London flowing beneath us I read a book about it.

A journey of some hours.

The Fleet river. Is it a flight?

That picture is erased.

You have to be quick, don't you, catch it all. 'I will journey over earth and water.' Now I get that too. I get everything.

Some hours.

Some hours.

There is . . .

There is . . .

A V.

A V.

Inverted.

A V inverted. Like an A without the little

The picture is forming from below.

Can I stop now. Can I hang on to the fame and money and stop now, like a quiz show?

It may be a star. It's an inverted V and above it there is a paragonal V.

Fine I can't. What's paragonal, like a normal one? That would make a cross.

It's not a cross, it's a figure.

Okay. You mean like a number. Is it a large number?

No not a number a figure, a person. Someone.

Right. Someone, finally. It was lonely in there.

This is another picture.

I see. I mean,

It's a man.

Tall dark stranger?

He is tall, he is indeed somewhat of a dark complexion, the veil is lifting. He is indeed tall, dark, and,

A stranger.

Well. He is indeed a stranger to you.

Does he have a name?

He gives no name. But he is always asking.

I'm sorry? He's always asking? Asking what?

He is always asking you to say . . .

YES.

Of course he is he's a man.

He is always asking.

I don't say yes, do I? Or do I?

You are always saying no.

Wrong girl there maybe.

You will say no to him. Receive these words.

'I will say no to him.' Good.

You will say no to him until the day you say yes.

What?

This is the Fourth Light. You will say no to him until the day you say yes.

Is that, I don't mean is that true I mean, is that what's there?

I don't see anything, I don't hear anything. I only mean, it's always a tall dark stranger in this, this sort of scene, isn't it? Can you see why I'm sceptical?

You will say no to him until the day you say yes.

Okay well that's original. 'I will say no to him until the day I say yes.'

Now it's moving. It's shimmering. The Fifth Light is shining. There is a shower of something.

Let me guess, confetti.

Now everything is shaking.

Wedding video.

It's shaking everywhere.

I think we should cut the cake.

On the next day you will die.

What?

What?

Receive it.

What did you just say?

I'm not receiving that. That's not there. You can't see that in there.

You have come to believe.

What?

You have come to believe about the fame, the money, the journey, the stranger, you believe these things.

I – no, I don't. I don't believe them.

You received them.

You – you told me to receive them.

You paid fifty pounds.

You – look, you can't tell me the day I'll die. You don't know it, it's not there.

Then why are you here, Susan Jane Mantle?

I – for nothing, because, for nothing, I'm not, I don't know why I'm here I was just passing the time and now I'm hungry I missed lunch and I'm leaving.

That isn't the door.

Look it is, it is, it was the door –

It's a door that goes nowhere.

Look, you're right, it's a cloakroom. Please tell me which door is the door.

Please tell me which door is the door.

Thank you. Thank you.

*

Thank you. That old bitch, and what I actually said was thank you.

She's already wrong, Suse.

Look I'm shaking just remembering. I meant to say piss off you old hag, you'll be dead forty years before me, why don't you save me a seat ya witch.

But you didn't say that.

No. I said thank you.

Thing is she's already wrong. About the money. You didn't receive any, you lost some. Fifty quid's worth. God! She has no idea how to do her job.

It's not a job Min it's a scam is what it is. I don't know, I must have wound her up somehow, I actually thought she liked me, she must have hated me, she's just one of those women-haters. Or just me, one of those Susie-haters you get these days. Maybe she was on one of my tours once. Telling me I'll – I know I will but not when she says, when I say. Or when, you know. Anyway. Bitch.

I know.

What a bitch.

Bitch is the word. Well there's others but it's one of them. But you know what I'm just thinking?

These drinks don't last long enough.

That's when it happened. You were in there with that total bitch when the news broke, because the news of the attack was at about 12.30. There was the original news of the attack, then the news about

Thomas, the false news of his, his alleged passing on, at 12.49, when you were still in that place. My boss had the radio on. He said Quiet Everyone. They got Thomas Bayne. They only went and got Thomas Bayne. Those words are printed on my, kind of, page of my mind. THEY ONLY WENT AND GOT THOMAS BAYNE. And someone said who's they and my boss was like. But we all knew it was terrorists. It was so obvious. And Pippa Candling from Accounts just started kind of all saying the names of his films, one after another, so we'd all remember them and never forget them. Hellfire High. The Reckoning 5. Whiteout. Scenario. Geek Attack. The Little Engine. The Little Engine 2. Desperation. Prince of Peace. Time of Angels. Time of Angels 2. Prince of Peace 2. Time of Angels 3. And she ended with The Book of Revelation, which was good, because it meant there was hope, that the film would be made, that we'd see him again if only in I don't know his, film self. And other films would be made but without him, but films would be made. It's like these people would never win. Every bomb would make like two more films rise up in its place, like the heads of, like, you know some monster of film. But a monster on our side for once! It was good of her to do that. It was like a moment's silence, like dignified? but with that film list as well, so there was something to listen to.

I can't believe that woman.

I get out, I'm on the street, it's very sunny, maybe no more sunny than it was before I don't have the faintest idea. But I'd been an hour in a very dark room so the light was really dazzling it was so bright it felt like flashbulbs as if everyone knew what had happened and everyone wanted a quote from me but my eyes accustom and there's no one. I just keep on walking it was just London in the afternoon, old buildings, new buildings.

No way was I going to work. Those Texas ladies could drift out into the Estuary and the North Sea looking at everything in their great mad sunglasses, I'd have told them about the edge of the world.

Wow.

And of course I didn't believe it, it's a sideshow at some village fête, it's vile gypsy bullshit I only did it for a laugh.

I don't believe in anything but it was hurtful that she'd done it, you know, spiteful. She was elderly, that witch, had she never met any children? She was old when I was a little girl, you can't treat people like that. I felt abused, Min, I felt someone had hit me.

Wow. Total cow I know.

I didn't know where I was. I kept saying London. I just walked with my head down and I watched my feet in my trainers trying to outwalk each other, really pounding along and I had them talking about it, sympathising, like two people power-walking, gasping out what they think. My trainers . . . but it isn't true, but it might be true, but it isn't true, but it might be true . . . And whenever I got to a kerb I just looked up a second and said Oh that way and went that way and there were thousands of feet coming the other way it was somewhere near Victoria but not Victoria I don't know where.

You, Suse, were walking, through Victoria, exactly when the news was breaking you're incredible! There must have been big signs at all the Evening Standard stalls and people gathering around! There was a spirit of the Blitz! That's what Ian Thoroughboard said there was and he was there!

I didn't notice anything. I didn't know what I was looking for. I just felt very, I don't know, very innocent, like I'd never once in my life, and it probably isn't true, but never once did anything so nasty that an old witch woman would do something so nasty back. I felt really wronged. Wreally wronged. I'm having another drink.

Are you sure?

Do I look like I'm mulling it over.

So I didn't know where I was, and until I heard these men saying I didn't realise I was crying.

Beautiful but crying!

They didn't say that.

What did they say?

*

Can you talk to us?

Is it a bad time? We know it's a bad time. It's a bad time for all of us

Don't take it so hard

(Don't say that Ron, she can take it hard) be natural, let it flow, sweetheart

Behave

That's good

Be natural about it, be true to your feelings

And then can you give us some words about your reaction?

No?

Steve, come in closer

Can you give us your name, sweetheart?

She's too upset

No she's going to say something

Steve good to go

Yussuf good to go

Lords on a Sunday

Tenerife

Disneyland

And rolling

Let's go for it. Sweetheart, what thoughts come to mind?

Death . . .

Yeah I know, I know

There there

Death.

It's the big one at the end of the day

You picking up that siren, Steve

Mm-hm just wait

Wait a second, love

Emergency somewhere

Thanks for that mate. Steve clear

Yussuf clear
Snowdonia
Gran Canaria
Vegas
And rolling
Rolling, death, sweetheart, yeah, and?

Death will,
Go on

Death will have no dominion.

Is that it?
Right, good
That was good, love
Bit poetic
Ask her to expand on that, could you
She don't need to expand on it, it means Death will have no power
Do you mean Death will have no power, sweetheart? Is that what you're saying?

Death will have no dominion.
That's powerful, repeating it
Not if no one understands it, Ron, then it's more like confusing. It doesn't illuminate so much as y'know, not, like de-luminate it if that's a word
Chick looks this good who cares?
Behave
I like it. I think that's well said
Dominion is land, gents. Death will have no lands, no property
Thanks for that, Yussuf
Course he would be the only one who knows

Death hasn't got any lands anyway
It's a metaphor you berk
I know that, I did English, got a B in the ol' retake. Better than a C anyway. What I mean is it was worth it
They can explain it in a sub-title

They won't go for that
Morons it's the Bard

I knew that, I just didn't know which one
I'm pretty sure it's Macbeth
You mean the Scottish play
That's right it's Scottish, isn't it, Macbeth, so that'll play well with the jocks
Is she going to say any more?
Fourteen years bad luck you just caused us, Ron
Don't believe in it
We're having 'em anyway
No change there
I'd just like to point out that you might as well say Death will actually have dominion, I mean if it means power, I mean it did today you could argue
Yeah it's got power today and lands
No but it's a religious thing, for people who think it won't, you know, in the end, have much, or any. Any say
I got that straight away mate
Are you religious, sweetheart? It's okay. We have viewers who are
Death will have no dominion.

Nah, that's the same thing three times. People are going to clock that as nutty
Not if we only run it once. Can we have your name, sweetheart

Put her down as F. K., Pimlico
F. K.?
Stands for 'We Don't Know'
Put down 'Jane Macbeth'
Seven more fucking years Ron that's twenty-one

It's a small 'b' in Macbeth
Christ will someone tell him

*

They must have been film students having some sort of joke, I didn't want anything to do with them, I just said the only thing that kept going through my mind and then I walked on and didn't turn around. They had too much equipment to come after me. I was light on my feet. I was weightless.

I walked a long way then.

I found a cinema. Finally a place it made sense to be, I thought I'll see anything I'll just sit there. They were showing Burn Time 4 and I got a family pack of Revels and I sat there eating them sort of helplessly following the story.

What happened?

It ended and I left.

I mean in it.

Well Minni in Burn Time 4 there are lots of fires and explosions and a man called Kurphew avenges his brother. People somersault out of buildings. People catch fire and stand around waving their arms like kids with sparklers. When Kurphew's brother catches fire the camera slows down and Kurphew screams Nooooo very slowly. I ate three Revels in the time it took him to say it and they were all orange. At the end some people applauded.

Did you?

No Minni I stood up and cheered. (Can we have more drinks please here like really soon?) So, that was, I don't know, 4.30. I'd missed the tours at one, two, three, four but I could make the tours at five, but I thought you know fuck it I'm fired anyway. I'm dead anyway.

You're not dead, she was lying!

Envious ugly thing.

No way you're going to be rich and famous!

Or die, Min.

Or die! No way!

Okay, so round that time, now you say, yes, I do remember a sign saying THOMAS BAYNE ALIVE! but because I didn't know he was dead I thought it was maybe a poster for a concert, and just about then, and this is ridiculous, I went to the cashpoint.

Cos you thought there might be a gig?

Min you're not getting this.

I've had a bad day Suse!

It's okay now, there there, Thomas Bayne's alive.

Yeah but he wasn't for ages kind of.

Look: she said I was going to be famous. Soon as I set foot outside her dump I meet a camera crew. So the way my mind's working, I think maybe that's all it was, maybe just, somehow, she kind of did glimpse that coming, or maybe she knows those film students, maybe they're always hanging around and I was bound to meet them, so then I think, she said I was going to be rich, so, if I look at my bank account maybe by some weird chance it's bigger than it was but only slightly? Something I've forgotten, or a computer glitch, I mean, maybe everything she says will come that tiny bit true, a short journey, I dunno, Tesco's or something, a relatively tall, vaguely brown stranger who I say 'whatever' to until I say 'why not' to.

Sounds like me on a Friday night!

Exactly, and then, she said the next day I'd,

Just what . . . pass away, but . . . only a bit?

Yes! Get a cold, a virus. Snuggle up with a blanket and a box-set of something. So I did swing by the cashpoint.

Omigod.

I knew I had about eighty pounds in the world,

Omigod you suddenly had more!

*

CSC BANK
ATM5
572 ST CROSS ST LONDON UK

CARD:	**XXXXXXXXXXXX7420**
NETWORK:	**PLUS-CIRRUS**
TIME:	**17.31**
DATE:	**20.10.08**
ACCOUNT#:	**64629456**
WITHDRAWAL:	**40.00**
NEW BALANCE:	**32.75**

*

You had me really scared, you know.

I'm not going to die, Min. I'm immortal.

No you're not!

I'm immortal. I'm going home.

*

######## ######## ### Hello?

Susan Mantle of 52 Hazeldene Avenue.

Susan Mantle? Anyone present?

Yes. Who is it.

You don't know. You do know.

Nigel.

Nailed it.

Hey.

Where are you?

I'm at home.

Sound like you're in a bar.

It's the TV. I'll switch it off. There.

Does it sound like I'm home now?

It's quiet. 'Yeah. Too quiet.'

I had a quiet day. I had a long day. It won't end.

They still don't know who did it.

Really. Hasn't anyone claimed they did it?

Just about everyone. Al-Qaeda, Islamic Jihad. Brigade of Islam. Christians from America. They say anyone who tells stories about the Bible is going to Hell. Say it was the Lord's work they just did. That's some crazy shit. Nah. Broken all records for claims of responsibility. Might issue my own statement.

Why would you do that.

Gallows humour. Have that brand as you know.

Well I missed it all.

I've a bit of a dark side. Where were you when you heard?

What does that matter?

Yeah. I was in Café Easy on the Royalton Road. Just bought the club sandwich with avocado I'm a big avocado man. About to take a bite, you know, classic, and the radio's on, and my mouth's open and I, am, literally starving, so though I hear the voice and it's Thomas Bayne dead, Kennedy Clover dead, Michael Vicksey dead, Marcus 'MC Meltdown' Johnson dead I'm slowly still eating, but you know, I'm feeling guilty about it seeing as other people aren't, you know, eating. Other people put their food down or didn't touch it, no ta, just sat there in remembrance. I felt I don't know, I did wrong somehow, didn't rise to it. Had, what do they say: a bad war.

So that's where I was. In Café Easy on Royalton. That was the first minute of the ninety-nine.

The ninety-nine.

Ninety-nine minutes it appears we thought Thomas Bayne was deceased if I may, we thought the world was officially without Thomas Everett Bayne. Till the news came in. Till it broke, you there Susan? Mind if I call you Susie? I mean, now we're, you know.

I don't care.

You don't care? That's harsh.

Okay I don't mind.

Like it. Susie.

It's very quiet here. I grew up here and it's empty. It's just me and Bonner.

Who's that then.

My cat.

I'm not allergic.

He's not either.

Never have been.

All my, old things are in the attic and now it's my attic. I feel I should go in there. I can't go in there that's mad. A madwoman's probably there already. Do you mind if I have the TV back on?

Go for it, Susie. Sounds like an old film. Ol' black and white melodrama.

It is an old film. Why did they think he was dead for so long?

Who. You mean Bayne? Stunt double.

Stunt double.

Stunt double's on set, right, someone sees him outside Bayne's trailer in the few seconds before blast-off, double's on his cell, dead ringer, spitting image, boom, no double. Witness jumps to conclusions. You would. Poor guy though, the double. Just, ceased to exist.

Yeah, I thought doubles could survive things.

No way. Not that.

They'd live on in the world. As singles.

No way.

All that training. You'd think he'd brush himself off in the wreckage, or step out of the inferno and say gosh that was close. Lucky I had my, I don't know, harness. Kurphew would have made it.

I don't think in a way it's quite sunk in for you.

Oh it's sunk in.

Takes time. Where are you, you're at home. Thursday's clear, you know. Could come up on the ol' Northern. Unless they bomb that again, of course. Don't know their plans.

You'd take that risk for me.

Otherwise you let them win. They don't know who they're dealing with.

You don't know who you're dealing with, you've only met me twice and never sober.

Thrice as you well know.

You could send your stunt double.

Don't have one. Wish I did.

Right.

Get him to go to the office. Get him to fix the car,

Yep

Get him to pay the taxes, fill in forms,

Etc

Free me up for my real work. So how about Thursday.

If I make it.

Meaning?

It's okay.

Like it, Susan Mantle. Susie M. Susanna Mantello. Suzanne Von

I have a question.

Fire away.

Is your hair naturally dark?

Good question yes it is, never touched it, been long been short been styled in fact but coloration no way.

Do you know what that means you are?

Means I'm, no, I don't know, well I do know, but what.

You're a tall dark stranger.

I am. But I'm not, I'm not a stranger, am I, I know you.

No you don't.

In the intimacy stakes come on, but in general terms? I certainly know who you are, and you could pick me out of a line-up, usual suspects type of thing, Keyser, you know, it's Kevin Spacey if you haven't seen it it's worth checking. What I'm saying is I'm no stranger. Tall, dark, guilty as charged: stranger no way.

All right so you're not. We're soul mates. There was nothing, then there was you. Big bang.

Huge.

So you might make the journey?

Will make the journey.

Do you need directions?

Got my A to Z. Very clear mapping.

You'll find me quite near Z.

Where's that then.

You go through Greenwich and then Woolwich and then you start to see looming up on the horizon this big towering sort of Z and that's sort of Mersham and I'm there somewhere, alone in a big detached house just sitting there in my front garden in a deckchair reading a book.

You really got your parents' whole place?

I do.

Someone's looking out for you.

You think? Feels like no one.

Maybe someone should, you know, step up to the plate. Baseball reference. Your phone's ringing.

No. It's in the film.

It's an old phone I'm hearing. Anyone going to answer it?

I don't know, I wasn't following the story. There's been a

murder. Maybe it's the killer with some vital clue.

Sounds like Hitchcock. Has he appeared yet?

It's on the stairs or something.

Phone's still ringing. I think it's real.

Shit so it is it's the landline. Can I put you on the chair?

Put me where you like.

I'll do that Nigel.

Hello?

Susan.

Mum?

Susan.

Mum I thought you were in the film.

Tell me you're all right.

I'm all right.

Thank God. (She's all right.) You heard the news.

Right I did but I live in London, Mum, and that news happened in Libya. London came through it okay on the whole except people are rat-arsed and acting like the world ended.

Thank God. (Alec, she's all right, bit stressed.)

Are you all right?

(She's all right, Alec, no put the tray down, make two trips, come back for the limes. No, it's on the side . . . honestly . . .) Honestly your father. He keeps banging his head on the door frame like some big robot who's programmed to.

Are you okay Mum.

Us of course we're okay. We're down here away from it all.

Mum actually you're five hundred miles closer to it than I am.

I don't think Ramparts-de-Guise is exactly in the firing line. France isn't even there.

France isn't where, Mum?

In the war.

I thought this was about the Bible.

Depends whom you believe. Some people are saying London's next.

We've already been next, Mum. Someone else can be next.

Yes, you've been next once, but then time passes and someone else is next and before you know it you're next again.

Well thanks for that Mum.

Susan, there was British money in The Book of Revelation.

About 20p and some props, I should think.

Four of the dead are British.

Nineteen are American, five are Italian and a hundred and six are assorted Africans and Bangladeshis working on the set, my friend Miranda phoned me to say so.

Miranda. Minni. The dim one from before.

We go back.

We all go back, Susan. What happened to all your smart friends? Your college friends?

They graduated. To things like marriage and babies. The music suddenly stopped and they all sat on each other. I was left sort of dancing on my own till I noticed.

Why are we talking about you?

I don't know, because I survived a bombing in Africa. By being in Pimlico. Smart move.

You don't believe it's close to home, but it is, Susan, we're the enemy to them.

That's right, you, me, Dad, Bonner. Sleeper cell. We do the terrorism, Bonner handles sleeping.

You shouldn't even say that, the CIA are listening.

Hello spies. It's an attack on America, Mum. And they tried to get Thomas Bayne because he's the biggest star in Hollywood, but he's from Calfornia Mum he's not from Mersham. There's Newsnight coming on.

You'll see what I said is true. London is a hotbed.

I don't want to watch it. It's just bits of burning towers in the desert and it hasn't even started. That must have been the film set. Still looks like a film set actually. They're advising viewer caution, so I'm viewing fairly cautiously now, with a sort of frown, sort of filtering things.

Do they show Thomas Bayne?

Yeah there he is beaming away, not dead any more.

(How typical to go on about that. Alec, Susan has Newsnight.)

Actually it's not Thomas Bayne it's the double. Well they did say to view cautiously. Wow. Good likeness. His name was Zbigniew Jackson, of Big Falls Idaho. He was a stuntman. Big Falls oh no that's too good to be true –

(He was from Idaho, Alec, no Idaho. The dead double, his name was Jackson)

No one's going to point that out, maybe I should, lighten the mood a bit. Big Falls will never be the same.

(Jackson like Michael Jackson's Thriller.) What's that Susan?

Now they're just showing Thomas Bayne's fans looking miserable in a pub, I can see they're still getting the rounds in. But apparently they all wept for ninety-nine minutes. Hey call the Guinness Book of Records. There they are, making a start on that. Five lagers please, sob, plus a white wine spritzer, sob, with chardonnay boo-hoo no make it a pinot.

They thought he was dead, Susan.

He isn't. I was filmed today but not about that. I just looked nice crying. I cried so much I was a girl in a wet T-shirt contest. I just stood there and won. Of course they wanted to film me.

Why would they, Susan, on a day like this? This is a huge day for news and what have you done lately, shown some girl guides Nelson's Column.

I didn't show them Nelson's Column, I just explained why it was called that and got fired anyway that was Dreamtours not Silverlines.

I'm sorry I couldn't remember which of those prestigious corporations was currently paying your McDonald's money.

I wish. Anyway, they've moved on.

Who's moved on?

They've moved on to a government minister. They're asking him what he's going to do to protect film sets in London. Are there any? He's saying they're doing everything that's necessary to win the war against whoever the war's against until whoever the war's against is brought to justice.

He didn't say that.

Might've. How do you know, you emigrated. Now there's a shot of Hugh Grant in Notting Hill. The film, not the district. It's been a long day.

We're an hour ahead of you. It's tomorrow here.

Blimey what's that like.

Mum?

Susan.

It's only, have you ever gone to, or visited a, like a, a fortune teller sort of

I'm putting your father on.

Nononononono wait!

Sukey!

Dad. No. Yes.

I hear we have nothing to worry about!

Yes, you have nothing to worry about. It's official. I was not the target. I hear you're having trouble with the doors.

Honestly this house was built for a tribe of midgets. If there was one thing I'd change, and there isn't, that would be the one.

You'll have to stoop Dad.

Stoopez-vous, s'il vous plait! I wish I could say join us for a nightcap, we're having a nightcap on the terrace, we can see the sea! We can see 'la mer'!

How is la mer.

It is très blue and très grande. Very grand!

So you're blending in.

In Ramparts-of-the-Geezer yes, tomorrow I'll be down to the village for my blue and white hooped sweater, and my baguettes, and my onions, and I might stop and

Play a game of tossing big metal balls in the gravel, okay yep.

And partake of a little vin supérieure.

Glad you're enjoying yourself.

You know they sometimes don't have corks these days. They have screw-

tops would you believe? It doesn't seem very classy, I used to think

Wine with screw-tops was crap but that's not necessarily true.

We speak as of one mind.

Okay. Good. Well, I might just go to bed now.

I can see the stars quite clearly. Isn't it strange to think

We can see exactly the same stars although we're far apart.

Indeedy! Les stars méditerranéane!

Étoiles, Dad. And anyway I can't see anything because it's cloudy and even if it wasn't it's polluted. Oh and it's raining. I can hear it on the roof of the lean-to.

The lean-to, ah . . . Just think, raining, raining in England! As ever!

Actually it was nice today. Always is when this shit happens.

Language!

Language.

(It's raining, Marie! Nice earlier, rainy now.) Typical

English weather.

English weather!

Bye then.

Take good care of the place, Sukey! The old homestead!

All right. Bye then.

Oh God Nigel.

Nigel are you still there? Nigel?

Dad are you still there?

☽

####### ####### ####### ####### ### Who the hell –

Suse! It's me!

Min it's what it's

You sitting down?

No I'm lying down in the dark I'm asleep it's what is it fucking 3:51

You'd better sit up!

Why

You sitting up yet?

Yeah okay okay

I just saw the news.

I know about the news. Black people died. Thomas Bayne's on a yacht. Night then.

No. You were on television.

No I wasn't.

Yes you were. Like the woman said you would be. The total bitch? You're famous.

Bollocks Min I saw Newsnight.

This is the 24-hour rolling Sky thing, I'm in a hotel. You're famous. And I'm talking to you. I know you.

Stop stop stop why are you in a hotel?

It doesn't matter, it was the bit at the end, or in fact in the middle before they do the headlines again, you know, when they do something on a lighter note? Well they do, it was that, it's like incredible, but you're famous. I hate you.

This isn't funny, Min.

I know. It was you. You were crying, it was those guys with the camera they weren't students they were only Sky! That's why the guy in the bar said that – beautiful but crying! He must have seen it on Sky, but the BBC doesn't have it. You're crying!

I'm not. And I'm not laughing.

No I mean on TV you're crying, but the voiceover says something like 'here's another broken heart torn in pieces, a pretty face in a state of shock' I think it goes I've seen it three times now, then it goes, wait for it, 'beautiful but crying! An ordinary girl, on an ordinary street in London, on an extraordinary day in history, beautiful but crying . . .' Beautiful but crying! Like the barman said at Arroyo's! You're crying about Thomas!

No no no no no I'm crying I was crying about that gypsy bitch, I told you. You have no idea what fraction of a fuck I give about Thomas Bayne. It was nothing to do with Thomas Bayne. Nothing's anything to do with Thomas Bayne.

Then you quote him.

Then I quote who?

Thomas! You quote Thomas!

What are you talking about.

You say how 'Death will never win' or something, which was great, you said it through your tears. And this expert said it's a line from Thomas.

I'm drowning.

That's why I said sit up.

I didn't. I stayed lying down and it's pitch dark and it's pouring with rain and everything's just sliding away.

You're unbelievable! I've never been on TV! Except at Make Poverty History and I was tiny!

I wasn't crying about Thomas Bayne and what I said wasn't about Thomas Bayne. I was crying about me and what I said was about me.

No but here's the thing. They had this timer running, and apparently, they said in the segment, you appeared in the ninety-ninth minute.

What?

I wrote all this down, here, on the hotel pad with this hotel biro. At 12:49, the news broke that Thomas was, that Thomas had passed away in the recent outrage. Right? (It's 12:49, I wrote it down for her, she's my mate from school, she knows me, shut up!)

Who are you talking to?

(Who am I talking to? Justin.)

Justin.

Okay.

At 2:28 pm, that's apparently ninety-nine minutes later, which is the figure that became the, you know, famous number, at 2.28 you said to the Sky people DEATH WILL NEVER WIN, *which is becoming another thing about the day which people remember, and you said it Suse, my best friend said it! (She's my best friend.) So a few seconds after you say* DEATH WILL NEVER WIN, *quoting from Thomas, the news breaks that he's alive! Not only alive, but in a yacht in (where was it Justin? Croatia) in Croatia.*

Okay. Look.

He's going to make a statement tomorrow, from that nation.

I don't know where to start.

You should take deep breaths.

I can't take any breaths.

Oh yes and they say she's a Mystery Girl, you that is I so hate you, because you walked away without saying your name, as if you'd simply, I don't know, the experts said it was like you'd waved a wand, kind of, you kind of turned the day round and instead of all bad news there was suddenly the good! You said DEATH WILL NEVER WIN, *and it didn't!*

It didn't get Thomas Bayne. It got everyone else.

But Thomas Bayne, you know! Can you imagine! What would we have done? That's what the experts pointed out. It's sad about Kennedy Clover, who was kind of always being talked about as a star of tomorrow, she was actually on the cover of Tomorrow, which comes out today, ironically! and it's sad about Meltdown, as his album's also up for the Mercury Awards, which are now going to be held in honour of his contribution to the music industry and may even be called the Meltdown Awards which is a bit unfair on the other nominees but Thomas Bayne! They're saying it's like they struck at I wrote it down on the hotel pad, at 'our very soul'. As if they just knew, the you know the terrorists. They may not like films much, but they know how to hurt us where it, hurts.

I thought this was mad Americans.

It said on the news, they could be terrorists too, it's not just Arab terrorists who might be that's racist. You or me could be one, easily, that's why they have to have the new laws.

What new laws? (Bonner get off my legs.)

And those mad Americans watch films. They watch religious films. Like the one with Jesus.

What one with Jesus.

With what happened, what they actually did to him in real life. I mean just seeing it in church with the cross and stuff is totally like okay if you're a believer, that was then and perhaps in a way it was meant to be. But that film. I saw a trailer it was gross.

Should have bombed that.

Anyway The Da Vinci Code proved it was all a story apparently. He was just like us.

Oh Jesus.

I know . . . but this day is just historical. You were also described as the ANGEL OF LIFE. You're famous Susan. And I know you. And I don't hate you but I kind of do. It's a time of honesty. That total bitch was totally right. And a bitch.

It. Is. A. Coincidence.

No I know, yeah, but it's the way it seems that matters. People are crying, people don't want to be, don't want the star to, you know, pass away, you know, you can see how it makes sense.

He wasn't even in my mind.

Well no, but they're saying God moves in mysterious ways.

Is that right? Thomas Bayne write that too?

No. I don't know. Did he? You're the reader.

Min. I won't be angry, we're mates. Tell me this is a joke.

You were on TV, Susan, on Sky!

Try harder to tell me this is a joke.

I'm sorry. You're famous. You were on TV.

Right, as an afterthought, at four in the morning, for no

one. Just you and Justin. Who's Justin?
He's right here. (Who are you she's saying.)

He wants to speak to you. Go on she's waiting.
What don't put him on

(Hey.)
No, no
(Hey. Listen girl)
No no no no no no
(Death will not win
Death will not begin)
You have got to be joking
(Death will have no dominay-shon
He is powerless against creay-shon)
I'm going to hang up, friend
(Death he frightened of your powah
You is the Angel of the howah
Death he bow down to your language
Death he never been to Cam-bridge
Death he sobbin' Death he sighin'
Cos you beauty-full but cryin'
You the
Go away.

You are going to be rich

######## *JOHN CORMIN. LEAVE A MESSAGE.* #

It's, um. Been ages, it's Sue. Susan it's nothing really. Have a nice, you know. Day. Bye.

Fuck. Idiot.

*

I am not going to be famous.

I am not going to be rich.

I will not travel over earth nor water.

I will not meet a tall dark stranger, and I will not say no to him until the day I don't say yes. I mean I <u>will</u> say no to him until the day I also you know what I mean.

The next day I will not die.

*

######## #### *Franck?*

No.

Susan?

Mum, hi.

A nice surprise, An evening call, a morning call.

Have you heard anything?

No, nothing new.

Has anyone called you?

No. Only Monsieur Oliveira about the doors first thing. Your father spoke to him in his schoolboy franglais it's so embarrassing in front of Monsieur Oliveira who's being so helpful. We're only changing the doors because he's such a bloody beanpole.

O-kay . . .

Why would anyone have called me, Susan.

I have forty missed messages on my phone. That's thirty-five more people than know my number. I don't want to hear them. I was on TV last night.

You were? No. On Newsnight?

No, on Sky. Remember we subscribed so Dad could see some pointless sports. But I'm afraid to switch it on. It's very quiet in this house. I'm in bed, listening to the birds. The chaffinches.

Why were you on TV? What in the background? (Alec, Susan was on TV last night! No on TV. Last night. In England.) That got him moving. He's sorting out photo albums on the terrace, he's gone absurdly brown.

They filmed me when I was upset, they thought I was upset about Thomas Bayne but I didn't even know about it, and I said . . .

Hello is someone there?

(Banged my blasted head again blast blast buggery!)

You okay Dad.

Sukey? Am I hearing my daughter is a star?

No Dad I was a vox pop that's all but it was a mistake

Did you tape it? Do you know where the blank tapes dwell?

Yes I know where their happy home is but I didn't tape it, I didn't know it was on and I'm sure it won't be on again

Someone must have got it, we can go tape to tape, they're in the third drawer of the system, we have the technology Houston!

Dad can you put Mum on.

I know who'll have it. Bob Trellis.

Is Mum there?

Bob'll have it, no worries. (She wants you. She says she was a vox pop, the Lady on the Street oh that didn't sound quite right!)

(Give me the damn thing) Susan? Why are you in bed? Are you not tour-guiding today?

No, I'm in bed Mum I'm just sitting up in bed listening to the chaffinches it's pretty amazing I've only been here twenty-seven years and I don't think I've ever done this. Did you ever do this? Are they chaffinches? Well I'm doing it. And they might be.

They're sparrows. Have you got yourself a cup of tea?

No, not yet.

That's what I'd do next.

Okay. It's what I'll do next then.

You sound quite strange, Susan, are you all right?

Yes. Well. However I say this it's . . .

You don't sound quite yourself.

It's just, I just feel, I don't know, like I'm sort of not alone.

Well you're not alone.

Right. I have Bonner.

Well, yes, that too. Is someone there? Did you throw a party?

No. I just feel, somehow, not alone.

We're certainly with you in spirit (aren't we, Alec, he's by the door nodding like some kind of gangly wooden puppet) we're absolutely at your side in spirit Susan and you know it.

Yep.

Get yourself that cup of tea. And you'll let us know about any future TV appearances.

There won't be any, Mum. That was my career, that was my rise and fall.

Your father's going to call Bob Trellis about tapes.

I think you should just enjoy your new life and not worry about me, Mum.

Not worry? Try stopping us.

I am.

Well you'll fail.

Okay.

Bye.

We're proud of you, Susan.

Oh. Why?

Mum?

*

Hey look. Look, Macavity. (I know it's you Bonner, we're playing a little scene here, your name is Macavity, go with it Bonner . . .)

Here comes someone.

Here comes a pretty young lady.

But I'm not pretty, I'm old, I'm ugly, I'm a witch. So I don't like her one bit. And she keeps saying crystal ball when I tell her it's crystal glass. What do you think it is? Exactly. She makes fun of my craft, my trade. She doesn't like you, Macavity. She lies to foreign tourists. I'm going to teach her a lesson. She'd like to be famous, wouldn't she, that's all anyone wants now. Done, and she'd like to be rich, she's shallow her eyes look shallow. Done. Oh and a journey, of course, she'd like to see the world. Done, and what's next. Sex. Sex. Tall dark stranger, of course, give this slut the TDS treatment. Done, I can flatter her, make her think she can put up a little fight, say no to him, hold him off, but sex is all any of them want, in their little tops and skirts these days, so she says yes in the end, some sunny day, somewhere. Look at her smiley face. Thinks all her dreams just leap from a frigging gateau. Next day, pretty one, next day you are going to ####### ####### ####### ####### ####### ####### ####### ### Hello who's that?

Is that Susan Mantle?

Maybe. Yes.

Bloody excellent. You don't know me I'm a pal of Mal Granger's.

I don't know a Mal Granger. So I'm, hanging up.

Gary Cornelius?

No.

Georgie Fleece?

No.

Sally Bendit-James.

No.

Beverly Makesmith.

No.

Natalie Payles. Ophelia Payles. Minni Kaye.

I know Minni.

I knew it. Minni's a fine girl.

Is that what you called to say?

She's a keeper.

I'm tending back to that earlier hanging-up idea.

Don't hang up. Do not hang up the telephone.

It's a mobile, you know, I just press this little raised area and you disappear.

Do not terminate this conversation.

Why.

'Why', good question. You're no fool, Susan Mantle.

So why.

You've not got all day.

Actually I do. Why? Who are you?

I'm Ed Hardhouse.

Well that's cleared that up. Why are you calling me, Ed Hardhouse?

It's the situation.

The situation.

Your situation.

My situation. Let's see how many sentences we can say with the word situation in them.

Your situation vis-à-vis Mr Thomas Bayne.

That's a good one, that had situation in it plus a recognisable star name. See how effortlessly I responded though?

It's not a situation I've seen before.

That sounded a little contrived, Ed, you didn't really need to say 'situation' then like I just did.

But I have ideas about it.

You lose. What word shall we do now?

You, Sue, are news. There, words of one syllable.

Is that the game? Syllable isn't a word of one syllable.

You, Sue, are in denial.

Nor's denial. You're rubbish at this. Hardhouse. 'Hardhouse'? Come on.

It's Huguenot. Came over with the Conqueror.

Huguenots didn't come over with the Conqueror, Ed.

No. No they did not. They stayed at home. No, I'm a state-school lad, Sue, University of Life though I have as it happens French heritage, if you can live with that.

Live with what.

Live with it, if you can live with it.

You don't know me, go away.

I'm looking at your headshot.

What?

No but on the level.

Where did you see my, headshot.

I'm looking at it now. It's on page 5 of the Daily Mirror.

Oh fuck off.

It's on page 5, with all that that entails. You near a shop?

No I'm at home.

Go to a shop. No don't. Sit tight and listen to me.

I wasn't crying about Thomas Bayne.

Ssh, ssh, that's your story, but just, just hush, Susie Mantle.

I wish he'd died.

Funny that's what Bayne says.

What do you mean?

He was talking about his stunt double, that's page 3, page before you. He, Bayne, says Big Jack died for him, but in a perfect world, which Bayne admits it is so very far from being, he, Bayne, would have died for Big Jack.

Zbigniew Jackson from Big Falls Idaho.

That's the dead gentleman, so you are near a shop.

I'm not near a shop. I heard it on the news last night, I thought it was really funny.

What part's funny?

Big Falls. Everything. Come on!

You're a wild one, Mantle. I like you.

Great! Result! Go Mantle!

I don't need to, bit unprofessional, but who's counting?

Who's fackin countin mate?

And so on, yeah, sshh . . . Any-way. The slant on this, is thus: Who the fuck are you, mind my Flemish. The headline is DEATH

WILL HAVE NO DOMINION. They've got this skeleton chap looking a bit down in the dumps, and there's a video grab from Sky of your lovely mug kind of half turned away and having a fair old weep as it happens, and it says WHO IS THE MYSTERY GIRL WHO UTTERED THESE POWERFUL WORDS? In the corner you've young Dylan Thomas, whose words of course these are, it also says when he died he had thirty-six gin and tonics the lightweight then there's a timeline showing how the news of Bayne's survival clocks in almost to the second at where you drop the quotation. And someone's saying SHE GAVE US HOPE, *and OUR PRAYERS WERE ANSWERED. You with me, Mantle?*

I can hear you. I'm trying to make some drinking chocolate.

Kim Jodrell of Epping Forest says 'Her words seemed to say what we were all feeling: there was no way Thomas was dead! And then he rose again.' It's very biblical, actually, a lot of people seem to be taking it in biblical mode: Billie Frowd of Bracknell is. Jonas Klipke, young man in from Munich, same viewpoint. Sharon Droves, 15. Lalla Silt, 24, dancer. John Gizzard, up from Cornwall, 46, same opinion, I mean in terms of stuff like the stone rolled back, the rising again, the eternal if you like.

You know Ed even then there was a bloke who thought it sounded like bollocks. Another Thomas as it happens.

Biblical allusion but they proved it to him, didn't they, silenced the doubters. The Mantles of this world.

Okay. Deep breath. Can you see who I am from the picture?

Absolutely. I saw that this morning I thought, wouldn't mind waking up next to that.

You know what Ed, I'm the person you're talking to.

Yeah! You got a boyfriend, Mantle? Sshh, rhetorical question, anyway . . . What else have we got . . . PITHY SAYINGS TO SEND DEATH PACKING . . . there's a kind of Best of: DEATH WHERE IS THY STING, that's one. DEATH BE NOT PROUD, that's good, that's another, and this is quite a long one: DO NOT STAND AT MY GRAVE AND CRY, I AM NOT THERE, I DID NOT DIE kind of mystical utterance and they have this kind of mock-up of a grave with THOMAS EVERETT BAYNE written on it but kind of Tipp-Exed out a little lacking in taste.

Oh d'ya think.

You can phone in if there's others in that vein, it's just people rising up, Mantle, the ordinary folk taking the Big Guy down a peg or two is what it is.

Bit of fun eh.

Then, what's this, page 8, they've got other famous people who people thought were dead erroneously, you know, meaning

Alive.

Alive. Mark Twain's one. Though obviously passed on now. Realm of books. Paul McCartney, realm of music. McCartney? Didn't know he'd been dead, or, you know, not, take your pick. Britney Spears, Jimmy Savile, Lazarus. Biblical again, see. I don't know, Mantle, somehow you caught the mood there with your poetical ruminations. I mean who'd've thought it? The ars poetica. Times of crisis all bets are off.

Is there anything in the paper about the hundred African people who actually were blown to pieces by terrorists?

Blimey Mantle it's everywhere, some of these pictures. I think they crossed a line with some of this I mean I'm not the actual watchdog. People are going to be looking over at your face and thinking mmm thank Christ for her. They've got a nice little portfolio of Kennedy Clover on 10 in her prime, but, you know, why do that, the girl's gone, it's over, leave it, let us grieve.

It's been nice talking to you, Mr Hardhouse.

You get your hot chocolate?

I got it right here. I'm removing the skin with a chopstick.

Nice image.

Shall I come and make you some, Ed? Do you live in a house or do you just slither about in the undergrowth.

Make me some, make me some, bit of a frisson, sshh . . . Anyway . . . as of now, these people – and so far it's just the Mirror with the redtops, but the BBC had it this morning, also CNN – these people don't know who you are, you're the Mystery Angel, so:

Let's do absolutely nothing and let it all die down.

Well,

Because it's all wank.

Edgy. You're the best, Mantle.

Is that your suggestion?

Well, now you say, not entirely.

Because if you have a suggestion, and it has anything to do with my receiving any money in any shape or form from any source whatsoever, I'm not interested in hearing it. That was your suggestion wasn't it.

Oi! Behave! Not entirely, there are ways to play this . . .

I'm listening. I can hear the birds, I can hear the chaffinches.

You're sitting pretty, Mantle. To coin a phrase, I'm going to make you a star.

You have to find me first.

You know what I like about you? Your sense of humour.

*

Like the shades, Suse, it's a good look for you.

I'm a star out in public, we all come to this café. What's that?

A decaf mochaccino with chocolate sprinkles! Have some!

(Another of those please with caffeine and a croissant.) How do you know him Min he's vile.

He's famous, he's been around forever. I don't know him. Well I do now! I know <u>two</u> famous people! Sean says he's the best.

At what? Who's Sean?

His, you know. He's a freelance presenter plus he's big in PR. Ed, not Sean. He knows everyone. He used to present Grin and Bare It, I was always out when it was on but he's still famous. His card says he's 'a pilot through the shallows'.

Why do you have his card?

Why? I've got lots of cards. I've got a section for them. Look: in my bag.

You should have called me first.

You didn't answer.

I was asleep. He was the first call I got. After him I put my phone on silent. It's still on silent. (Please can I have my mocka-chockacino please.)

What are you gonna do about it Suse?

Sort of stir it, probably with this teaspoon.

Come on! Everyone's waiting to see what your next move is!

You can see what it is it's lunch. I just walked four miles all morning you should try it I saw London. I hadn't noticed it.

Four miles you did not! You so didn't.

Why do people only believe things about me they made up?

Come <u>*on*</u> *Suse! What next?*

Nothing, I said. Nothing. I'm just going to make a statement to the Daily Mirror how I'm thinking of the loved ones of all those who died in the attack, and I wish Mr Thomas Bayne well in his job, such as it is, but I was actually crying about something else so it's a mistake and I wish to be left alone.

Oh. My. God. And that's it?

Pretty much.

Ed Hardhouse suggested – <u>*that*</u>*?*

Hell no. He said I should talk to Richard and Julie.

Omigod. I am <u>*actually dreaming*</u>*. Also it's Judy.*

I should do some chat-shows, set up a website, release a track called 'Death Will Have No Dominion' on a webspot, blogcast, whatever, call myself The Mystery Angel. Get downloaded to Number One by the British people. He says they can do that. He told me to get rid of any boyfriends, I said I was managing that okay. When he mentioned the tasteful swimsuit pictures I hung up, but it was all quite entertaining. (Thanks. Actually could I change this for a pain au chocolat?) Do you want it Min? (Thanks.) I'm going to do nothing at all ever. Except eat this. First thing I've eaten all day.

I can't believe you Suse.

No it is, I live alone, I forget to buy food. I buy it for Bonner then I forget there's someone else.

I mean it's like I hardly know you.

I don't mind if you hardly know me. I hardly know anyone. I just curl up in my chair and read, or I tell tourists whoppers in the sunshine.

I can't believe you're passing up this like this one shot at stardom. I know it's like weird stardom, not like something you're brilliant at or like a talent, but you do only get one shot. Eminem says that in his lyrics. You only get one shot. He himself only got one shot, but he took it.

Was that Eminem you were in bed with?

No. He's taken. No it was Justin 'Cool C' Breeze. His real name's Justin McClintock, he's at Durham University doing like a module. Did you like his rap? I tried to stop him.

Try harder next time.

If there is a next time.

Oh did <u>you</u> only get one shot?

Ho no! I got a little more than <u>that</u> Suse. Suse! Mm-hmm! What was I saying. Yes, it's unbelievable! You could start a whole career on this, you'll do an album then you'll probably move into film, I could like help you with those decisions.

I don't want any money. (Or these crumbs go away crumbs.)

What, cos of what that bitch said?

Fame, money, journey, tall dark stranger. Not doing it. It's a trap set for me and I'm standing still till it goes away.

What?

It's a trap set for me and I'm standing still till it goes away.

I know you said that, but . . . but you're famous!

Barely. And I pass on the money.

But if it's just about the money, you could give someone else the money!

You!

Me! No but you could, like a charity, you could give it to Prince Charles to organise or Bob Geldof, then there'd be a concert with like, your mates coming on to sing with you at the end in a chorus and people in tears and then Suse, just have the fame!

I don't want the fame.

Please have the fame!

Please have it! PLEASE!

I don't want it.

Omigod want it please want it! For me please want it! Want it for people who know you!

Fine you have it. Just walk out of here up to Leicester Square, find a bench, start bawling your eyes out, works every time.

I just, I can't believe you. I'm sitting here seeing you, one to one, like friends, like even you know like <u>the</u> Friends, like Monica and Rachel but it's like suddenly they're in a film and it's not them at all if you see what I mean, it's like they're someone else, like their acting names. But you want to call them Monica or Rachel.

Or Phoebe.

Phoebe yeah if you met them. I want things back as they were.

No one knows who I am. I'm going to lie low for three days and it'll all be gone.

This just actually makes me depressed.

Not everyone wants what everyone wants.

They do! That's why it's everyone!

What?

Suse, don't you want to be known for something?

No.

It's unbelievable. It's like, everything I believed in, turned round, on its head, like, smashed. It could be like God himself giving you this chance and what are you saying to God?

Bog off God.

Sshh! no but you are.

It's not God. It's Death.

Suse! I thought you didn't believe what that total bitch said.

I don't. But maybe Death does. Maybe he thinks he has a contract.

Eh?

Look. There's been a coincidence, an accident. That bitch sort of had enough weird psycho-power to see it coming, I can believe that's possible,

It is, I saw a programme,

They read what your eyes are saying,

Yeah, they see the future there!

Er, right. So it's possible. Bravo lady. So accidentally I'm very slightly 'famous'.

What's that?

What's what?

The thing with your fingers when you said famous. Someone did that in that sitcom.

What, 'this'?

Yes that!

Quotation marks. Sort of, qualifies what I'm saying. You know, undermines it.

I might have a muffin.

Go for it. Okay, now if I cooperate with your sleazy Ed Shithouse man then some way, by hook or by crook, someone will give me money. I'm in the paper, it's what happens next. Soap star, gangster, murderer, model, drug addict, pop star, politician, all the same and no, I don't think because of that I'll go on a journey, and on the journey I'll meet a tall dark dickhead and say no a few times and then say yes and die the next day,

Suse!

But I don't want a single syllable more of that bitch's shit to come true, okay? So I'm not cooperating, not playing, not doing what I would do. I'm doing the opposite every time. End of story. Oh come on don't look like that. Eat your yoghurt.

Unbelievable. Just, you can't just hide from fame! Not when it comes knocking!

Mm, top croissant.

Unbelievable. Just . . . how are you going to lie low then.

At home.

Do you want me to come round your house tonight? Why not?

Because I'm fine. I walked four miles to this café to tell you I'm fine.

Why didn't you phone?

Because every time I switch it on it rings or it says I missed more messages. It's just telling me that all those people didn't want to talk to me till this happened. Forty-six people.

I think a lot of them are me, Suse.

Whatever. Fuck the mobile. It felt good to make it go dark

and just walk alone along a busy road. You don't even believe I did that, which makes it all the more precious.

You're getting more and more weird. You should learn how to text.

Nope.

Someone said it's the new talking.

I liked the old talking.

I text everyone except you.

That makes me feel special, don't spoil it. Nigel Pilman's coming round on Thursday.

But he's a tall dark stranger!

Maybe I'll shag him till he isn't. I'll shag him till he's a short blond mate of mine, it worked with all the others.

It didn't work with that John the tour guide.

Never heard of him.

I don't think you're over him.

You know I think there's still a spot on Neptune where that matters.

And now it's all about Nigel!

He can take my mind off things. Him for example. I don't know Min, maybe I'll cancel.

You know what you sound like? You sound like the woman in this film I saw and what her friend says to her is like something like: 'You, honey,' she calls her honey in the film I'm not calling you honey, 'are, afraid of life.'

Ah, there you have it. May as well bring the doctor and the priest in their long coats, running over the fields.

More Derek Thomas!

Yup. More of the master.

Mmm. At a time like this it says we need his wisdom.

*

CSC BANK
ATM1
10 ROSEMEAD AVE LONDON UK

CARD:	XXXXXXXXXXXXXX7420
NETWORK:	PLUS-CIRRUS
TIME:	12.19
DATE:	21.10.08
ACCOUNT #:	64629456
WITHDRAWAL:	20.00

NEW BALANCE: 12.75

*

Mrs Dawn Sage you are a fat dumpy swindling lying piece of shit and I have just enough money for a sandwich.

ALLO ALLO. NOUS SOMMES PAS CHEZ NOUS. LAISSEZ-VOUS UNE MESSAGE, S'IL VOUS PLAIT. HELLO HELLO. WE ARE NOT AT THE HOUSE OF US! LEAVE YOU A MESSAGE IF IT PLEASES YOU!

Hi Dad. A bi-lingual answering machine. Very organised of you. Message for Mum. Someone's probably told you by now, but because I was on TV I was also in the newspaper. You might have been trying to call but I switched off everything so no one can get through. People are trying to find out who I am, and find out where I live, and maybe someone might be tempted to tell them, but I just wanted to say I don't want that to happen, so what I might do is just lie low for a few days. Something else happened which*is a bit and now some sort of beep has gone and that probably means I'm talking to myself.

I'm talking to myself somewhere in the French system de telefones. Allo. Allo. Mum, ma mère, ma mère, an old woman told me some things would happen and at the end of them I'd, I'd die Mum and that's another thing I don't want to happen, but now it's been said I can't help . . . I can't help bearing it in mind and it makes me feel I'm being watched. I look out in the garden and it's like whoever was there just dipped behind the hedge, Mum, and he only can't be seen because I'm looking where I'm looking. Everyone else can see him. And they all think it's the beginning of a movie and it really can't get going until he turns up his collar and advances on the house . . . It's just, suddenly, very*look there's another one, another bi-lingual beep now what does that one mean . . . Not even the machine is listening now. Everything I say is turning round on dead tape . . . flick . . . flick . . . flick . . . flick . . .

*

####### Pilman.

Nigel. It's me.

No way.

It is it's Susan.

I repeat. No way.

Well I'll go then.

You know what I'm saying, don't you?

Not as such.

I'm saying, my meaning being, you're like: totally someone else. Not that which whom you were.

I'll call you back shall I.

Stay right there. I know you're you, I know you very well, three times I do, three times a lady, but not the lady I did believe you were. In former times. In a bygone

You saw the paper.

The paper? Saw the clip it's on YouTube. 'Death will have no dominion.' I've learned the whole thing.

What? You've learned the poem?

Sure. 'Death . . . will have no dominion.'

Go on then.

Go on, let's hear it.

Eh? I just did it. What do you want, blood?

Look it's a misunderstanding.

Half a page spread in the Mirror and it's a misunderstanding she goes. You need managing, Susie.

No I don't, and if I did I already have some arsehole lined up for the gig he's called Ed.

Nice try! nah . . . you need a friend at this juncture.

Don't call me 'Suzi', I'm not on a calendar.

Wouldn't dream. Just, still cannot believe my girlfriend is a famous person.

Oh you've a girlfriend.

Ha! Funny. Like it. What's with your cell, you switched it off?

Yep.

Good move. Sort of thing I can assist with. You know, paying out misinformation, travelling alternate routes, outrunning paparazzi, switching cars, you got a motor as they say?

Look I called you because I can't see you tonight.

Hey . . . guess what. Baz just left.

What?

The office, Baz went out to get his bacon roll, I'm all alone, this is a private conversation.

Okay, anyway, so I can't see you tonight. I'm

What are you wearing, Susie?

What?

Shit, he's back, he's only forgotten something. Baz. (Baz, bit of privacy here, eh?) Baz is such a waster. In his new shirt.

I think I might hang up now.

No I'm listening, you postponing me you big star celebrity diva?

Hell yes.

Not sure that's possible. I know where you live! Joke.

I know you know where I live, I told you where I live.

Found you on satellite, got you on GPS, 52 Hazeldene. Saw the Z, zoomed in, you meant a building in a Z shape from a plan view, right? Useful landmark. It'll be pointed out on coach parties. I'll be standing there in my shades at the edge of the property saying: 'Don't even think about it, losers.'

I don't want anyone here. You included.

Hey. Hey. Baz has gone . . .

Fuck Baz.

No one wants Baz, him and his, really reckons himself, thinks that shirt's gonna make the difference, he doesn't believe I know you. You, um, feeling lonely out there Susie?

Jesus.

You are so doing the celebrity act. Lucky I know the real you.

Look I can't see you while this shit's happening.

I can see you, though, here in the national newspaper, and you are one stunning sight to see.

I'm crying in that picture.

All part of the effect eh? Mascara gone wild! Quite like it.

Look. I'm crying because an old witch told me I'd die soon so fuck off.

Eh? She did what?

A fortune teller told me I'd die soon. Then I added fuck off but it's okay, once will do.

What do you mean soon?

Soon.

What, this week? I mean you're famous enough already. You kick it you're gonna spike like crazy. You're all over the radio, I say bit of hush lads, that's my chick they're talking about.

Don't know where to start with this.

I'll come right by after work, get some wine in, a movie, and we shall face the music together.

I don't drink, I don't watch movies, and I never face the music. You don't know me at all.

Who knows anyone in this fucked-up world? Man. You're my business, Susie, you're my problem you big celebrity star-vehicle diva bitch. Are you in your clothes?

What? Am I what?

Are you dressed? Baz has gone.

What do you mean am I dressed? Are you dressed?

Could be. Fuck me it's Baz (Baz what's your problem? Private chat and all.)

I can't see you tonight.

(Female client, big-guy, going over the details . . .)

I can always see you tomorrow.

Eh? (D'ya get me a salad mate?)

But I can never see you today.

Eh?

*

ALLO ALLO. NOUS SOMMES PAS CHEZ NOUS. LAISSEZ-VOUS UNE MESSAGE, S'IL VOUS PLAIT. HELLO HELLO. WE ARE NOT AT THE

HOUSE OF US! LEAVE YOU A MESSAGE IF IT PLEASES YOU!

Hello Dad, hello Mum, hello Provence. I'm just sorteying out for some

Sukey!

Dad oh hello a person.

I don't know how to stop the machine! Our whole conversation will be recorded for the ages!

Right, good well we'd better make it a good one.

A corker! Une corquerre!

Is Mum around?

Your mater, is, at this moment, would you believe, achetaying une bicyclette.

Mum's buying a bike.

Oui. Exactement.

That's good, Dad, it's good exercise.

It's very good exercise. You should try it!

No. So anyway. Everything okay?

Oui!

Bien.

Très bien. How's Blighty?

Cloudy.

Always is, you see. Except when it's raining!

Or sunny.

Changeable, that's the thing, it's all down to the

Gulf Stream

True! What's on the box?

I don't watch the box.

I have to watch 'Antenne-Deux'! Garbage!

Do you miss London, Dad?

Not in the slightest! I'm sitting here right now, with a newly poured glass of chablis in one hand and well, the phone's in the other, but it's usually a delicious fresh-baked croissant you'll find there! and I'm looking out over the roofs of all our new neighbours down to the sea, la mer, and I might even glimpse your mater in the distance, riding her bicyclette in and out of the shadows! I can see the fishing boats. I can see the bay, the silvery bay. Not at all! Beats working, I should flamin' coco!

Mum says you have a serious tan.

I am indeed the couleur of chocolat!

Be careful in the sun Dad.

Got my hat, got my trusty panama. Now, what I want to know is: have you kept the clippings?

What?

I'm in touch with Bob Trellis and he did say a pal of his at work, Norman Drilling, would probably have recorded Sky that night, so not to worry! Norman Drilling's on the case.

I'm lying low, Dad, it's meaningless, people forget. I'm walking along Hazeldene, it's the first time I've been out all day.

Ah Hazeldene . . . on a sunny morn.

Cloudy but hey, go for it.

And do you have more future television appearances lined up?

No Dad. I just stay in and look out at the garden. This is my first exciting trip, I'm walking to the cashpoint.

Money eh.

Root of all . . .

Things!

Evil, Dad.

So they say! Funny you should mention the garden, I can see the garden in my mind's eye. How's it looking?

I've gone out, Dad, I'm walking to the shops.

Grass a bit hairy I should think!

No I mow it every hour.

Have you not called Jim Flitcher?

He's coming next week. He's in the Bahamas.

He'll sort it out, green-fingered Jim. How are the roses?

The roses. It's been a good year for them.

And the azaleas?

Doing their thing.

Nothing quite like an English garden.

Nope. Maybe the one next to it.

An English country garden!

Uh-huh in Mersham.

I can see it in my mind's eye!

You mow it then.

Are you eating properly Sukey?

Not right now. I'm crossing over Brookham Road.

Look right, look left,

And right again I did that Dad, I made it. And yes I'm eating properly. Knife in right hand, fork in left, mouth shut, ask permission to leave table. But no one's there as you know so I just dine in the cobwebs like Miss Havisham.

Ah, well, now was that 'a poetic reference' . . . passed me right by of course!

It's okay.

Funny to think of you on your own at that big table!

Yep.

You must invite people over! You should

Ask the Happenhursts.

Happenhursts.

It's okay Dad. I know people under sixty.

Or the Sandimans.

Or Bob Trellis.

Bob Trellis is another.

Do you want to know about Bonner?

Oh yes Bonner how's Bonner doing?

Bonner's well. The sun just came out and he's staring at the sunbeams. When it goes in again he just sits there wondering where they went. A packed schedule.

Good old Bonner. But if I was organising a dinner party, which God forbid! No more o'that! I would probably invite Tim and Mandy Happenhurst, Bob and Weenie Trellis, and you know who else?

The Trawlinsons.

The Ripleys. You know why?

It's been on my mind.

Because yes I know they seem a little on the wild side, and they don't exactly blend in, but I find them and I don't mind saying this: bloody interesting!

Yes. Indeed.

But you know interesting people Sukey. You probably find all of our friends a little on the boring side!

Absolutely not. Outrageous.

Maybe just a tad? Maybe just a tad, come on . . .

I love them all.

Hmm. Where are you now?

I'm at the cashpoint, Dad, by the shops on Rosemead.

Busy at the shops?

No, Dad.

People going by . . .

Did Mum tell you about the fortune teller?

Fortune teller?

Never mind. (What's my stupid number . . .)

I went to a fortune teller once.

What did she say. (Don't be any money . . .)

I have absolutely no idea.

CSC BANK
ATM1
10 ROSEMEAD AVE LONDON UK

CARD:	XXXXXXXXXXXXX7420
NETWORK:	PLUS-CIRRUS
TIME:	17.03
DATE:	22.10.08
ACCOUNT #:	64629456
WITHDRAWAL:	10.00
NEW BALANCE:	581,233.41

Dad.

Sukey.

Dad, I . . . can you just hang on a minute.

I can hang on many minutes! I am a whole time zone ahead of you. I shall whistle!

CSC BANK
ATM1
10 ROSEMEAD AVE LONDON UK

CARD:	**XXXXXXXXXXXX7420**
NETWORK:	**PLUS-CIRRUS**
TIME:	**17.05**
DATE:	**22.10.08**
ACCOUNT #:	**64629456**
WITHDRAWAL:	**10.00**
NEW BALANCE:	**581,223.41**

Dad.

Dad.

Present! Are you still at the shops at Rosemead? The Bickerdikes live opposite and their son's about your age.

Right.

Nicholas Bickerdike. But you know what? He's a complete tosspot!

Uh-huh. I'm just,

I'm going to put this card in again.

There's some kind of a,

CSC BANK
ATM1
10 ROSEMEAD AVE LONDON UK

CARD:	**XXXXXXXXXXXX7420**
NETWORK:	**PLUS-CIRRUS**
TIME:	**17.05**
DATE:	**22.10.08**
ACCOUNT #:	**64629456**
WITHDRAWAL:	**10.00**

NEW BALANCE:581,213.41

Dad.

The most boring man I think I've ever met and he drinks sherry at his age at least he did last Christmas.

Is Mum there?

Bicyclette, off at the magasin of the bicyclette!

Can she call me when she gets back to the house?

If she ever returns!

I'll leave my phone on, I'll know if it's you guys.

I like that: Us Guys. You'll know if it's Us Guys! You'll have Us Guys to deal with!

Bye Dad.

Au revoir Sukey! To the re-seeing of you!

*

######## ######## ######## #### *Hello?*

Who's that.

Hi John.

Oh hello. You all right there, Mystery Angel?

You saw.

Sorry, couldn't resist it. But talk about speechless.

It was all a mistake. Not why I phoned you, why I –

They going to come round to me and get the dirt on you?

What? Is there dirt, John?

They going to start waving chequebooks? 'Hey John, tell us about your ex, tell us about the real Sue Mantle' and stuff?

No I don't think that's going to happen.

Oh. Oh well. Funny to hear you. You sound just the same.

I am.

Headline news and she's just the same.

That's right.

Did I make a big mistake, Sue? Did I blow my chance of fame? The reflected glory? My life with the Mystery Angel . . .

No.

I don't know anyone famous. Only you. And I don't know you. Do I? Been a while. Did I make a mistake?

I don't, well no. It was something you decided.

Not really. Didn't know the future, did I?

You didn't, no. I do though.

What's that Sue?

I do know the future. I haven't got very long. Are you able to talk?

What, are you ill? Tell me you're not ill.

I need to talk to someone, John, and I know we're not together, and it's been two years, but what's happening to me is very strange and serious, and I just

Yeah, that's right Barbara, we should probably be concentrating on the Wingram stuff. More on the Wingram stuff.

What?

We should be prioritising Wingram at this point . . . I know, that's what I keep telling him. You with me on this Barbara?

You're not alone, are you.

I think the other contracts can wait. In the light of, you know, what's arisen.

Can I call you later?

Tell him I'm gonna think about it Barbara, I'm gonna sleep on it. But you know my feelings on this. Wingram all the way.

Bye then.

Will do Barbara. Catch you later.

Bye John.

####### ####### ####### Hello? Yes? Mum? Oh shit I didn't check

Mantle

Oh no no no

Mantle Mantle Mantle Hardhouse listen carefully

I don't know you you just call

Been thinking about the situation

Well don't, just . . . wait. Wait. While you're there. Did you do this?

Working down my list here, what did I do, Mantle?

My bank account. Did you transfer money into my bank account? Like a lot. I mean for some creepy reason.

I'm here to help you, Mantle, I don't pay for that.

This is to do with you.

Nor do <u>you</u> pay for it, this is gratis, pro bono, con leche.

I don't understand.

That's why the likes of me

Why is this happening?

Mantle. Mantle. You okay, love?

No – no no I'm not –

It's not fair –

Hey don't cry hey now I can help you, I can find you a comfort zone but don't cry, love, it's just life

It's not life, it's death

Hey now, hey now

I'm not going on a journey

You're staying right where you are, you're going to sit tight there Mantle and the mountain can come to you,

I don't – I don't –

Hey hey. Hush. Hush. Trust Ed. Sshh . . .

I don't understand.

Let me help you Mantle, what's on your mind?

I was . . . wondering why I haven't switched you off.

Because you trust me Susan.

I don't at all. So I don't know the reason.

And where does it say that matters?

Well nowhere.

Nowhere.

Look no: wait. Why don't I switch you off?

Have you ruled out deep attraction?

Yep. I know why. It's because it's – it's absurd, and so are you. You come from its world. You're mates with it, aren't you.

Hey now. You go home, make yourself a cup of tea, count your blessings and I'll be over later with a game plan on my clipboard.

Okay. Yes. Okay. A clipboard.

You know it makes sense.

What colour's your clipboard.

It's a mental clipboard, Susan, a clipboard of the mind.

I said what colour is it.

What colour it's lime green.

*

Suse?

Suse?

Hi Min.

My God thank God it's you!

It's me.

I know and thank God it is! Where are you?

Here.

Where's here?

I'm at home. Something happened. So I'm just obeying orders. I've run out of willpower. I kept it on the top shelf in the fridge then I looked and there's just hummus.

People are asking, Suse, I've had calls from people, people saying wasn't that your stuck-up mate Susan in the paper (it's them saying 'stuck-up' not me) there's people asking where you live. Did Ed Hardhouse get hold of you? He's fielding calls from twelve media outlets! He's being a total star! They all want to know where you live and he won't tell them!

He doesn't know.

Um . . .

He does know.

He's very professional. He's all that's standing between you and, like,

Life being normal.

Life being terrible! Like for Marilyn Monroe! Like a, like some downward spiral of doom!

Is someone feeding you lines, Min?

What? No!

Anyway it's nothing. No one cares.

But they do, Suse! They're offering money!

Money.

To find out who you are! Someone said it's like Cinderella!

Cinderella was skint.

I know, I saw it on DVD!

And her godmother was kind.

I know and had magic powers.

Yes well they think I have magic powers. That I had an effect on something.

You don't have magic powers but you did have an effect on something! People are saying like the National Mood! You can get T-shirts saying DEATH WILL HAVE NO DOMINION!

That's, some sort of breach of copyright.

No, SUZY SAYS: DEATH WILL HAVE NO DOMINION!

That's, some sort of breach of everything.

I've got one, Suse.

Uh-huh. What colour.

Mauve with black writing, there's also black with white and white with green. I'm wearing mine, it's a medium but it's perfect.

Medium ho ho.

There's other ones you can get with Death's kind of you know, face.

You mean his skull.

His skull-face, but with a red ring round it and a line through it like meaning, you know, NO DEATH ALLOWED. *Stupid! I didn't get one. Becky Trapton did, in Funds. Oh yes and are you sitting down?*

I'm turning cartwheels in the garden.

You will be! Someone told Thomas Bayne!

Stop.

Yes hello! It's in the paper! Someone told him all about it and how you said the Words of the Poet, and people believed he was dead and then they didn't because he wasn't and he said you were 'a wise soul who spread rays of hope at a time of great evil'.

No no no no no

A wise soul who spread rays of hope at a time of great evil. You were! Come on, he says that! You know Thomas Bayne. He knows you. He knows the name Susan Mantle. If someone said 'Susan Mantle' to him he might look up from his, you know, his thoughts or yoga or learning his lines or something. Because he knows you. And I know you. I am one living person away from Thomas Bayne. If you were standing there one minute and suddenly not, for whatever reason, just suppose, there would be . . . there would be Thomas. I could probably call him Thomas. Our eyes might meet where you used to be! He might say can you join me in special meditation please, or like, could you help with learning these lines? you could read the other person's lines, like the ones Scarlett Johansson has to say or someone. I wouldn't know what to say. I'd probably say something stupid! I was once right next to someone who touched Jude Law's arm. I just froze.

Suse? Don't hang up, it also said

*

GOOD MORNING. WELCOME TO CSC BANKING SERVICES. IF YOU'RE A CUSTOMER, IN ORDER FOR YOUR CALL TO BE ANSWERED MORE QUICKLY, PLEASE ENTER YOUR BRANCH SORT CODE, OR FOR CREDIT CARD ENQUIRIES, YOUR 16-DIGIT CREDIT CARD NUMBER.

I don't know where those things are.

I'M SORRY. I DID NOT UNDERSTAND YOUR RESPONSE. IN ORDER FOR YOUR CALL TO BE ANSWERED MORE QUICKLY, PLEASE ENTER YOUR BRANCH SORT CODE, OR FOR CREDIT CARD ENQUIRIES, YOUR 16-DIGIT CREDIT CARD NUMBER.

Be a person. Grow a personality. Evolve. Please evolve.

TO ASK TO SPEAK TO A REPRESENTATIVE, PLEASE STAY ON THE LINE.

Come on, grow fins, something . . .

PLEASE STAY ON THE LINE AND A REPRESENTATIVE WILL BE WITH YOU SHORTLY.

Just separate into two cells, for me, for Susie . . .

PLEASE STAY ON THE LINE AND A REPRESENTATIVE WILL BE WITH YOU SHORTLY.

PLEASE STAY ON THE LINE AND A REPRESENTATIVE WILL BE WITH YOU SHORTLY.

PLEASE STAY ON THE LINE AND A REPRESENTATIVE WILL BE WITH YOU SHORTLY.

Darwin you're full of shit.

PLEASE STAY ON THE LINE AND A REPRESENTATIVE WILL BE WITH YOU SHORTLY.

PLEASE STAY *Hello how can I help you.*

My name is Susan Mantle. My branch is on Rosemead Avenue in Mersham. I'm on the line. Help me.

Right, just getting you up here on the screen . . . great, there you are. How about we kick off with your account number.

I can't find my chequebook right now and I don't know it.

The eight-figure number.

Oh, well, is it 00000000?

Not possible I'm afraid!

Okay is it 00000001?

Again I'm afraid not.

Because I just told you I didn't know it, didn't I? So it's pointless asking me. So I might as well try everything.

Righty-ho. Then I just do then need to ask you a couple of security questions.

Look someone paid an enormous sum of money into my account.

Oh. That's handy.

Yes, very, but I'd like to know who it was.

Yes of course, I'm sorry, if I could just ask you a couple of security questions.

I don't want any information about anyone else's account, just my own.

If I could just ask those security questions.

Ask the security questions.

If I might just have your mother's maiden name.

Carpenter.

Excellent.

Thank you.

And the name of your first pet.

Mike Bridges.

I'm sorry?

Mike Bridges.

Mike –?

Bridges. We had a ginger cat called Michael Bridges.

'Michael . . . Bridges', good; righty-ho. And if you could let me know of any standing orders connected to the account.

What?

Any standing orders going out on a regular basis.

Yes. Right. Amnesty International. Five quid or something.

And finally if I could just have details of your most recent transactions.

What?

Any recent incomings or outgoings.

That's what this is about. Someone paid five hundred and eighty-one thousand two hundred and thirty-two pounds into my account today, without asking. That was what was incoming. And I just, funnily enough, want to know who it was.

Now I'm afraid that won't have shown up yet on our system. And without the account number –

I drew out forty quid on Monday.

Could you give me the terminal details?

The, terminal details. I don't have the balance information thingy statement in front of me. I don't have anything in front of me I'm not really here at all.

You see that's what I'm looking for, that would tell you, any recent incomings or outgoings and all the numbers we could possibly want.

The numbers.

Recent outgoings.

But not that recent.

Now we are getting our system upgraded.

I paid in four hundred about a month ago. I don't know where the statement is it's in a drawer. You said you'd help me, the voice said you'd help me.

Could we have an exact date on that 400, it is a security requirement.

Can you not see the five hundred and eighty-one thousand two hundred and thirty-two pounds on my account?

I'm afraid that won't have shown up yet on our system, but we are getting our system upgraded.

Carpenter. Mike Bridges. Amnesty. Four hundred pounds about a month ago, for fuck's sake. You want to know what colour's my underwear?

If you'd like to tell me. We are a personal bank.

Righty-ho, I tell you one thing, strictly off the record, that figure rings a bell.

It was you, wasn't it, you sent me the money because I sound so helpless you fell in love with me you simply got too personal.

No! Well, joking aside! No, no well it happens to be pretty much exactly today's exchange rate for a million dollars US. It sounds like an American donation, a very generous one.

Donation? Donation to what? There's nothing wrong with me.

Oh I know that!

You don't know anything.

I'm really sorry to be not more helpful. My name's Alastair.

Righty-ho. When will it show up on your system <u>Alastair</u>.

Oh I <u>should</u> think in the next twenty-four hours or so.

And you'd be able to tell me the name of the donor <u>Alastair</u>.

Well then I'm afraid we're in the area of the donor's privacy rights. If the donor wishes to <u>be</u> anonymous

Go away Alastair

Goodbye Ms Mantle though I do hope

Go away

*

####### ####### ## *Hello who's that.*

Sue?

Can you talk.

At this point.

It's okay to be seeing someone John. I am. I was.

I know but, that said . . .

She might not be okay to have you talk to me?

I didn't say that.

I need to talk to someone, John, someone who knows me.

Pressure of fame type of thing.

Well, no, not exactly. It's more like, a weird turn of events.

Fuck!

What.

Trying to put out my cig, burned myself like a twat.

Poor you.

No but, shit. Go on. I've stopped self-mutilating, go on.

Do you, do you believe at all in the supernatural?

Kind of, ghosts and that.

Ghosts and that. Seeing into the future and that.

I dunno. Try me.

What do you mean try you.

I dunno, just wasn't sure what to say. I guess I mean be more specific.

Okay. Well you know I was filmed by those people the day of the bomb, when Thomas Bayne wasn't killed?

Well yes it had caught my attention, funnily enough.

Mm, well what also happened is that a huge sum of money just appeared in my bank account, and both things were foreseen by an old woman I went to in Victoria.

That's what I told him!

What?

I told him, Karen, I said Look, Geoff, these Wingram people want answers and they want them now!

I want answers now.

I know, but Geoff's saying they can wait, it's not a business in that sense, there's not exactly shareholders involved, you know what he's like.

Yeah, I do, typical Geoff, but the old woman also said I would die. John.

I know, I know, but some of those people they'll say anything Karen . . .

Tell Karen she's not going to die, John.

No way is that the case, Karen, absolutely no way and I made that crystal clear at the meeting.

Thank you John.

I respect that, Karen, and I think that when we meet we should bring all of this to the table.

When could we meet, John?

I have to get back to my calendar on that Karen, to be honest with you it's chocker.

Do you want to meet, at all.

Let's sleep on it, Karen, but my message is the same. The Wingram project is key and it's where we should be focusing.

Is that a yes.

Essentially yes but I'll get back to you on details. About your earlier question regarding the Victoria account, I'd just chalk it up to experience and move forward Karen.

Yes?

Will do. Will do. Will do. Bye.

*

####### ### Min.

Omigod thank God we got cut off! I thought you hung up!

I did hang up.

Omigod you did? You hung up?

Wanted quiet. So I'm sitting in my attic. Working on the Wingram stuff.

What? You're sitting in your attic?

With a torch.

Ugh! Spiders!

Bring it on, who cares, I'm in the hands of Mrs Sage.

No but yuk. And it's the wrong kind of thinking at this time, Suse, you need people like me we're batting for your corner.

Batting for my corner. That sounds like Ed Shithouse talk.

But he's right, well it is, but he's right Suse, we both are!

You told him where I live.

That is <u>so</u> not true. It's almost like the total opposite. If anything I didn't. As if I would, when I'm only your oldest friend and there's just no way. I'm leaving work in about eight seconds.

Everyone's going to come here.

Again, totally not true. If Ed did find out where you live, and he will, it's his kind of business to, but I won't tell him but he will, he'll what he'll do is look after your interests and no one else's he stresses that Suse it's win-win.

Win-win what's that a fucking panda.

Your language! How can you lose?

How can I lose, I can lose by going with what happens. Weird shit has started happening to me and I can go with it and things can keep coming true on me, or I can swim against it so different things come true and I get my life back.

Wow. I think you're losing it Suse.

What's the last thing I'd ever do on a nice day like today? Sit in the attic in the dark with a torch, surrounded by spiders and boxes of dead toys. So here I am. Living my life.

Here's what I think. I think it's not a situation really where you can you know run away from your kind of like duties. I mean, it's a situation you in a way created and I'm not blaming you Suse but still. This whole Death thing's like a craze, how it won't this and it won't that, I mean other people were just crying, they say tens of thousands of them it was a moment of . . . National Outpouring it said in The Times! like Di in a way but more as if she hadn't, you know, been there that night, hadn't gone through that revolving door towards those, what happened which was like her fate. There were people who, you could say, passed away, but it's like you, <u>you</u>, put a stop to it. You were the one who, what they're saying is looked it in the eye. Fate, almost. You looked it in the eye and said it would have no dominions which means it would have no lands by the way. What did you mean it would have no lands? I can ask you as your oldest friend.

Miranda. I'm rich. Someone put a million dollars in my bank account.

No. Way.

Someone put a million dollars in my bank account.

Shut. Up.

I think it was Thomas Bayne.

My. God. The cards, the cards!

Crystal ball.

The crystal ball, the crystal ball! She didn't use cards!

I don't know how he did that. He needs to have known all the code numbers. The bank won't tell me anything. But they can't just let him to do that. Can he just do that because he's him?

I, am, totally, just, I was standing up, I'm not now, I'm just, here, on the floor, like, spread out like you know, people are totally looking at me, someone's calling an ambulance almost.

Stand up again, Minni. Cancel the ambulance. Talk to me.

'kay.

Fame. Then money. Then a journey over earth and sea, and meeting a tall dark stranger, I say 'no', I say 'yes'. Then I,

You . . .

Exactly.

Die!

Thanks Min.

That total bitch I can't believe her.

Right. But there was something about the money. There was a condition.

Thomas oh it must have been! It says here on page 9 he said in a statement: 'she' meaning you! 'is a wise soul who spread rays of hope at a time of great evil'. I'm taking incredibly slow breaths right now, I'm going to breathe into a paper bag if I can find one. Can you wait a second?

There was something about the money. There was a catch but I don't think I wanted to know, because I don't know, I can't remember. I'm going to sleep in here tonight.

If it's anything like a film I saw with Helen Blockley not Helen Blockley Laura Hacknell that time with all those teenagers who should have died and didn't, did you see that? They all had accidents anyway so Death got what he wanted in the end there was a girl in the kitchen that was gross I thought with the wires I was just I was totally not looking. But she didn't deserve the money in the first place.

I didn't deserve the money in the first place. No one deserves money in the first place.

Keep out of the kitchen Suse. Or don't try making waffles when you're wet is one moral.

I wouldn't enjoy the money? Well I don't. Mrs Sage said I'd have it and I do and I don't want it.

But Suse! Just cos one little thing came true! There's still things that didn't!

Yeah I didn't die yet.

I. Know. A. Millionaire. Just saying the words!

Just because the fame came true, and the money came true,

It doesn't mean it all will!

Why doesn't it mean it all will? In a story it all would.

Well I dunno. You're the reader.

No. In a film it all would. You're the filmgoer.

I am, you know. I suppose! But it's not a film is it or a book or anything it's life, no one like pays to watch it, no one eats popcorn while it's going on!

Everyone eats popcorn while it's going on.

I'm talking to A Millionaire. About popcorn!

I wouldn't spend the money?

You have to! Wow. What was next. The tall dark stranger!

The journey. I would journey over earth and water . . .

Well, don't! Stay there and wait for us!

Us?

I mean me. Don't set out on a journey.

What if I have already? I was thinking, what if my tours were the journey? they take some hours, over earth and water.

But you got fired, you don't do that any more.

What if the order's wrong, I mean the sequence? What if it's just a rough thing, maybe the journey's been and gone.

That's not the journey.

Maybe It thinks it is.

Maybe what thinks it is?

The, well. It.

But there's no such, you know, you said that in your famous quotation.

I didn't say there was no such thing. And it's not my

No it's Derek Thomas no but you said It wouldn't get us! You did say that or you meant it.

Min. Listen carefully: I'll only say this once: It, will, get us.

But

It will get us.

But that's almost like you're just chucking in the towel Suse like saying it will have dominion when in fact you said it wouldn't. It's your claim to fame!

And you have it in green and mauve so it must be true.

Mauve and black but no. I'm not saying that. You can't go around believing what you read on I mean come on. Earth to Suse!

If, if It thinks that was the journey, that means the next thing is the tall dark stranger I say no to till I say yes to. Nigel Pilman wants to come round. I told him not to, I dumped him but he might anyway and he's a tall dark stranger.

But he's not a stranger. You got off with him! I can't believe you dumped him.

Maybe It . . . thinks he's a stranger. Maybe It . . . is not that bright you know? Or maybe It . . . is an alien and doesn't understand. Maybe It missed that part, maybe It was getting a round in, maybe It, is a bit like us and was pissed and can't remember how it went. Maybe I'm in the hands of something that's a bit . . . useless.

Woo. Scary. No. No I don't think 'it' – now I'm saying it! – I don't think 'it' drinks, cos, because, if you think, the drink would just all spill right out between his bones. Plus he's got no liver so he can't sort of . . . I mean, that's if he looks like people say. In legend. I don't believe that for a moment.

It was just a coincidence and I know that, I do. I was crying because Mrs Sage was so nasty and I'd done nothing wrong. And they happened to be filming, they were looking for people crying.

Everyone was crying. (I was but behind the scenes.)

Everyone was crying. But about something else. They put me on the news. So they put me in the papers. So someone showed it to the film star, and the film star is a jerk so he sent me money. Why would he send me money?

You just said Thomas Bayne was a 'jerk'. When he knows your name. He knows of your existence and you called him a 'jerk' that's like stop the world.

Why would he send me money?

Like, as a thank you.

For what? Does he actually think I brought him back to life?

One thing I know, Suse, in these difficult times, is that Thomas Bayne is a deep, complex person, and a very loving one.

And a very rich one.

A very giving one. He's very spiritual, there was a thing about him like a pullout.

What do you mean there was a thing about him like a pullout.

Like a sixteen-page glossy free pullout this morning. In this is it in the Mail: he's so spiritual, where is it. Not religious, cos that's about telling other people what to do and how to live and stuff? but spiritual which is totally the opposite. You can do like whatever and so can anyone else I mean good deeds, you can't do bad deeds that's like letting down the Elders but there's no rules about how you actually live as long as it's according to they have these twelve kind of laws?

Who has twelve kind of laws?

The, where is it, here it is, The Foundation. It used to be called the Order of The Gift but it's not called that any more, cos some of the people in that did some I don't know they let down the Elders. I'm just walking out of the building.

Who are the Elders?

It doesn't say. It's mysterious. Thomas is not one of them, he's at a lower level which is incredible in a way but he is. There's people higher but their identities are kept secret. On the lowest level it says there's like a million followers. You wear a pale blue wristband. But at higher levels you have other colours like indigo, magenta, and ultra-marine (meaning really marine, or really blue) there's a pyramid of colours. There's an eye in the pyramid. Don't go on a journey Suse.

If <u>It</u> thinks I've made the journey already it doesn't matter what I do.

Then you have to worry about the next part! It's like a great big kind of – game! But not obviously, any you know, fun.

Min. I need you to do something.

Yes! What?

Find Dawn Sage, go and find her.

I don't want to know –

Min –

I don't want to know I'm going to die –

She's not going to tell your fortune, I just want you to ask her why she said that to me. If you need to pay her I'll pay you back.

I'm not paying her! She'll start seeing stuff!

Tell her I want to know how to make the things not happen.

Make the things not happen?

Make the things not happen.

I don't think you can do that, Suse.

Tell her I'll pay her more.

But it's like, you've already had your go.

Tell her I'll pay her a million dollars to make the things not happen.

What? Then you won't be a millionaire any more!

Yes and you'll drop me.

I would so never drop you, Suse. You can't see but I've got my hand on my heart. My right hand on my, well, one heart.

Look. Just tell her. Tell her I understand I upset her in some way, which is why she said those things, but let her know I don't wish to go down this road any further, I want details, I want to know more, and I can pay, and I will pay.

I'm writing this all down, as there's quite a lot.

Take your hand off your heart, Min, it's easier.

I had done that.

Thank you Min.

This is so like a movie.

No it isn't.

It is for me, I'm like the friend, I'm in loads of scenes.

Please just find her Min. She's on the corner of St Anne's Street and Adair Road, there's a sign.

With the spiral curtains.

The spiral curtains.

*

ALLO ALLO. NOUS SOMMES PAS CHEZ NOUS. LAISSEZ-VOUS UNE MESSAGE, S'IL VOUS PLAIT. HELLO HELLO. WE ARE NOT AT THE HOUSE OF US! LEAVE YOU A MESSAGE IF IT PLEASES YOU!

Mum. Or Dad, but this is sort of to Mum it's Susan. It's just to say I – try and go with this, Mum . . .

I went to this fortune teller, I was trying to tell you. The fortune teller said I'd be famous, then the thing happened with the mistaken identity and the, you know, crying, and television footage and there's T-shirts and shit. Sorry that just slipped out.

She: said I'd be rich. And now someone, and I think it's that film star who I wasn't crying about, someone put a million dollars in my bank account. I'd no idea you could do that. You don't believe this, of course I don't either, but it's true I've got the bank slip in my, in my hand and it's only . . . then there's also a thing about a journey, meeting a stranger and, agreeing or something, saying yes and . . .

The next day she said that's it. The fortune teller said that's it, it's over the next day. For me. So. All I want to say, or ask I suppose, is * does this and there goes the bell to say no one in the world is listening to something they'd be laughing at if they were.

ALLO ALLO. NOUS SOMMES PAS CHEZ NOUS. LAISSEZ-NOUS UNE MESSAGE, S'IL VOUS PLAIT. HELLO HELLO. WE ARE NOT AT THE HOUSE OF US! LEAVE YOU A MESSAGE IF IT PLEASES YOU!

Just to finish, is there anything about this that makes any

Susan.

Mum!

Just walked in, heard you rabbiting on and I thought I'd pick up then I thought well she'll only rabbit on again from the start, so I listened till you ran out of tape.

Okay Mum thanks for that. Did you get a bicycle then?

I beg your pardon?

Dad said you went out to buy a bicycle, I'm making conversation.

Oh yes a bicycle. No. Fermé.

Bloody French.

No it's very civilised, I should have known, that's all.

Okay Mum.

You know what you just said sounds like total tosh, don't you?

Does it?

As for having a million dollars I'd suggest that the honest thing to do is report it to your bank as a computer error. Sorry.

Would you not like me to have a million dollars, Mother.

You don't have it, pure and simple. You haven't earned it. Mind you, I can't think of any millionaires who have earned it.

Still getting your European Guardian eh Mum.

Well can you?

No. Okay. But I have got it, Mum, somehow, that money and I'm frightened, I feel helpless and powerless and sort of lonely, can we call that a sub-text, would that help you to maybe, care a bit?

Susan. Whatever the whys and wherefores of how you've been credited with this windfall, I'm not sure a single late-night appearance on a satellite channel really constitutes fame, do you?

I'm in the newspapers Mum.

You're in tomorrow's chip paper Susan. Is anyone advising you through all this nonsense?

There's some sort of TV guy who keeps calling, he's so sleazy, but, people are coming here to find me and I can't go anywhere because it's a journey, so I think I'll stay here but I'm trapped Mum I'm trapped I feel cornered I feel cornered I spend time in the attic I sneak around the house I –

Susan, Susan

I just want you to say it's nonsense!

It is nonsense, Susan, it's shit. Shitshitshitshit okay?

When the bomb happened I was upset, but it wasn't about the bomb, it wasn't about Thomas Bayne. I was crying about the fortune teller, I said, and they just think I – didn't I leave a message?

Well it's not exactly why we came out here, you know Susan to hear messages.

No. No. No I suppose it's every day there's a picture in all the national papers of your only child crying, and I'm sure you get used to her being called a Mystery Angel who brought the most famous film star in the world back to life and now has some sort of weird hold over death in the national consciousness. I'd find that pretty tedious after a day or two.

Now you're just upset.

I'm not upset. I'm upset but I'm coping, I don't need anyone to fly back I mean truly, don't fret. You can stop packing now.

You know,

Put away the cases. Passports in the dresser. Cancel the limo.

Susan, if I thought for a second you were involved in anything you couldn't cope with I would be on that plane faster than you can say

Zbigniew Jackson

No I think it's delightful that your picture is in the paper, and that your face popped up on a satellite show. You know what the news is like when there isn't much to say.

A Hollywood film set was bombed by terrorists for the first time ever and over a hundred people died including two and a half film stars and everyone's claimed it and no one knows who did it. There's a bit to say.

It takes their minds off things. If it's all about death and bloody faces and bits of people, no one's going to buy the damn paper are they? This is so obvious I don't know why I'm telling you. I forget that you were once an 'A' student at a top university.

Was I. Blimey.

It's just been a very long silly season.

Note to hostile civilisations of the future. Avoid attacks during the silly season, no one thinks you mean it.

This is so like you.

It is me.

I'm sure someone's pointed it out to you ad nauseam that it's 'Death shall have no dominion', not will have. Death shall have no dominion. It's not a case of whether Death wants to have it.

Thanks Mum.

The Poet Laureate says that on page 26.

The Poet Laureate is in the tabloids?

No this is the Guardian. There's a whole section of articles about how absurd the tabloids are to even give this 'Mystery Angel' house room. I have to say I'm with them. They say it's medieval, like a weeping virgin or some such.

I was weeping, Mum, they're half right.

Makes me really quite uncomfortable Susan this picture. I thought I might see you in the Guardian one day, but, well, not like this. I mean you're crying, but you also look focused and intelligent. Perhaps they think you're a Guardian reader.

Death shall have. Shall I write it a hundred times.

Their expert thinks you're twenty.

That's nice of their expert. Is he tall and dark.

No, he's an old gentleman with glasses. He thinks you're probably a university graduate.

Not much gets past ol' four-eyes.

Well you know a line of poetry. You're thought to live in south-east London.

Out of date Mum. I'm known to.

They think you'll be easy enough to track down.

So do I.

It says Dylan Thomas wasn't actually a Welsh speaker.

I know that.

The Poet Laureate reckons this may give poetry a bit of a boost. He says it's about time. There's also an Anglo-Caribbean male here who says it might be the new 'Hip Hop'. MC ReeJekt is his name big R big J too many Es. Mr and Mrs ReeJekt must be very proud.

Do you mean a black man, Mum?

He says he's a huge fan of Shakespeare. He's certainly huge there's a picture. He's got a regular column now. No it's a nine-day wonder, Susan. Not even a nine-day, how long's it been,

Three days Mum, it's been forever.

A five-day wonder at the most. Then come out here for a, I was going to say holiday but it's all holiday to you so perhaps I'll say a change of scene. And by that time it will just be a silly memory, an embarrassing thing you did that unfortunately everyone came to hear about.

Thanks Mum I'll look forward to that.

Your father is dying to speak to you. (I told you Alec I'd be gone at least two hours.)

(You did indeed I'm all over the shop but look she's in the papers!)

(I know she's in the papers.)

(Marie can you get me some – Marie? Marie! Never mind! It can wait its turn in the queue!)

Hello? Someone?

Sukey!

Dad.

I'm a step ahead of your mater! Monsieur Oliveira went by the shop that sells the British dailies! I read three articles back to back! I'm told I did a little waltz on the terrace.

Dad.

Now what's this about a fortune teller. It seems the plot is thickening.

Dad she said I'd be famous. Now I'm in the newspapers. She said I'd be rich and there's a million dollars in my bank. She said some other things, she was quite exact, then she said I was going to die. I wanted Mum to reassure me but she went out to do her hair.

She's on some expedition or other!

Multi-tasking great that's vital. Look I'm only in the paper because this old hag made me cry.

Ma fille de la paparazzi! Don't let anyone drive you through any tunnels eh?

What?

Only joking! Get him breathalysed first!

Good one.

Hm, I'm going to get these articles laminated, Sukey, otherwise they'll just perish in the heat. It's very warm, but not abnormal for the time of year. La belle Midi, you see! Now, look at this, this is a deal of rum, what do you think of these statements . . .

What statements?

From your friend, Mr Thomas Bayne! Will we be meeting the famous Mr Bayne any time soon?

No. What statements?

Right here in the Review section. Monsieur Oliveira brought the papers, he's being very helpful. Bit of a charmer in his français style. Full of good pointers for living in these climes.

What's Thomas Bayne say?

Well, let me find the right page, it's always the

Last page you look at.

It is it's . . . it's not what one would say. He's in Sardinia it says it says he would have been in Libya to meet the survivors, 'but for security concerns'. ***I would like to express my sorrow at the loss of my dear friends and beloved co-workers in this appalling atrocity****. That bit's up to snuff. That's what the Queen called it.* ***I would also like to express my gratitude to the perpetrators of this act, who have unknowingly transported my dear friends and my beloved co-workers through a portal to a place of dazzling light and simplicity.*** *You hear that Sukey?* ***They had reached their time and have been fulfilled in the force of the Bestowing Sublime.***

You what?

I wish all of you Lightness. *Then there's a squiggle that must mean his name.*

Does he mention his next film?

Er . . . not here, no. But the Torygraph has a jolly nice picture of Keira Knightley and says she may feature. Where'd I put it . . .

I don't need to see that, Dad, I'm a straight female plus this is a phone call.

That's rather a queer statement isn't it Sukey?

I mean I can't see what you can see and I don't need to see Keira Knightley.

I mean Thomas Bayne's statement, is it a religion?

No Dad it's spiritual.

Ahh . . . Well it seems to give him great comfort.

It's got Elders and there's an eye in the pyramid.

Yes I'm looking at it now. It's looking right back!

I need to ask Mum something.

She went off with Oliveira for some damn thing. Air-conditioners maybe, he's our local fixer. Gives us good pointers.

Okay Dad I have to go.

And I have to . . . sit on la terrasse, sipping a little chablis perhaps, reading about my famous daughter! Not just a pretty face!

Close.

And I wish you the Bestowing . . .

Sublime

That's the feller!

Hello? Suse?

Did you do it.

Yes. I did.

And?

The spiral curtains are there like you said and it looks like someone does live there or did but there's no sign and no name and no one was in and we've tried three times.

We?

I mean me, I mean I've tried three times.

Three times.

It looks like the witch might be dead!

Or on holiday.

Yeah or on holiday. Or, and this is weird, but I've been thinking, can I run this by you?

Run it by me.

Or, third thing . . . she never existed . . .

What?

She never existed . . .

She existed.

You hear what I'm saying Suse? Or: she never existed . . .

She existed.

Are you sure?

Yes.

Okay. I'm just checking all the, the angles

*

####### ####### ####### Dad?

Well. You know what.

What, Dad, what's up?

I've been thinking.

What, Dad.

I've been listening to your message all day and now I'm sitting out here at the cocktail hour and you know what I'm doing I'm cogitating.

Which message Dad?

And it won't happen like that.

What won't?

This is the thing: she caused you to cry, am I right?

Yes she did that Dad.

She caused that to happen, so she herself, she affected the, time-space, you know, stream of, continuum kind of chappy, she influenced it herself, which I think is probably cheating in that lark do you not think? though I imagine that's not the term they use.

Hm.

Not playing fair, you see. Moving the goalposts.

I like that, Dad, that's good, you're right. If I hadn't gone to see her I wouldn't have cried, I don't cry often, do I?

Well obviously when the lion died in that wardrobe book

I mean this century

No, true, true, and of course he comes back to life! You were happy then, more tears!

And if I hadn't cried I wouldn't have been filmed, no one would have known who I was, no one would have sent me money, I like that, Dad, you're right, she can't mess with life like that.

No she can't do that at all, I'm sure it's a rule of the guild.

Yes!

He does come back to life, doesn't he? I know he's around at the end, the lion.

He does, he is. Okay. Okay:

So I'm sure the thing is to not think about it! All the trouble's been caused by thinking about it! So don't think about it!

Okay Dad I won't.

Promise?

Promise.

Okay.

Good on you Sukey.

What shall I think about?

I don't know! Les garçons, I suppose!

That's amusing.

Hm.

I'm in the garden, Dad.

Ah. La jardin.

Le jardin.

It's not a boy or a girl it's a bloody garden! So there!

I need to talk about old things. I'm thinking about you and I making bonfires Dad.

Bonfires, yes, we did in olden days. You and I, you and me . . .

You did, and I helped, getting sticks and leaves.

The Lion, the Witch, and the Magic Wardrobe.

That's the chappy, Dad.

Time for bed, says Zebedee.

O-kay . . .

Whereabouts are you sitting?

On the little bench at the end. Watching the lights come on in other houses. I can see Bonner in my bedroom window, big fat round silhouette. He's staring at me, he's wondering why I'm not fixing him his tuna morsels. He's quite puzzled by that. Not offended, just puzzled.

Good old Bonner. Wish I was back there sometimes! Not often though. It's very beautiful here Sukey. I'm going to have a G'n'T on the terrace in a minute! It's that evening hour of the day!

No clichés for you eh Dad.

Just a slice of lemon, ice, chink-chink, chin-chin. We're an hour ahead of you lot!

Us lot. Other thing is, now I look,

What's up, Sukey?

It's the street, Dad, our street, Hazeldene Avenue.

Old stomping ground!

It's, what's happening there's, there's hundreds of headlamps, Dad, there's,

What's that?

There's a floodlight shining from across the road. God it makes it light as morning. Or like, lightning that's, stuck here, it's just,

What's going on there Sukey?

Everything Dad. The doorbell's ringing and ringing, like there's no one left but children.

Are you going to answer it?

They're coming round the side Daddy they're laughing.

They're laughing at everything

You will journey over earth and water

*

<u>*Plum Chard, Assistant Manager, Silverlines Tours:*</u>
'She was a super girl in and of herself, Susan Mantle, a super girl. But I would have to concede there were rumours about well, her work practices. There was perhaps it's fair to say a shortfall in terms of her responsibilities as to the client I'm trying to think of an example. Yes. Oh yes yes yes. It was to do with Tower Bridge. That's it: I think she got her bridges mixed up because she said that there was residential housing once upon a time all along Tower Bridge, when I think she meant London Bridge, which is true, but she said Tower Bridge, which is not, and that twice a day, morning and evening, it's actually quite amusing in its own kind of silly context, but of course not so very amusing for the client paying good money! is that what she said, is: twice a day the people would have to evacuate their houses so the bridge could lift up, you know, as it does, in the middle, for the boats, and the houses would lift up with it, and everyone's furniture would slide down their living rooms and crockery would get smashed to absolute smithereens, and pets would be terrified, it's absurd if you think! And then after a while the bridge would return to its level position again and people could go back on to the bridge if you're with me, and start clearing up the mess. She said the houses could be rented very cheaply because of this inconvenience, and our Japanese friends are busily writing all of this down and of course, needless to say, it's an absolute fabrication and totally unacceptable in a reputable company such as Silverlines. Either that or it's well, if it's not malicious it's well it's sloppy. On the credit side, Susan Mantle was always prompt and punctual and tidily dressed. But, well; really; what's the word, what, an old-fashioned word, what folly.'

*

Stuart 'Stew-boy' Gable, former lover, student days

'I must say it's, well it's pretty bizarre to see her suddenly shooting to fame, I say fame albeit a certain kind of, it's odd, I must say, well, we did, objectively 'have' 'something' I think from this distance I can say I can also say yes, it finished insofar as it had a beginning and an end, well, yes, it had an end, I am very much, well, I've made a, my peace with that insofar as there was anything there to, well, as Stein has it in another context, insofar as there was a 'there there', because I'm looking at these old photographs, um, Ed, I see these old photographs and one is hard-pressed to remember we looked quite that way, 'we' as in the two of us, here, this must be in the cloister at, at Kings, when 'we' were 'together', quotes, you see the human body renews itself every seven years or so as I'm sure you're aware, um, Ed, what do I mean; well: that person who was what the person you call 'Susan Mantle' was, or did, in my company, here in the Fellows Garden this must be, at sunrise, or the company of what I refer to as 'myself' many years ago, many hundred of weeks, millions of minutes, billions of seconds is, now I look at these pictures of 'us', is not there, not; there; not in the images created by ions of silver and chlorine, not on the digital image you show me of a contemporaneous individual with that name, not in what we may conveniently term the mind. The memory of this particular person may persist or or or endure as a psychological event on a mental plane in a certain subjective space for example, 'mine', at times but at the end of the day, you can't, you can't live life like that it's, you know, it's nuts. Utter, you know, one has, one has a 'life', um, Ed, I mean, a life.'

☽

White, no sugar, right,

What was I going to say,

I'll just set it down here for you at your side.

What was I going to say, oh yes. 'Who are you?' was a question, and oh, 'What exactly are you all doing in my house' was a sort of supplementary.

You know what Mantle I'm telling you, some of those people down there I have never in my life set eyes on.

That's reassuring. Anyone seen my cat?

Ginge? Yeah, Ginge is good. He's down in the living room with the sound boys.

The sound boys.

Sshh, it's okay, Steve's a cat lover. Yussuf's allergic. Tosser.

Oh and of course you know Miranda Kaye.

How's that?

You've no idea who Minni is. Ed.

Oh, Mini-girl, course I do! You having a go? Oh yeah, Mini-girl is special. Going places.

Do you think before she goes to those places she might come up here? In her sort of capacity as my newest oldest best friend.

Yeah, sshh, everything's cool.

Is there someone called Nigel Pilman here?

Pale chap in the kitchen, could be him, could be.

Could someone throw him out please thanks he's a mistake.

It's kind of an ambience we got going down there. And then there's you up here, it's really beyond cool, Mantle, that you just stay in here. I think it redefines cool. You got Twiggy, bit before my time, you got

Julie Christie, that's my era, you got Kate Moss, can't last forever, you got Mantle. Beauty is freakish, it can never be foreseen.

Well thanks for that Ed. Is The Simpsons on down there?

That's right, just started.

It's all about Lisa.

There you go.

That meal was really good, where did it come from?

Some local Thai, the lads are on it.

I mean, you're really looking after me, Ed. And I appreciate that, but it also makes me sad, because it's all a misunderstanding and a waste of time.

Time itself is proud to pass with Mantle. Time itself.

Yep. I'm trying to think how I might put this in a way you might understand.

I welcome those guidelines.

I want to be able to say things that enter your brain in shapes you can recognise.

You can only try, Mantle, you're the one with form in lit-er-ah-ture. All them books on all them shelves, must have taught you something.

Mm-hm. So. Can you, 'level' with me?

I can.

Maybe we could both be 'on the same wavelength'.

I read you.

We could even 'talk each other's language'.

You know I reckon we're starting to. Exciting.

So Ed. Eddie. Ed Hardhouse. We do all understand, don't we (fine tea, I have to say) that my picture was in the paper because I was mistaken for someone being upset about Thomas Bayne. Yes?

You were a sight for the ages.

I'm still going, okay? And that, okay I'm not, maybe, an atrocity to look at, which means I'm like those same two blondes who are in the paper every year getting their A level results.

I hear what you're saying.

Good. You're three feet away so you should be picking it up. So I was crying for my own reasons, about my own troubles, and I said a line of poetry that made me feel better. And then, by coincidence,

I hear what you're saying.

It got filmed and it got scrambled up with this Thomas Bayne stuff and many thousands of mad people who adore this man

It's millions Mantle but I hear what you're saying

Millions of mad people think I had something to do with him surviving this bomb.

Sshh, quick rewind. It was Bayne who stated that you spread rays of light at a time of great evil. Now, no one thinks you magically got him through the danger Mantle they're not idiots the British public, but people take their cue from Bayne. If Bayne says you spread rays of light at a time of great evil then I'm sorry, rays of light at a time of great evil was what you spread. He's a star, Mantle. Look I hear what you're saying. But no one at this moment in time wants to know why you might yourself <u>believe</u> you were crying, Mantle. It's truly moved beyond that realm as of now. It's about timing. You know what it's about it's about time. It's about the right words at the right time, the right attitude at the right time, the right face at the right time. And at this very moment I'm gazing upon that face, Mantle, here we go. Just on the desk Roy.

Why is a man called Roy bringing a TV screen in here?

Sshh . . .

Why are you doing that, Roy?

It's okay Sue, it's okay Roy, sshh it's all good, it's all good . . . thanks Roy.

Could your friend Roy go and bring my friend Minni up from downstairs.

He'll do that, won't you Roy? See, off he goes. Now, because you're gorgeous, Mantle, and exceptional circumstances have brought me into your holy of holies, I shall explain all, or, or: as much as is humanly possible. I am yours for the grilling of.

I think you mean I can ask you questions.

Fire.

Right. Fire. Is this going to be on television?

That I can tell you. Yes.

Do I have to do it.

No.

So go away. Switch off The Simpsons, switch off the lights and all fuck off. Actually leave The Simpsons on. And the lights.

I think I'm in love with you Mantle. Not lust, as your expression would indicate: love, as mine would.

Actually can I get The Simpsons on that screen there?

Mantle. Recap. You say you're in here for your own reasons.

I've come in here because it's safe and warm. And I don't mind you downstairs because it was just so quiet in this house and I was feeling strange and you keep bringing me nice things. Could someone clear this tray away?

Wish. Command. (Roberta.)

It's like being ill in the old days. Whole world's at school. You know, you could see the time go by as you sat in bed, it was the only time you could ever see it, the time go by. Cost you a sore throat maybe, or a hot shivery feeling, or sometimes just pretend, but you'd actually witness that, sort of procession. Nine. Sun shining in. Ten. Blimey it's quiet. Eleven, cup of Lemsip, hello Mum look: a programme about maths, that beardy gent he knows his fractions. Bus goes by. Shadow cross the wall, thermometer in your cheek. Twelve. Little children shouting, little triangles of toast, tomato soup you spill getting comfy. Susan's Midday Garden. No one looks after me any more.

What is this genius on about. Hey meanwhile someone to see you. Couple of minutes tops. Mantle, here's Mini-girl: Mini-girl, you be a friend to Mantle she's rambling, rambling . . .

I'm home ill from school, Min, it's the only explanation. Are you all right? You look pale.

You don't know, do you Suse?

No. Whatever it is, same answer.

I don't know either, but they said I can't say a word!

Who's they.

The crew! Sky! Ed, who's making this all happen for you! He doesn't need to! This is real, Suse, this is going to be on TV! Ed holds the rights!

To me lying in bed in a jumper. I don't do porn, you know.

I'm sworn to silence!

Shut up then.

I . . . I can't!

I know. Can you tell me how many people are downstairs?

I don't think so!

Is it between five and fifty?

You can't tell him Suse!

Can't tell who what?

Whoever comes!

Whoever comes?

You were crying for him! I didn't say that!

What's the TV for?

I can't say what it's for!

It's okay, Min, don't say what it's for. It's just nice having it in case something comes on.

Something might come on. Omigod I've said too much. Don't tell them!

Don't tell them what?

That something might come on! It might not come on! Nothing might come on! Or nothing might not oh God!

Mini-girl what's wrong?

Ed I've had my two minutes, I've gone, I've gone!

That's one wired-up pal you got there Mantle.

Hardhouse.

Mantle.

Hardhouse. Is there something I should sign?

Do you want to sign something?

Not really.

It's the reality genre, Mantle, it's organic. Signing stuff, that's for people who want to make the same old chess moves, who don't believe it unless it's documented, duplicate, triplicate. Automatons, friend.

Sounds a bit negligent.

Yeah it is.

Are you looking after my interests?

Yeah. Me and the Mini-girl.

That's good. What are my interests?

Well your well-being, Mantle.

No. I don't have any interests.

Love, love . . . You got a load of books.

I can't reach them from here.

You want me to pass you a book Mantle? There's very little I wouldn't do, you know, I'm that smitten. Any special book? Any favourites?

No. Don't pass me a book. They're all. They're all very old books now, they look so far away.

You okay there love? This moving a bit fast?

Nothing's moving at all. Only me, sort of, west, adrift . . .

You just wait, gorgeous, you just wait.

What's Roy doing now?

He's setting up a camera. I just want you to be happy.

It's facing me.

That's right.

There's nothing on that TV.

That's right too.

Someone's outside the door.

Roy, could you palm the door open I think there's a visitation.

Nigel. I said our date was cancelled.

(Date. Right. Charming. This is warped, man. I come here, quiet night in, up the garden path, no one tells me you're, no one tells me it's, just no one tells me, someone's having a pop.)

Ed, Nigel has to leave now.

(She's not serious, Ed, she's under pressure and I'm here to take it off her. You know what: I just met Graham Forming. Forming on Five he used to do, he used to go totally awol on the commentary like Maradona. He'd say 'Goal' but it would last several seconds, so it would sound like this: 'Goaaal', but longer, I'm not doing it right, like 'Goaaaaal' and I just met him. Not a bad bloke, a professional. He's working on this show.)

Ed I want him to leave.

Come on son, let's go.

(Man, you're not serious.)

You heard. Roy, little help here.

(This is a total error of judgement.)

Mantle wants some privacy.

(Sure, but with me, yeah? We've done it five times, you ask her, in three ways.)

Out we go, son.

(I'll catch a beer with Forming, nobody's heard the last.)

And, exit.

That your beau, Mantle?

What do you fucking think. I want him out of here.

You can probably sense the relief in me, it's palpable. The lads will take care of it.

Who's the cover-girl on the landing Ed I keep glimpsing someone.

Make-up. Come in sweetheart, she's ready. Make an entrance.

(Hiya.)

Hello. You look like a nice girl. Can you protect me from this?

(No.)

Okay.

(You'll be fine.)

Okay.

(I'm Roberta De Coex. Hello! Do you need the bathroom?)

No. Do you?

(No.)

We're good then. Sisters don't need to do it for themselves. Should I tell you when I do?

(Yes.)

Okay. And you'll tell me?

(They want you to wear the T-shirt. The one that says SUZY SAYS.*)*

Okay. Which colour?

(This one, here you go.)

Oh. Lovely. An unbirthday present.

(Alice in Wonderland. It'll be over soon. Powder.)

What will?

(Close your eyes.)

Mmmm. That's nice.

(Do not go gentle into that good night.)

O-kay.

(Rage, rage, against the dying of the light. Fluff it up a bit, that's good.)

There you go.

(There we are. You're perfection, Susan.)

Thanks Roberta De something. Goodbye.

(Goodnight sweet ladies sweet ladies goodnight goodnight.)

Very literary crew you have Ed.

Hand-picked Mantle all over my head personally look, I think I'm getting the signal go go go. Sit up, it's not a game now, angel. Sit up and shine your light because you are a sight to see. You are prime-time, you are water-cooler, you will leave men weeping by the wayside for what's been. I'm going to sit right here and feed you lines, okay, but we'll cut around it in the mix. So just go with it, angel, it's reality, okay? it aspires to the haphazard.

Has anything started? I'm looking at a blank screen. Who are they on the landing?

Sshh, sshh . . .

Fucking poetry.

Don't do that angel. Don't say poetry.

What's going to appear?

Sshh . . . and:

(Steve clear.)

(Yussuf clear.)

(Stringfellow's.)

(Norfolk Broads.)

(Sydney Harbour.)

(Track it.)

(And we're rolling.)

Susie.

Susie. (Say something girl we're rolling.)

Oh I'm sorry. Yes?

Say you're Susie Mantle.

I'm Susan Mantle.

We're from Drop Dead Gorgeous on Sky, and nothing escapes us, Susie, and you're the girl of the moment, so we thought we'd come and pay you a call in your own back yard.

You did.

(That's the monitor, love, this is the camera.)

Hello there then.

But we find you in bed, Susie, what's that about, can you tell us?

Why am I in bed?

Why are you in bed.

Can I ask instead why are you all in my house. No I can't can I. Silly.

Why are you in bed Susie.

It's night time. Here's where I go.

And this is since Monday, when you made a most memorable contribution to a most terrible day. We'll then cut to the Dominion footage, probably dissolve into your weeping face.

Sounds good.

Everyone fine?

(We're good to go, boss.)

(Ayya Napa.)

(Lords on a Sunday.)

(Stamford Bridge.)

On we go. Now you couldn't have known what effect your words were going to have.

They had no effect at all.

A very modest girl. (Close in on the T-shirt.) And you couldn't have known, you couldn't have woken up on Monday morning knowing that the world's most bankable film star would know your name by Wednesday and that you yourself would be a TV star by Friday.

That is very true, Ed. I both could not and did not know that.

Well there's something else you don't know.

I thought there might be.

We have him on the line.

Oh for fuck's sake.

We, have, Thomas, Everett, Bayne, star of Hollywood, THE star of Hollywood, on the line, right now, from a secure location somewhere in Europe.

That's what this is? That's the secret?

Girl's in shock. (Close in.)

That's what this is.

Look at the monitor.

I can see him.

He can see you.

Fuck off.

(Tone it down a tad love it's less work for us.)

He can see me?

He can see you. You can't see much in the background because as I say, he's in a secure location, having survived the recent attempt on his life but that is Thomas Bayne himself, in the flesh, fresh from his ordeal, he's now finishing off his glass of I believe guava juice from his own estate and we understand he's ready to speak to you. Thomas?

Thomas?

Hi there is that Ed?

Loud and clear, Thomas this is Ed Hardhouse from Drop Dead Gorgeous in the United Kingdom of Great Britain, we have a girl here who I think you may know.

I think I do, you know, am I talking to Miss Susie Mantle of Mersham, London, England?

(She's a little speechless right now, Thomas . . .)

Miss Mantle! How are you my friend! Can you hear me?

Er. I'm all right.

That's fantastic.

How are you.

You know what I'm okay. I'm okay I really am.

Good. I'm. Sorry about your colleagues.

I'm sorry?

I mean, about the, what happened in Libya.

Well, I know, yes, but you know things happen for a reason, Miss Mantle.

Really.

Things happen for a reason. Things manifest themselves.

That's, comforting.

All you and I can do is allow them to reveal their purpose. Because you know I also feel that you and I have been brought together like this for a reason.

You think that.

How about that? You know Susie I think we're standing at a crossroads, you know in terms of reality, and history? I mean you spread like a whole ton of light into the world with what you said. It's kind of off of the scale.

Well, it was, it was a terrible thing that happened to all those people, and I hope the survivors, you know, get better, and if I cheered anyone up I'm glad. Now we can all move on maybe. It's just a line from a poem by

I've been hearing you're a modest girl, and I'm noticing that for myself!

By Dylan Thomas.

You don't have to cry any more, Susie.

I'm sorry?

You don't have to cry any more. The time for tears is past.

It is? Okay; thanks for that.

Death will have no dominion.

Yes it says so on my top.

You're a poet, Susie!

I'm not a poet.

You're a poet of the soul.

Excuse me, I'm not, and also: did your foundation place a million dollars in my bank account?

(What???)

There's a million dollars in my bank account and no one else could have done it.

(Bale out Mantle you can't ask that)

Hello? Can you hear me Susie?

Did you or your foundation put a million dollars in my bank account because I didn't want that.

Hello?

You can't do that without asking. I didn't need it.

Hello? I think we lost the connection for a moment there Susie but you know what? I have a proposition for you.

Susie?

All right what is it.

What is it, well maybe Ed there can bring you up to speed, can you do that Ed?

(Sorry we had a little glitch there yes I most certainly can Thomas. Take a deep breath there, Susan Mantle of Mersham London England, because we're flying you out there, read 'em and weep, to the Colosseum in the Italian capital of Rome, where next week the cream of the rock and film worlds will be coming together – and this is all being put together by Thomas's organisation as we speak – to raise money for the victims and survivors of 20/10. You'll be there as Thomas's personal guest for the evening, first-class flight paid both ways as well as accommodation in Rome's finest hotel. – Close in on her face. Come on Mantle work it.)

Did you tell her, Ed? Is she up to speed on the project?

(I told her, Thomas, she's gone a little quiet. – Stay close. Say something Mantle. Say oh my God, say fuck, jump up, dance, strip, do something fucking <u>watchable</u>.)

I want to go home but I am home.

(Death of me, this one, absolute death of me)

What I'll be trying to do in Rome is harness together many sources of lightness from the worlds of film, rock, fashion, really all the separate and connected worlds so in the process we manifest a kind of beacon of pure light.

(Mantle, you'll be there with him, at his side, in the photos. React, ya nutjob)

Death is an illusion, Susie, we all know that. And what you represent to me, Susie, is how one voice howling in the wilderness can speak louder than words. Or like, louder than, than

actions as we saw. And you have that power. It's about power. It's about love. It's about the power of love. The two kind of melded. And peace, world peace at this time. And the truth, and you, are kind of like an ancient speaker, or soothsayer, of truth.

I, look,

You know what, Ed, it's probably kind of a load for the young lady to absorb at this point in time, you can let me know

No I can let you know now, I really can't, I really don't feel I can go anywhere right now. Like Rome or. Anywhere. Thomas.

(She didn't just say that. Someone tell me she didn't just say that)

You know what, Susie? It's just incredible the lightness coming off you it's as if I can read you it's like reading Thomas Bayne in a re-gendered form. We are so, alike in so many – we're like it's off of the scale. And you know you could really, you know, have what, kind of, in the old way of thinking that we are very much beyond, 'insulted' me?

Kind of crazy, to think that, that that, that I, I could be 'offended', by you! You just would not have insulted me, would you, no way, probably not for the world, because you know Thomas Bayne simply does not traffic in those negativities, and even if he did, you have not, if you see, because, in this hypothesis, he, does not really allow those kinds of negativities into his space, but if you did, if you did, by your words, do that, he, I, would still only see lightness coming at me like you know some things are kind of like beyond words themselves. In many ways it's a time to return to the source, you know? and this little humble house of yours is, for you, in the confines of, of you, the source, so, okay. That bridging of lightness will have to wait for another time, another age. So thank you for that decision.

I'm glad you understand, Thomas. If it had been another time. There's you know I have a cat and I have to feed him.

(Jesus Christ someone shoot her, shoot her cat, do something)

You know, I have a cat too, Susie, back in LA, and I know exactly what you're going through. It's like. You know, cats . . .

(Someone fucking say something)

Cats are, you know, they're, they're almost they're it's like they're . . .

Kinda wise. Look: I am rendered very, you know, both in the old style of words 'disappointed' and also at the same time I'm kind of overcome with empathy relating to your reality, and you know, yeah okay, we thought it was possible this might happen, as Ed there was telling me you are a mysterious lady and I respect that, I respect all mystery, so I'm afraid we've been telling you a little kind of an untruth there, Susie, talking of truth, if anyone can. Jesus, for example, the Middle-Eastern male spiritual leader, was asking what that was in real terms.

It's a good question Jesus.

Are you looking at me, Susie?

Yes. Or no. An image of you. You're not actually a head in that box, are you?

Look very carefully Susie, can you see my pal here removing the blue background?

Yes. Is he your bodyguard? He looks like – she looks like – no no no no

Does she look like your best friend Mandy? Does the room behind me look a little like your kitchen Susie? Does this ginger cat look a little like your ginger cat?

Shit you're in my house. You're in my house you're holding Bonner

Hey there cutie,

He doesn't like being held by strange men, Ed, what's happening, help

('Safe house in Europe' Mantle, didn't say whose)

You brought Thomas Bayne round to my house

(Looks that way, soldier)

For a TV show

(You're a star, Mantle, ask the man up, tell him to bring the cat in)

Get him out of here.

(Someone get the cat out of here)

Not the cat get Thomas Bayne out of here.

(Are you fucking out of your mind? What did you just say?)

Thomas, can you hear me?

I can, you hanging in there young lady? Ed I guess that might be shock setting in

Look I know you've come all this way, I know you've been through a lot, Thomas, what with not dying in the attack and what with being on a yacht and so on, but, you know, I'd like you to leave now, all of you, everyone, please, please leave.

(Mantle, Mantle, take fucking five, Thomas Bayne is downstairs in your kitchen girl, feeding your cat. Get the man up here, he's a megastar, snog him, we'll have every paper on earth are you out of your mind?)

Go away, Ed. Go away, Roy, Steve, Yussuf, Roberta De something. Go away Nigel Pilman and the man who says goaaaaaaal go away Minni, go away Thomas Bayne, go away Thomas Bayne, my house is not a safe house. I'm going to sleep now for a long time and when I wake up I need there to be no one.

Ed?

It's okay, Thomas. (Cut. Switch it.)

Ed? Who can hear me? Can he hear me, is this working? Thomas Bayne does not do this. This is not what Thomas Bayne does.

Did that just happen?

Talk to him talk to him talk to him

Five's gone dead boss

Did we just witness

Shut up. Yeah Roy what's she doing

She's under the covers boss

Did we just witness

Roy can you maybe

Leave it leave it leave it

Can she do that?

Can she do that?

Team focus it's history cut to three Roy we need to see her face, Roberta, Roberta get Roberta to talk to him, we got a bit of a, where is she find her

He's what? He left? He left
Three's gone dead boss
Roberta find Roberta
They're both saying
They're saying Bayne split
Just close up on the sheet
Bring him in bring him in Ed says bring him in

No mate he's gone, they just pulled out the drive. We got it all tyres squealing everything he never said a word boss, what the fuck do we do now?

Fuck. Fuck. Fuck. And then again . . . Magnificent. Absolutely fucking magnificent. You see that daft cow lying in there? She just crapped on Elvis.

*

American tourist Randy Flosser of Sanction, Ohio, shot this film with his mobile phone on May 29th this year. You can see a girl standing with a microphone on the upper floor of a Dreamtours London tour bus, we've circled her, and Dreamtours have confirmed that that is indeed Susan Mantle obviously shot prior to the present time. We've added subtitles as the soundtrack is corrupted:

[MRS LORELEI FLOSSER:] WHAT'S SHE SAYING RANDALL?

OH NO THAT'S NOT RIGHT, THAT'S JUST [GASPS] OH NO. OH NO. THAT'S WRONG THAT'S JUST PLAIN WRONG!

WHAT'S SHE SAYING RANDALL?

[INAUDIBLE, TRAFFIC NOISE] LIKE KIND OF A [INAUDIBLE]

I DIDN'T KNOW THEY MADE CHURCHILL THE KING, RANDALL.

OH MY, THEY DID NOT. OH MY LORD THEY DID NOT DO THAT.

Randy Flosser:

'I do my research when I visit a place, I read up, I'm prepped. I do not expect to be told that Trafalgar Square is called Trafalgar Square on account of you could stand by Nelson's Column and hear the guns of the Battle of Trafalgar. From there, like from the Column. Like across the ocean, which is not to even get into the whole thing of, like, why would there be a Nelson's Column at that point, you know? There's a kind of a surreal, like it's unhistorical what's going down there. And

the whole thing of the tube. You know I read up about the tube I know all about the tube. It does not originate as a very narrow tube that the Victorians used for shouting vital information to each other. Not so. And it got 'expanded over time'? Well with respect, Ms Tour-Guide, (A) it's impossible, (B) well there's no B it's just not the case. I have examples here . . . we were on that goddamned bus an hour, you can hear on the recording what kind of distress my wife had to endure on account of this, of the actions of a single, what's this, here, Nelson was standing by something called the Grand Arch when he heard the guns of the Battle of Trafalgar and decided his country needed him. He was overheard to say to his friend Mr Hardy, who he had just been, what does that say, kissing? 'England expects every man to do his duty.' Oh and yes, they were playing marbles, so now it's the 'Marble' Arch. And this Mr Hardy went home to the county of Wessex and decided to become a novelist and you know what? We paid good money to ride that bus. That is one very screwed-up lady. You check it out. Go to Wikipedia.'

*

Minni Kaye, best friend:
'When he left, I was like, left in a total dilemma. Cos we've been chatting, and he's got to know me, and that was only totally ruined by what she did. People were totally polite to him, and when I was talking to him we had quite a few laughs me and him! I was nervous, but after a while I was put at my ease by Thomas, which he didn't mind at all me calling him and it was only her who was like, who did, what she did to him. I've still got this mug that I had a cup of tea in that he made! I don't think maybe he'd made any tea before. I've got clingfilm over it so there's no . . . y'know.

'People say he's like a bit mad with his philosophical you know beliefs, but he's a very complex and very deep man, and he does so much good in the world with his films, which tend to totally have a positive message, and he's very charitable with all his millions, I can say his millions cos they are millions.

'It's like, any other girl in the whole entire country or world would have been in that car with him like, in my mind's eye I was there in my mind, in the passenger seat in the dark I'd be asleep while he was

driving, or actually no we'd both be in the back, he'd have his own driver: 'No comment' he'd always say.

'It was not to be, but I think it maybe was, to be. There was a joke I was in like the middle of. He might never know the punchline, he might think I was just saying knock-knock which is ridiculous. Knock-knock. And then nothing. Unbelievable. He had to go and choose her I think she just like totally hates famous people.

'We were at school together, me and her, so it's not so much like we were friends as more like you know old friends. And now she's, now – things change in life, Ed, I've learned from this experience. I mean who does she think she is? She's turned totally into this girl who just stays in bed and doesn't care if we all die in a way. Which is uncanny, it's like the power of, you know, the show, your show, it's like it's bigger than things.'

*

University friends Chris Clamberton and Dr Lucinda Phipps-Clamberton MA PhD (Cantab) with their twins Rael and Malory

'Between you me and the gatepost a bit of a fruit-and-nutcake. In a good way.'

'Out of her gourd she was, the Mants.'

'And we miss her, we used to see her more.'

'The Mants was cool.'

'I cherish Susan Mantle, if that's not too strong a word, but having said that I should add that many of us did wonder what exactly she was going to, I should say . . .'

'Do with herself.'

'With her life Clamps yes.'

'Bright girl in a bright year. Thing is with our gang, and this is the thing, Loops, five years on, a lifetime in a way, what with the new arrivals, thing is: we did rather kind of pair off in a sense, there's us, you got Robs and Bernadette, you got Blabs and Alicia, you got Jills and Galen . . .'

'Brian and Mike.'

'Brian and Mike, they count.'

'Of course they count.'

'I'm saying they count, Loops, but you could also say in a kind of way we all paired off.'

'The Mants had Stew-boy though.'

'Yeah but she dumped Stew-boy. Which is so like the Mants. Yeah we all paired off.'

'I don't think we all paired off, did we Clamps? I know <u>we</u> did.'

'"For better or worse."'

'Pardon?'

'It's in the ceremony Loops: "for better or worse".'

'It wasn't in ours. You wrote ours.'

☽

Suse.

Suse. Suse can I come in.

You are in.

I did what you said Suse.

And.

There's nothing there. There's like twelve pounds something.

Really?

There's nothing there. You must have imagined it maybe. Here's your card though.

I saw it. It was whatever a million dollars is.

There's twelve pounds forty-five, or twenty-five, something five. You imagined it. It's gone anyway. So now you're not rich, you're not a millionaire and see? I haven't dropped you so you were wrong about that big time. Ha! You're still famous though, we both are, I'm famous! So it's like that came true! I mean no one said it would, but I knew it would happen in the end so it's still like mystical. I have a section in the show where they ask me what I think you'll do next. It's called With Friends Like That. I abbreviate it to Friends, then I can say I'm in Friends! Which I am.

You abbreviate it.

It means shorten it, yeah. They ask me why you just lie there in bed. Why I think you did what you did, to, what you did to him. He's cancelled work on all projects. Including The Book of Revelation. Which in a way means the terrorists won in the end.

I'm not saying they did, or that it's the end, it's only certain people and they're entitled to their opinion. It's just that, he, that man you did what you did to, him, is very much against the terrorists, and what you did was very much against <u>*him*</u>*, so in a way, and I'm not saying this Suse, in a way what you did was for the terrorists. Someone told me someone said that but I think it's total rubbish. To even mention the terrorist agenda.*

It's I suppose lucky for you they don't watch programmes like Drop Dead Gorgeous cos it's against their beliefs but they might, they're not living in the Dark Ages.

And apparently they're everywhere. All I'm saying is: film work has stopped on The Book of Revelation, due to what you did, and it was a film that was going to finally reveal the truth about everything and that might have ended the terrorism, who knows? There were rumours it was going to, just, tell the truth. I don't know I'm not a philosopher like Thomas I'm just an expert on a top-rated show and I'm entitled to my opinion, which is, that now it won't. Terrorism will go on. And I'm not saying you're anything to do with that because you're just not. You're so not.

But you are in the public eye at this point in time. There's people phoning in asking to feed your cat. There was one man wanted to eat catfood in front of you but I think they took him away. There are people standing outside in T-shirts with things about you in an organised group. Your old university adopted you as a mascot, but you don't have to dress up as an owl, it's honourable. Also there was that twelve-year-old girl they found in your garden with an axe but they promised her PlayStation3 and she handed it back.

The world's gone mad and I'm right in the eye of the sort of hurricane of that.

The eye's the calm part by the way and I'm surprisingly calm. I say surprisingly because I've just been told what they're going to do next. And you don't know.

And I'm saying this as your old friend: another person is coming.

Everyone loves this person. He was voted fourth coolest human on earth but that doesn't give it away. It was only one of many polls. If you turn this person down, or treat him like you treated Thomas Everett Bayne and I give him his full title, star of Prince of Peace 1,2 and 3, I will have some real trouble staying your closest friend and I say that.

I say that with Ed's full support, and Ed is looking out for you always Suse. This person, this mystery person, is a good person. He supports what you did to Thomas Bayne, that's his political position, he's an ico, an iclono,

Iconoclast.

Yeah apparently. He supports good causes a lot of which are green, and he wants to show you his support for you. He thought it was really funny what happened to Thomas, and I don't at all, I'm an iclonocast about that, but he called Thomas 'that Hollywood shit-for-brains' he said that not me on the radio and it was everywhere. He said what you did was an 'action'. Was it?

Anything could happen now Suse! You could become friends with him, the mystery person, we both could even, and I don't have any problem with that actually.

Miranda.

Suse, Susan.

I won't do what's expected. I can't. You know why.

I think Suse, I think this is bigger than that.

Bigger than being told I'll die Min.

You have your own show, Suse, your own segment in Drop Dead Gorgeous. I have a section in your segment called With Friends Like That. Ed asks me questions about you, your secret hopes and fears.

That I won't die. That I will die. Tell him.

It's not that kind of show, Suse. It's entertainment and it's life-affirming. People want to see you with this mystery person. Not in a relationship, no, definitely not. Ed and I talked about that and it's no way, it wouldn't work.

It's not life-affirming.

No it just wouldn't work. I'm thinking very much of, you could be friends with him and we'd hang out with him maybe as a threesome but not in any sense of, you know, he's a very moral person. He's a star, he's been through a lot. That court case, but he didn't do it.

I thought he was supposed to be a secret.

Oh, yes . . . no he is, he's a mystery, he's totally mystical. He may not have been through much at all, and no court case, and maybe he <u>*did*</u> *do it. I was just saying.*

Is he a tall dark stranger.

Is he a tall dark stranger.

Is he

Yes.

Is it Klaus Fold out of Vermin Jones.

God! No! I mean it might be. But no, not necessarily.

He's tall and dark, and I have some of his CDs, and he was in court, and it's pretty much exactly what they'd do next.

It might be but it might not be. It might well not be.

And he's a stranger to me.

Yes, but there are no strangers!

What?

There are no strangers, only strangers who are not yet friends.

What?

No wait: there are no friends, only strangers who haven't met. No,

Miranda.

Suse, wait,

Is it Klaus Fold out of Vermin Jones?

If you have a relationship with him it will spoil everything and I will never speak to you again. But it may not be him. And if you do to him, whoever, what you did to Thomas Bayne I will also not consider us friends any more in a real sense, Suse. Those are two, kind of, I've said my piece.

So what you'd like is for me to welcome him into my bedroom and hug him for the cameras like Ed wants, and then have biscuits with him and introduce him to you, like you want.

I'm not saying that <u>should</u> *happen. I'm not saying it shouldn't. I'm saying I would not have a problem with it. He is a moral person, if he's the mystery person, a poet and he may not be, he may not be on his way at this moment as we speak. All I want is I want things back as they were. Or quite like they were, but with perhaps you and me, like the friends we are, Suse, and have been, obviously knowing this mystery person and going to his concerts with him in his car. I mean, if concerts are indeed what he does. He may be a film star, then it would be film premieres, or the Oscars, and we'd take it in turns to be the one on the, but it may well not be. It may be more like a sportsman, or a vet. Then we'd take it in turns to pass him the, whatever, scissors please, or eyedrops. So: I'm going to just put this mobile phone here by the bed, and, leave you in peace for now, Suse, and is there anything you want?*

No, so, good. We're all depending on you Suse!

*

Cassidy Plume, Co-Presenter, Drop Dead Gorgeous:
'Well of course DDG has been a smash, particularly the Snoozie Mental strand, and I'm absolutely thrilled to be brought in to help at this point. It's still very much Ed Hardhouse's baby and I wouldn't dream of treading on the toes of that, well, Ed's like an institution these days! I think the idea was that after the, after what happened with Thomas Bayne which was so extraordinary and out of the ordinary, all eyes rather swivelled round to take a good hard look at this young lady. This, this girl who has this dream-come-true just walking into her house and tells him to, well, it's TV legend now and it's only been a week, it's a shoo-in for Telly Moment of the Year on Boxing Day I would think, over the old cold turkey remains! and of course Ed went for the same trick again, as anyone would, I mean hats off to the man, that's what thirty years in television can do for you, he still has the instincts in his old age! Keep giving them what they want. That never fades, you know. Sometimes it's not about brilliant ideas, sometimes it's not about being imaginative, sometimes it's about doing the same thing again and again. Getting right inside that box and thinking inside it! Sometimes. Me I'm fresh in this business, you see, sure I've had some monster hits, Blind Brother, Balloonacy, the list goes on, but sometimes one needs an old hand to just, you know, damn well do the same thing again! Which is how we get to Klaus Fold, who was the coolest man in rock till he set foot in Hazeldene Avenue.'

*

(Klaus, Klaus mate, let's get you home old son.)
She's up there
(Come on, it's over, son.)
She won't see me Ed she's up there laughing

(Love and war, mate, love and war, put it behind you.)

She knows my every move but she doesn't know me, sir, she doesn't know me, how can she judge me, how do people judge people, Ed? What gives them the right, you know?

(Oh I know)

I come here in good faith, I come here in good faith Ed

(Roberta, get the lad some black coffee)

I come here in good fuckin faith Ed, this is the girl, I say, this is the girl I say, the girl to set us right

(I know she's quite a madam, isn't she Klaus)

No, no, she's the girl to set us right, Ed, she, this, this note is not writ in her handwriting.

(You don't know her handwriting Klaus, you've never met her.)

In a dream I did, sir, it's between her and I, sir, in a dream I met her by a rock-pool sir

(Here comes your espresso son, how about you take a gulp of that?)

In a dream she wrote a note this is not writ in her hand

(Let's hold it up to the lens again shall we)

Let's do that, sir, let's do that, let's let the people be the judge of it, let the people's tribunal speak, speak, o ye men of truth, speak out loud and long ye men of virtue for we are few and we are, get out of my face you bitch

(It's okay Roberta, go and get Roy, no go and get Roy)

It's the handwriting of a man of hatred sir and I want to know which one, is it you, or is it you, you have the eyes of a polecat, you have changed a day of brightness to a day of cloud and you will not be forgiven nor forgotten on high

(This is the note that dropped out of that window about seven minutes ago and we've been staying live to get Klaus's reaction to what does seem to be bad news . . . pull in a bit Steve)

You are gentlemen of hatred, you speak in tongues of paper, and the ink is the ink of oilwells get your fucking paws off me you man-cub

(Steady old son, take a breather)

I'M SORRY I DON'T LOVE YOU

(That looks fairly final to me, mate.)

It's not final, it's not fine, it's not fine by Klaus, it's not the end, it's not, it's not the beginning of the end, it's not even the end of the beginning Ed, it's the beginning of the beginning. Open the fucking door thou article of nightmare

(Come on, let's leave it)

I'm a fucking rock star I'm the *fucking rock star I'm outside your little fucking castle lady on my horse with the sable feather*

(Yussuf, Roy, little help here)

In a dream by a rock-pool, in a cleft by the look I'm fucking composing here get your fucking hands off me ya bastard trying to pluck out my soul-source

(It's raining son, let's get you in the van)

It is a van to nowhere, to the nests of the moon, in a cleft by the rock-pool, to the only girl, to the only girl,

(I'm Ed Hardhouse, believe it and weep: the Mystery Angel who slew the Death Dragon, who pushed aside the Pride of Hollywood for the sake of a cat called Bonner, has now barred the door to the Bard of Britain . . .)

Let me out of this fucking van, I don't love her, she loves me

(And eradicated the Voice of Vermin Jones: what will she do next? WHAT WILL SHE NOT DO NEXT? I'm Ed Hardhouse, and after the break we have the Mini-Girl With Friends Like That trying to make some sense of this with my lovely new assistant Cassidy Plume, stay with us!)

She loves me, yeah yeah yeah she loves me, yeah yeah yeah

(Not a moment we thought we'd ever see)

She loves me, yeah yeah yeah she loves me, yeah yeah yeah

(It brings us no joy to show it to you believe me)

And with a love like that:

(But it's reality, and this too, my friends, is reality)

You know you should be glad, yeah yeah yeah

(And I'm Ed Hardhouse. And cut.)

I'll drain him dry as hay:
Sleep shall neither night nor day
Hang upon his pent-house lid;
He shall live a man forbid;
Weary sev'nights, nine times nine,
Shall he dwindle, peak, and pine.
Though his bark cannot be lost,
Yet it shall be tempest-tost.

Ed.
It speaks, it speaks . . .
Could you come in here a minute.
(Steve, we're going in)
Without a cameraman.
(Okay, hold that for now.)

Mantle in all her nightly glory.
Shut up Ed you can't see anything. What time is it.
Small hours Mantle, small hours.
There are people out on the lawn.
Thought you were asleep for keeps, like when my lot were babies. Wouldn't have disturbed you for the world.
People are on the lawn though.
More precisely on the roof of the shed.
The witches from Macbeth are on the lawn.
Roof of the shed. The army's on the lawn. Come and take a look, girl. They came all this way. And you're not supposed to utter its name . . .
Macbeth. I think I'm beyond that. Who came all this way?

Come and see them, it's my gift to you ya reckless angel.

What?

Come to the window, wave to them, they're the finest thespians of the realm, they drove all the way from Stratford-upon-Avon.

Ed . . .

That's right, sit up, come back to life Mantle, come back to us, take that first step towards home.

I am home. I'm in bed.

They drove all the way to see you in their caravans of glory.

Ed, did you get the Royal Shakespeare Company to perform Macbeth on my lawn in the middle of the night?

Just savour that Queen's English as spoken by masters . . .

To get me out of bed?

Shakespeare in her garden. What more can I give the girl . . .

Answer my question, Ed.

Mantle, Susie, Mystery Angel, wrong-place-right-time lady . . .

Answer my question.

Look it's my last chance, girl. They brought in Cassidy Plume, she's the Queen of Reality.

Slow down, Ed. What?

They hired the Queen of Reality. They're going to take my format and give it to Plume. They said I had one more chance to get you out of bed and I said I'll take it. Because I know you, Mantle. I admire you. We go back. Why should you roll over for the fake jewels of a jumble-sale world? You are a creature of quality.

Get on with it, Edward.

So I look at your bookshelves and I spy volume after volume, Shakespeare far as the eye can see, used volumes, tattered volumes and the Scottish play's the most tattered of all and I say No. No more stars of tinsel, no more preeners of pop. You'll move yourself for what matters. So. Hence. The Royal Shakespeare Theatre Company Players are serenading you, angel. And all you need to do is move to the window and lights will go on everywhere and the world will get the message: do not bring me trivial sweet things scraped from the bowl of the present. Bring to me the bitter fruits of the centuries.

Ed you are just this supreme necromancer of crap.

Dammit I tried

Get them out of here, 'caravans of glory' Jesus

You can be out of this game Mantle, you can be left in peace, you can life live as you want, but you do not want to mess with the Queen of Reality.

I don't want to mess with anyone.

She's poisoned the Mini-girl well'n'good and she's working on Roberta. There's no one I can trust.

I won't do what's expected, Ed, I have faith in what a witch said.

Babe you don't know what a witch is, you've not met Cassidy Plume.

Bring her on, I don't care, there's nothing I want but this.

This is madness, my girl!

It is waiting for a mistake and it's a mistake to leave this bed.

It's Shakespeare, in your garden, with a light show for the ages.

Please, Susan Mantle, or I'm televisual history. Step to the window, Susan, thou lady of, you know, in keeping with . . .

Well. If I have to go.

At least you struck the blow, girl.

Jesus Ed get a grip.

I know, I'm sorry.

I mean,

I know, I'm going, I'm gone

####### ####### ####### What is it, Dad.

Eh?

You called me, Dad, my phone says your name, it says DAD, I checked, that's why I answered. What is it?

Been, been out all day, all her many interests as she calls them. But, been out all day.

Who's been out all day? Mum?

Mum, yes, your mater, yes.

Can't you call her?

Dad?

Had a bit of a, funny thing, what are you up to now?

You all right Dad?

No. We are worried.

So am I, what's up with you?

Reading all sorts of things!

Forget my crap, Dad, it's showbiz, it just goes on.

Your mum won't answer the phone, won't let me either. Has a French telephone-mobeel now, just for what's his name.

For Monsieur Oliveira?

The paper's full of polls about you you're slipping badly Sukey.

It's not an election Dad. It's a reality-TV show and I just lay there and they didn't know what to do with me, so they decided to gang up and make everyone hate me. Gemma Rand did that twenty years ago in the sandpit and I seem to have survived. Don't worry. Who's this Oliveira?

You do get some shockers. Rock stars!

Forget it.

Vermin!

Jones, that was the name of his band, Dad, don't worry.

And the Royal Shakespeare Theatre!

Dad, try not to worry.

And the blessed England football team training in the garden!

So I'm told.

The lawn must be a mess! But I have all the articles, I have them laminated. 'The Babe In Bed Forever'! That's what they call you now! It says and I quote: 'Snoozie Suzie Mental was offered a place on the books of . . .' um,

United Premier Models

'along with the likes of . . .'

Jenna Binkley, Nadja Tresor and Mel 6. Ten grand a shoot. Did you laminate that, Dad?

Mel 6 is a funny name.

The other five were taken. They're running out of ideas, Dad, they know they're beaten.

Oh I don't think that's true Sukey. Not since this woman took over.

What woman? The Queen of Reality?

She says she's just warming up, it's in the Telegraph. There's a photomontage, Sukey, a photomontage

Photomontage

Photomontage, of her dressed up like a witch, and she's brewing up something in this enormous cauldron, hubble-bubble it says for some reason: PLUME TO MAKE SUZIE AN OFFER SHE CAN'T REFUSE.

She can fuck off. Sorry.

No you're right! Fuck her! Fuck her!

Jesus Dad.

But if you do, Sukey, if you do do that, if you do what the Queen of Reality wants, won't all this nonsense be over?

Possibly.

Why don't you do it Sukey? I don't think you're enjoying it much!

I can't do what's expected and I can't go anywhere.

Ha! Sounds like me . . .

What's that Dad?

Dad?

Do you know, they now say that we should all have the diet of Mediterranean folk?

They've always said that Dad.

Well I have it, I have that, it's working for me!

You have shed-loads of vino and the odd olive. No wonder you bang your head all the time.

You know me

Like you know yourself.

They

Broke the mould. No they didn't break the mould. You mean something about apples not falling far from the tree.

The apple harvest. God I hate it here.

What did you just say? Dad?

It says you've insulted virtually every demographic. There's a chart of them by way of, here,

Is that the Guardian?

A pie chart, an apple-pie chart. This columnist chappy reckons training with the England team was, and I quote, 'this strange woman's last chance to show some solidarity with us ordinary Brits'.

I'm not strange, Ordinary Brits are. They played out there for hours.

Sukey.

Yes Dad.

Show some solidarity with ordinary Brits it's not a bad old place. Just go and have a kick-about, you can bend it like Beckham! Is he there?

I didn't look. It was last week, Dad.

Probably not. Footie on a Saturday afternoon! Traditional! One-nil! Score draw! Match abandoned, bad light!

Come home Dad, you hate it there come home.

Hate it? Sacré bleu! Incroyable! This is our new life! This is my home! I am chez moi, I am at the house of me!

I just heard you say you hate it.

We have scrimped and saved. What <u>is</u> scrimping anyway? I scrimp, you scrimp, he scrimps. Scrimpez-vous? Oui, j'ai scrimpé. I have scrumpy *yes please it's a good harvest. There's still people sticking up for you. Couple of writers here, a black one and a white one, they seem to admire your rebel inclinations! Prince Charles says you're like him, a dissident. That's the heir to the throne coming through for my Sukey oh no, that was before, no he says the Shakespeare thing was an insult to our heritage with what I don't know castles and there's a picture of Nelson and oh there's the Shakespeare cast somewhere in costume looking disappointed sponsored by someone it says an Englishman's home is it kind of, malarkey, well, yes, I'm rather happy here it's always sunny sunny sun sun beating down but she's always out all day anyway and Sukey, there's a picture of you sleeping Sukey, Sukey, Sukini which is what the Americans*

Courgettes.

Mm, but it's spelt some other way it's with a zed, with a zee as they say stateside with a zee . . .

Dad can I ask are you really drinking a lot.

You can, I am, right now, good for the heart, next question?

Can you call when you get hold of Mum?

Oh well, yes, call, yes, you'll be lucky, you'll be fuckin' lucky.

You swear a lot Dad. It's weird.

I'm old!

You're not old Dad.

Dad? Alec? Alec?

Alec, a goal to Alec, one-nil to Mersham in extra time! Are the footballers still playing?

Jesus Christ.

☽

Susie. Lady Susie. Princess Susie. Are you awake?

Yep. Am now. And you are?

I'm Cassidy. I know you know. Twelve-o-twelve Show, Blind Brother, Balloonacy, Drop Dead Gorgeous. The Babe in Bed Forever. The greatest hits . . . No? You're not a TV watcher, are you?

No but sit down, feel free, everyone else does.

It's such a joy to meet you finally. Look I brought you a Bloody Mary.

So you did.

I didn't have to, you know.

But you did anyway so we're best friends. What time is it?

I'm trying to understand you.

I wish I could say same here, but I can't. Is that your salad?

Yes, you requested the risotto.

I did. Where is it? I mean sorry but, come on.

You have another show tonight, Susie.

Excellent.

But it's probably the last.

Shame.

I wanted you to know that. You have ridden the luck of seven lifetimes, Susie. You slung a film star out of your kitchen, you reduced a rock genius to a gibbering wreck, you lay there snoring while the finest actors of their generations performed Shakespeare on your lawn, and you wouldn't even wave to the most brilliant strikers of the land.

It was only England, Cassidy.

You took every little girl's dream of a top modelling contract and you spat on it.

That's a dream that should be spat on. In fact it should be pooed on. Nobody makes it.

Jenna Binkley made it.

Only because she's three stone in her shoes.

You turned your back on everything ordinary people care about. People are starting to publicly ask if anything matters.

Are you leaving the tomatoes?

A piece in the Independent today: 'Does Anything Matter?' Jeremy Paxman argues that it does.

How can you not like cherry tomatoes?

My blood group. You're a celebrity, Susie. Dirty word in a dirty world, but it's the currency we buy and sell in. Ordinary people care what you do. They want to know why you won't do what they would do. You have to prove to them you share some dream of theirs, some aspiration, otherwise you're what, in the eyes of the world?

Er, someone who doesn't.

You do share them, I know you do, I know you're playing us all for fools and I have news for you: the British people are not fools.

Why doesn't anyone listen to me? I won't do what's expected of me, it's not rocket science, we've been through that.

No one believes your tale of a crystal ball.

Well I do I was there.

I asked your best friend and she thinks it never happened.

Well. Maybe she was never my best friend. Maybe that never happened.

She thinks you've been under pressure. She's worried about you. She said there's something in your past.

Really.

You're lying here in bed to make some sort of twisted point about modern life. What's the point of rising to the top if no one treats you differently? You are making the entire youth of this nation feel their dreams are meaningless. Films: pap. Music: crap. Theatre: pointless. Football: puerile. Fashion: trivial. Money: filth.

You said all of that Cassidy I didn't say any of it.

You are single-handedly undermining the confidence of a culture. A vibrant culture.

Well. That was the tarot cards on the table.

It's just I feel you ought to tread softly because you're treading on their dreams.

Roberta told you that one.

Look. Okay.

It's Yeats.

I know, the poet Yeats. Death shall have no dominion.

That's Derek Thomas, idiot.

You're the idiot excuse me it's Dylan.

Time holds me green and dying, but I sing in my chains like the sea.

I beg your pardon?

Cassidy, new best friend, you might have been welcome in here when I was fourteen. We might have had a school science project to do together, S. Mantle and C. Plume: Our Study of Worms. Method, Result, Conclusion. 'Method: 1. We took some worms. 2. We boiled some water' hang on, that is what you're doing

It's funny. It's painful actually more than funny because I agree, I feel you and I are really very alike. In certain circumstances I might have done the same. Gone for it like you have.

I doubt it.

You don't know me Susie.

Well all I have to go on is that you come into my bedroom in your cool boots to present a show about what a bitch I am because I don't chew on any of the bait you bring in. And now the camera's off you try and play on some deep sister-love you think I should have.

I know you do have.

Okay. Perhaps I ought to be sort of in awe of your great achievements.

At least I do something.

Well. Touché I suppose.

You ever hear of Blind Brother?

No.

Expect me to believe that?

No. Okay I've heard of it but I never watched it. They had

a documentary about Dostoevsky on the other side. Must have been a spoiler.

Very witty. Anyway you're not supposed to watch it. It's post-ironic. It's cult viewing. It's not all market-based in my world.

What was that your show?

Yes I devised it. I intended it as a comment upon reality television. I actually intended it to put a stop to the whole screwy circus.

No half measures for you eh.

Decent ratings <u>and</u> the Turner shortlist. Don't you follow anything from your crow's nest?

Okay what happened on Blind Brother. You can tell me since I'll never watch it.

No one will ever watch it. It was a one-off.

Okay.

We auditioned thousands of people.

Good, more dreams through the grinder.

We chose twelve. We put them in a house we built and put enough food in it for three months. We told them the winner would win a hundred thousand pounds.

Er. This all sounds a bit familiar Cassidy.

I know. We filled the house with cameras.

Yes, and the kingdom of Shakespeare watched a dozen people thick as goat-shit burping and snogging all summer. That was you?

No. The cameras were fake. We just went away. We didn't film anything. We never told anyone where the house was. They'd been driven there blindfold. Every few days we said something through the loud-speaker like 'Talk In Falsetto All Day' or 'Make A Coat Out Of Pasta' or 'Hold Some Kind Of Olympics' then we switched the thing off and went away again. Every Thursday night we drew two names out of a hat and told the residents through a loudspeaker which two were nominated for eviction. We still didn't film anything. Then on Friday night we tossed a coin, Gazza or Shazza, and the evicted person climbed the stairs to the door which we briefly unlocked. Then they went out into the world waving their arms and there was no one there. Sometimes it was raining. The person had to get a bus home.

Bet you filmed that.

From a distance, kind of film noir, you couldn't see the face of the evictee.

Isn't that a bit cruel Cassidy.

Sure they'd've liked a close-up.

I don't think I meant that.

Then we went away again, and the eleven still in there went on fighting and fornicating for eleven more weeks until there was only one person was left. Then we let him out. His name was Munky. I'm the only person who's ever heard of him.

Did Munky get the dosh?

Of course he did. Who do you think we are? He bought a season ticket for Chelsea.

So a dream did come true. Eat your heart out Disney.

Well they won a cup that year.

And he wasn't even terminally ill?

No, that was No Greater Love on ITV. Which was a train-wreck thank you very much.

Blind Brother. And that was you.

That was my calling card. Then I did Balloonacy.

Stop right there! It's coming, it's coming . . . a hot-air balloon, yes, and inside it, a couple with a wretched marriage?

We screen-tested that, but in the end we went with teenage love triangles.

Floating over the landscape in misery.

Strapped in though. And then came this, The Babe in Bed Forever. Who could have seen that coming? That's the joy of Reality. The girl who said no to Thomas Bayne. The girl who wouldn't get out of bed to meet the coolest rock star we have. Or even to watch the RSC in her back garden though she'd gone to Oxbridge. This is cutting-edge reality and I'm the go-to girl.

'Go-to girl' bollocks those were all Ed's ideas. Is this my risotto coming . . . Thank you Roberta. How are things downstairs?

(Do you want to know.)

No.

(Parmesan?)

Hell yes.

I was in on all the discussions. I was totally opposed to the bloody RSC. Real people don't know what it is, it sounds like an insurance firm. I brought in the England lads: Ed was opposed to that. Ed was opposed to the modelling contract, said it cheapened the concept. One of us had to go.

Fine, law of the jungle, I'm not moving, do what you want. Set fire to the house. Let the little girl with the axe in: The Babe in Bits Forever.

Look I'm afraid for you, and I'm afraid of the wider effects.

On what? The morality of the nation? Bit late for that. You think I'll crack if we make friends, that's your plan B.

I'm afraid for you as a person. You've been voted Most Hated Celebrity by Under-15 Girls.

Shit that's a key demographic.

You really have no clue how serious things are getting. You've lost the mainstream filmgoers. You've lost the cool rock kids. You've lost the highbrow playgoers, the football fans, the fashion wannabes . . .

So what it's just traffic wardens and the homeless.

People matter, Susie. This is one of the most popular British television shows of the twenty-first century. The century. People are watching, people are talking, people are texting, people matter.

What have you done with Ed?

Mr Hardhouse will not be appearing on this show again. He said something extremely demeaning to me on live television.

Isn't it all demeaning, live television?

He said the unsayable.

Is anything unsayable?

Did he call you the c-word, Cassidy?

There are still, touch wood, some standards.

Glory be.

There's someone coming to meet you.

Let me guess. Hello Prime Minister, can you just wait an hour while I do my toenails.

No. Someone you know.

Really.

Yes. He's arriving any minute.

And this is surprising why.

No reason. No reason it would surprise you, were a gentleman from your past to reappear on the scene. Such things happen.

Well. Okay. No.

He's extremely excited to meet you.

Narrows it down to no one.

We've been trying to get to the heart of what might make you happy. What might allow you to rejoin the race of feeling creatures. You would hear the general sigh of national relief.

What, like a wankathon? Did Channel Four buy you out?

So we asked around a little, old friends here and there.

Sure, why ask me?

We don't trust you, Susan.

Good. And?

I tracked the gentleman down. He feels your relationship didn't really have its day in the sun, Susan.

Sorry, who are we talking about.

He feels that circumstances were against you.

Cassidy, there's no cameras running, there's no buzzers, no prize money, I'm not the fucking weakest link, can you just tell me who you're talking about?

He thinks you were meant to be.

Your face!

I know who you're talking about, and he finished with me, so fair enough, that was his choice.

How strange love is. He thinks you finished with him.

He does? No he doesn't.

He thinks you two had a beautiful thing. Which you ended.

It's, hard to see how he'd think that.

He thinks he made a mistake. He keeps saying he did something wrong. And I think he'd like to put it right, Susie. Tonight. For us.

Oh, right, sure, now he gets to be on television.

No.

No?

No. He's happy for us to film the two of you reunited. After that, with your blessing, we will withdraw the cameras. Everything else is up to you. If you agree to leave this bedroom with this gentleman, I will regard our game as over, the programme will cease to exist, and we will vanish from your life. You will have your life back. And you will have a special man to share it with. I'm the Queen of Reality and I say: Yes, there <u>*are*</u> *second chances in life!*

You know what,

What, Susan?

I happen to know this person has a girlfriend.

And I happen to know he doesn't.

He doesn't?

He doesn't now. He doesn't yet. He's unattached. He thinks he made a mistake. He's on his way.

I have to think about this.

You do that. I'll take your tray, here, and let's dim the lights, there, and you can have a little snooze and think about how far he's come, and how very much he wants to see you again. Yes?

Just leave me alone Cassidy.

I can tell him it's off, I can tell him not to bother his pretty head about you, I can tell him you're gone forever. I do have his mobile number.

Give it to me then.

Oh well I would, Susie, but I left it on the side in the kitchen, and that would involve you dragging your little self downstairs, and then you wouldn't be The Babe in Bed Forever any more, would you, and no one would give a shit, so will you see him when he comes?

Do I take that as a yes? No? I'll tell him you're too tired . . .

He can come in here. But that person left me.

You can tell him that. You can have a lovers' tiff.

This is sick. I spoke to him.

Ssshh, you rest now. It's been a long lonely day. And it's all about to end.

*

John Cormin, former lover:

'Sue Mantle is really a bit of a big puzzle to me, Cassidy. I think about her and I think, well, first up this girl is a real stunner, I mean, when she bothers, and I think, more importantly, she's bright, I mean more than bright, she's like an intellectual again, I say, when she bothers. She has books and stuff, she quotes things, we'd be walking in the park, which we did a lot, when we weren't in the pub to be honest, and I'm not stupid, some of my mates might disagree there, but I'd go like: was that you speaking, Sue, or a quote of some kind? I wouldn't have a clue. It could be quite poetic and I'd think hey: nice one. Maybe she thought of it, maybe she didn't but I'm still like: it's something of a treat to be the one who gets that, said to, I'm all in a tangle, sorry. Again please? Yeah, in bed, well again, I mean, great. Good company. Funny, which is important: funny. Sexy? I mean, yes, no worries, things did what things do in those situations sure, and – what? Again please? Well. Certainly. I'd ask, people do, I'd ask: you like that? And it'd be yes and we'd do it, sometimes it'd be no and I'd, I would, you know, I would forebear. What? Again please, special things? What, in bed? Well she quite liked, she liked to have, you know, everyone does, hugs, it's good to hug, good for the system. What else? Eh? No, she: no. Actually she did quite like being, hang on, we both quite liked being the one who gets, you know, you know . . . You know Cassidy I suddenly had this weird feeling it was actually none of your beeswax. Sorry. You can cut that if you want. I just really liked her very much indeed, she's a, cool person. I just: I didn't want her around all the time so I suppose I didn't love her and I don't know why. I feel like, low, to be saying so. I feel like low, not loving her. It feels like an insult, if this makes sense, to, like to, nature or something. We'd kind of, touch each other as we dropped off to sleep, we were always a little sheets to the wind, however it goes that phrase. But in the morning I'd, I'd just, you know like, turn away. Choose that way to face and that. And stick with it. And I wish I could wave a magic wand because I'd never leave her if I, you know, felt different in the mornings. But then I suppose I'd be, well . . . can you stop it now. Oi.'

*

I'm extremely excited.

I must say that I'm extremely excited.

Can I use that bathroom, please?
(No it's busy right now. Keep moving along.)
All right.
(Are you a bit nervous then?)
Yes. I am nervous and excited all at once! I don't know if she'll remember me!
(Of course she'll remember you, you mean a lot to Susie. Everything's going to be fine.)
(Okay then.)
(Is he miked up?)
(He's good to go.)
(You good to go, sir?)
(You good to go, sir?)
(You good to go, mate?)
Yes I am.
(He's good to go.)
(We all good to go?)
(Graceland.)
(Alton Towers.)
(San Siro under floodlights.)
(Track it.)
(And rolling.)

(And rolling.)

(And rolling.)
I am an old friend of Susan Mantle's from her school days. We were at one time quite close together but that is not true now.

(And? Why aren't you so close now Arthur.)
We are not so close now because in their lives people have to move on.
(And Susan moved on, right, after you and she left school?)

That is right. Susan moved on, after we left our school. The Sir John Stanborough Secondary School in Mersham, London.

(Pulling teeth.)

(What's with this cove?)

(Medication.)

(Boys get him some coffee.)

(Yeah right.)

(What do you mean?)

(You can't Cass. No coke no coffee no sugar.)

(Oh good grief. Now, okay . . . And you did not – I mean, you didn't move on, Arthur?)

I did move on.

(Good, that's good, but things haven't been so great for you lately, is that fair to say, Arthur?)

Yes.

(Can you tell us about your problems at all, Arthur.)

Yes.

(Go on then. Arthur.)

My name is Arthur, Paul, Border. I am also known as 'APB', because of my initials being 'APB', which in the work of the police force in the course of their duties refers to: 'All Points Bulletin'. Because of that, I was known, at school, as 'Points'.

Or, sometimes . . .

'Bulletin'.

(Oh for fuck's sake)

I am an old friend of Susan Mantle's from her school days. We were at one time quite close together but that is not true now. We are not so close together now because in their lives people have to move on. That is something you learn as you get older!

I did not know that Susan was famous until I saw her picture in the Daily Express, the Daily Mirror, the Daily Star, the Daily Mail, and the Sun! I also saw her on telly and I jumped right out of my skin! She was always very attractive as a younger woman and she has lost none of that attractiveness. I heard her say once in an interview she did once that death would have no domination and that has been an influence on many people in these dark times of terrorist bombs, me for example. I have known some people who died of old age when I was working in the hospice, and I think it would have been a bit of a comfort for them to hear that from an intelligent girl like Susan Mantle. Because death is of course very troubling to the more elderly folk, who might think it might be dominant after all. So her words would have great powers. Superpowers!

I consider myself very lucky to have known such an attractive person. Some might say that she and I were actually 'an item' for a short time! Meaning that we were going out together. That might seem impossible now that she is famous and a 'mover' and 'shaker'!

We went to see Die Hard (With A Vengeance) with Bruce Willis and for some parts of the film we were holding hands, for example during the big explosions. And not just because of the excitement! After that we went for a pizza meal in Leicester Square; and I had a margarita pizza, but Susan Mantle had a chicken salad.

(Hold up the photo, Arthur.)

(Hold up the photo, Arthur.)

(Arthur, the photograph, you brought it all this way.)

(Hold up the – cool Arthur.)

Here.

Here it is. A picture of us in Leicester Square. It was taken by a coloured lady.

(Mark that Steve.)

In the background you can see the pigeons if you look carefully.

(Got 'em Arthur.)

Feeding!

I wish Susan very well in the future, and I am very grateful to Cassidy Plume and the Sky team for helping me to have this chance to meet my old 'girlfriend' in the flesh again.

(Beautiful sentiment Arthur. Are you nervous, Arthur, that she's somewhere in this very house?)

I don't want to disturb her if she's sleeping.

(You know all about her, Arthur, all about her recent troubles, she just lies there waiting for something to happen. She's like a Sleeping Beauty, isn't she! Maybe she's waiting for Prince Charming, who knows? But you've seen all the shows. Do you think you might be the one to make a difference?)

Well I don't know about that.
(She knows you're here, Arthur.)
Oh! Oh heck.
(Oh heck says Arthur. You know what else Arthur?)
No.
(She's upstairs in that little room up there! Waiting for you!)

(What do you think about that Arthur?)

(What does that sign mean Arthur? You're making a gesture. He's making a gesture Steve.)
(His pills he wants his pills.)
(Jesus Christ.)
(Is she ready?)
(Steve, is she visible?)
(Negative.)
(Is she saying anything.)
(Negative.)
(Is she sentient Steve.)
(Dunno what that means sorry Cass.)
(Oh come on!)
(It means conscious Steve.)
(Thanks Yussuf. Yeah I reckon, she just moved her leg.)

(Feeling better now Arthur?)
Yes. A bit better.
(Can you tell us a little bit about your problems.)

Well. It's only that sometimes I did used to get a bit, a bit down. I used to get a bit down about things.
(Right. At school, do you mean?)
No. Not at school. School was a very good time for me when I was there. Some people say that your days at school are 'the best days of

your lives' and I think my days at school probably were the best days of my life for me.

(And your trip to Leicester Square with Susie, that must have been up there, right, at the top of the charts?)

Oh yes!

(Yes?)

Yes. My trip with Susie is right at the very top of the charts!

(You still remember it very well to this day.)

There was a smoking section and a no-smoking section, and we sat in the no-smoking section.

(Uh-huh, this is in the restaurant.)

Because although in those days, Susan Mantle was a smoker, she did not want to smoke, because I was not a smoker.

(That was nice of her, wasn't it, it's stayed with you.)

Her kind of cigarettes was Dunhill.

(Okay, so she must have quite liked you Arthur, to think of you first like that.)

Yes.

(So if that was the happiest time, can you tell us a little bit about the unhappy times? In your own words Arthur. Was it girl trouble?)

Oh. Yes. All right. Well. I suppose I was quite unhappy when Susan Mantle said she had changed her mind.

(About being your girlfriend?)

Yes. I was unhappy when she said she had changed her mind. It was in the canteen.

(Because you loved her, Arthur?)

I,

(You wanted it to last forever, didn't you?)

Yes.

(That was a few days later, wasn't it?)

(So it was a short, sweet, passionate romance?)

She said she didn't want to have a boyfriend at that time. She was carrying her lunch on a yellow-coloured wooden tray. I remember she had tomato soup with cream in the middle of it in a spiral shape.

(A spiral, which is of course eternal Arthur.)

Soup. And: she had three triangles of Dairylea.

(The triangle of – she had protein.)

And a metal cup of water.

(Okay. – Arthur: we all had those sweet passionate romances at school, didn't we, I know I did! I expect you had lots more after Susie, didn't you! Can you tell us about some of them?)

(Arthur?)

She said she had changed her mind, and that she didn't want to have a boyfriend at that particular time, but only four days later than that I saw her in the queue for Batman Forever with Val Kilmer, and she was up to all sorts with Colin Berry.

(Well. We know that Susie's had her ups and downs with the opposite sex in the last few years Arthur, but I'm more interested in what happened to you!)

She later went out with Eric Minns, Gareth Harvey, and Trevor Bourne.

(Right . . .)

No. Gareth Harvey, then Eric Minns, then Trevor Bourne.

(Three, count 'em.)

No, Gareth Harvey, then Eric Minns, then Gareth Harvey for the second time, then Trevor Bourne.

(Arthur, you never found love again, did you?)

(Whereas Susie had a two-year sexual relationship with Stuart 'Stew-boy' Gable at Cambridge University which included at least three other partners during that time, possibly at the same time we just don't know! And an intense and darkly kinky sexual affair of seven months with John Cormin, a very good-looking fellow worker at Dreamtours! it can't be easy to hear that, can it Arthur.)

(Because love's been hard to find for you would you say that Arthur?)

(Arthur?)

I have been shown a lot of love by my family and people, especially during the bad times.

(You mean your depression Arthur.)

It's a medical problem. I went to the clinic and I was told it was a medical problem. So that's how I got much better. All credit to the staff at St Tom's!

(Right, of course, but it's fair to say that in terms of, you know, what we were discussing, those sweet, passionate, romantic, sexy moments even, that really stopped with Susie, didn't it.)

(Didn't it Arthur.)

It's very exciting to meet Susan Mantle again, in the flesh so to speak.

(You must be a bit nervous.)

Oh! Just a bit! Yes.

(Just before we go in Arthur, and I've got the signal that she's awake and ready for us Arthur, and I know this isn't easy, but you've been having a few problems lately with very serious depression, haven't you, can you tell us a little bit about that?)

Well. You don't want to know about that. All that stuff!

(Actually we do Arthur.)

It isn't very. It isn't very nice that.

(These things have to be faced, Arthur.)

I don't want Susie to know.

(She wants to know. She needs to know. What is he doing?)

See my wrists here are covered in bloody marks from when I

(No no no no Arthur, it's okay, just tell us, no need to show us.)

It doesn't hurt if I have my loose jersey.

(You attempted to end it, didn't you Arthur. You'd had enough.)

Well.

(And then, the overdoses Arthur.)

It's not very good medicine.

(What's that Arthur?)

It's not very good medicine. Cos you all lose control in your bowels and you start to

(But no we want to think about a happy image, don't we Arthur a happy image from the past that could wipe away all that pain? Can you think of what that happy image might be?)

(Hey, here's a clue. Explosions? Bruce Willis? Holding hands? Pizza?)

Margarita pizza.

(Holding hands with a certain someone? . . . Might chase the blues away, do you think? . . . Do you think we should go and meet someone now, a special someone, Arthur?)

Yes.

(Now, while Yussuf is escorting Arthur Border into the private chamber of the Only Girl He Has Ever Loved, I'm going to, let me unclip this, hang on, got it, I'm going to stay out here on the landing, give them some private time, and I ought to stress for those of you who have concerns that we do have the channel's medical supervisor on hand here the beautiful Cheryl give us a wave, yes! and she'll of course step in to help Arthur if the emotion becomes a little too much for him, as well it might!)

(Is she awake?)
(She's under the duvet Cass sort of propped up. Definitely awake.)
(Hold it . . .)

(Okay green light, go)
(Green light, go, go)
(Caesar's Palace)
(Mount Olympus)
(The new Wembley)
(Valhalla)
(Are you in?)
(We're in.)

(Tell him he can speak to her.)
(I did.)
(Tell him he's got to.)
(I did.)
(Tell him he's got to or he's going home.)

Good afternoon, Susan. I hope you can forgive the first name terms! It's Arthur, from the Sir John Stanborough Secondary School in the old days. Good afternoon.

Looks like she's forgotten about me.

Um . . . Cassidy? She's forgotten about me.

Hello Points.
Nickname!

Nickname, me old nickname! 'Points'! Said by the voice of Susan Mantle, also known as 'Susie', or 'Snoozie Mental'! Well! The television company, I'm, I'm, I am just lost for words.
(Tell him he can't be.)

This is like a dream come true.
You mean a lie that's happening.
Pardon?

How are you, Points.
I am very much okay!
You don't have to do this, Points.
I do, or I'm going home!
I mean you don't have to be here.
I want to be here. I've been a bit unwell.
O-kay. Sorry you've been unwell.
Nothing I can't handle. All credit to the staff at St Tom's!
Sorry I'm not dressed and so on.
No. Yes.
It's not real, Points, it's just TV.
It's my TV debut. Hi, Mum! Talking to me mum there, with the magic of technology. But you're an expert! It's amazing how easy I am finding it is to talk to you! I thought it would be quite difficult because of our situation in the past, but it's actually quite easy to talk to you. You put me at my ease!
Points . . . Arthur . . .
Cassidy Plume and me were talking about the time you and me, that is, 'we', went to the Odeon Cinema (Screen 7) in Leicester Square and saw Die Hard (With A Vengeance) with Bruce Willis.
I see.
I was thinking about our date!

Oh Points . . . oh Bulletin.

Our meal of pizza.

Yep.

In the no-Smoking section.

Stuff of dreams eh.

We were just talking about all your many conquests Susan, for example: Gareth Harvey, Eric Minns, and Trevor Bourne.

Look I never went out with Eric Minns I did have some fucking standards.

Oh. I'm.

I'm always wondering what I did wrong.

What?

I'm always wondering what I did wrong.

No no no no no no no

Because I think back to our happy time together, and I am always sometimes wondering what I did wrong, to make your love go away like that.

No no no I can't do this I can't do this

I think it must be something I said!

It's not anything you said

It's hard to read the mind of Susan Mantle!

Good. Look: Points, I'm twenty-seven. You're twenty-seven.

I'm twenty-eight.

I'm twenty-nine, I'm thirty. See how fast it's going? These are things from ten years ago Points, they mean nothing, I'm sorry, Ms Plume knows they mean nothing, those men know, it's just none of them care. I'm sorry, it's not you.

Me? It is me! It is me in real life! It is, it is, it is, quite, it is quite, disappointing to be told that the times we had, between us, mean nothing to you.

I said I'm sorry. You're okay, Arthur, and cut.

When I think of how you looked at me!

Oh come on.

You were just as beautiful as then. I mean now.

The wench is dead. The one you knew is dead.

Um . . . yes. Who is it who's dead?

The girl in the cinema, me, her, dead, buried, gravestone, flowers.

Oh no, because she's very much alive and kicking, and her name is Susan Mantle!

Help me someone

Do you sometimes dream about the past?

Cassidy it's inhuman

I sometimes dream about the past.

Sometimes I dream about you, and we're still together, we're still an 'item' after all this time! but we're in a house I used to know when I was small. It was in 80 Marford Close in Bromley the dream takes place. It's not a house you ever went to! How could you be there? But you seem to know your way around. I don't need to follow you, because I see you all the time, but I follow you anyway about your daily business! It's always sunny outside and we have to go to the circus tonight. But we don't have to go until later. Sometimes we star in an acrobat show and it's time to get in our costumes.

Then I'm not sure which room you went in, and I think to myself I think: Points, you don't need to be in this house now. You don't live here. Then I think to myself I think: Points, you haven't lived here since you were six. And Susan never lived here! And then I think, of course, because I'm waking up now: Points, Susan never lived with you anywhere! And then I open my eyes. Or I sit up and it's visiting time.

Another dream I have is

(And CUT. Okay that's lovely Arthur, we've gone to a break okay, so we'll give you a sign when we're back.)

I'm quite glad about that, because I badly want to go to the WC.

(Fuck. Roy. Quick quick quick quick quick)

It's funny talking about my dreams with Susan.

(You go, Arthur, you relax.)

*

Cassidy.

My God it has a face. How are we doing there Susie?

He calls himself Points.

Oh I know.

He calls himself, by a nickname, in his own dream.

He's a character, this is going well.

It's hideous, what do you want you bitch.

What's it to you, Susie, you won't do what's expected, that's your thing, isn't it?

You want me to hold his hand, right.

Obviously. Go for a walk, pizza, a movie, I've got the listings.

You want me to kiss him.

Obviously but it's icing. I'll settle for the walk. If you're really that cold.

I think I'm going to be sick.

I'm the Queen of Reality baby, I'm the go-to girl, it's not like I didn't tell you. I got you, didn't I Susie? You're desperate not to touch him, but, if you don't, he is just rather going to be crushed.

Depression's a disease not a magic spell you can wish away you piece of shit

Roberta, Pepto-Bismol to 101

And a Bloody fucking Mary

And Susie's tipple of choice. Look I know what depression is, I've had it, Susie. Try getting out of bed with that, you freak. I also know that you, because of me, the Queen of Reality, have a chance to do a beautiful deed before the eyes of the world and you're desperate not to do it. And because of the person you've become, it's by no means certain you <u>will</u> do it. Who does that make a piece of shit? Don't you feel the force of the moment? The eyes of the world on you? This is high-end reality, Susie: the dying gladiator awaits the choice of the empress . . .

Why should I do it I don't love him, I didn't love him then. I didn't even like him, I was sorry for him, I'm sorry for him now but we don't have to console every sad pitiful tosser on earth.

No, Susie, <u>we</u> don't. <u>You</u> do. Right now. Death will have no dominion. Death wants to know what you'll do! Oh God you're 24-carat. Right they need me on the landing. Where the hell is Arthur?

(In the bog, Cass, big time.)

Christ.

(You told him to relax.)

Go to Carl's recorded bit with the polls. Standby. You, Mantle, heavenly creature, stay there.

(She's gone under the duvet boss. Standby.)

I know. She knows she's beaten. Nailed her with a fairy tale! It's frog-kissing time!

*

Susan.

Susan.

Go away.

It's Roberta De Coex, I have your Smirnoff and t.j.

Leave it and piss off.

I just need a word. I don't need to see you.

What, where's Cassidy

Sshh, she's live, on the landing. I only have a second.

Where's Points

They were talking about your decision.

Who was, what decision?

To stay here.

It's not a decision.

Just now they were talking, Steven and Roy, in the kitchen, about your staying here and not going to Provence.

I'm not going to Provence it's a journey of some hours and it's over earth and water. It's what the witch wants me to do.

Then someone said for a joke, Has anyone actually told her?

Told me what?

And Roy said surely, and Steven said sure. But they looked at me. Then I said well who told her? Someone said it's okay, Cassidy's on it.

Cassidy? Told me what?

Oh crap you don't know. They think you know, they think you've actually decided not to go to Provence. That made you sound such an awful person and I didn't think it rang true.

Why would I go to Provence? It's only my parents.
No, it is. Your father had a stroke today and he's very very poorly.

I'm so sorry Susan.
No he didn't.
I'm so sorry.

*

Susan, in another dream
Fuck off Points I'm leaving.

You will meet a tall, dark stranger, and you will say no to him until the day you say yes

☽

ALLO ALLO. NOUS SOMMES PAS CHEZ NOUS. LAISSEZ-VOUS UNE MESSAGE, S'IL VOUS PLAIT. HELLO HELLO. WE ARE NOT AT THE HOUSE OF US! LEAVE YOU A MESSAGE IF IT PLEASES YOU!

Mum. I'm at Gatwick okay it's five in the morning. I keep trying your number but no one's ever there. I only got the message last night and there wasn't a night flight so I spent the night here and my flight's at eight I'll be there by lunch I come into Nice. No one has to meet me I'll get a taxi someone lent me some money I have the address.

Look Mum I only know he's alive because I got through to a hospital, like the fifth one I tried and all in French how resourceful is that? That was pretty horrible Mum. It would've been nice if you'd, well, anyway.

They said he was asleep and you'd gone home for a rest but I tried and you weren't there, I suppose you had the machine on mute or something. Please try and call me if you get this message. Please make it a sort of priority for you.

I only didn't pick up the phone because the TV people picked it up but that's all over like you said, it was a nine-day wonder. Well, twenty-nine but still. I'm just going to come down and help okay? Okay. Bye.

*

####### ##### Hello? Hello who's there? Hello?

It's me, Min.

My God! Suse! It's so, actually I have my agent on can I put you on hold?

What?

Can I put you on hold I have my agent on!

No. Get stuffed.

####### ####### ####### ####### ####### ####### ####### ####### ###### What.

Suse.

Min.

I finished my other call.

Okay. Well done.

It was from my agent.

I've got an agent.

Where are you?

Gatwick.

With the show?

What?

To do with the show?

No. My dad's had a stroke. I'm going to the south of France. Fuck the show.

Oh.

But he's okay, to answer your next question.

Thank God! Wow, bloody hell thank God for that!

He had an 'ischaemic' something, I wrote it down. It happens to people his age. Well, him anyway. He's asleep in hospital in Nice. My mum's . . . somewhere.

You must be so relieved Suse.

I saw you on the show.

Right. How come you didn't know about my dad then.

They didn't mention your dad.

What?

They didn't mention him.

Okay. Well they didn't give me the message for five hours so that's par for the course. What did they say.

They said it was over.

Drop Dead Gorgeous is over?

No, your bit, The Babe in Bed Forever is over. They just showed you walking out of the door with that girl

Roberta

Roberta de Coex, with your suitcase.

She helped me pack, she gave me a lift. She was crying, I just stared out the window. It was like, cue the rain.

They showed the car going into the distance, and through the rain on the windows that big fat bloke you know your ex?

Oh for fuck's sake

He was rocking back and forward

Points

Yeah Points he seemed pretty down. They faded to commercials. The new segment where your segment used to be is going to be called Kiss of Life it's all about how he's feeling.

Points.

Yeah.

You mean whether or not he hangs himself.

They didn't say that.

Did they not.

Apparently it's about his Quest For Love.

Classy.

Apparently they already have these two party girls want to meet him, you know cheer him up?

Go Points.

And there's a number you can text if you want to be involved.

Involved how.

If there's a kiss I think they get to stay on the show? Or you phone in your vote.

Hey either way.

Isn't it gross? I know. Anyway . . . Everyone thought you were going to talk to Cassidy at the end, like when housemates are evicted.

Evicted, right. Even when it's their own house and their own choice and one of their parents might be dying.

Yeah, it was weird you didn't say a word. It was like when Thomas walked out on you. People are saying it was real drama and only I know the real truth!

I know I should have stopped for a natter with ol' Cass, because as far as I knew my dad's brain was maybe mostly still functioning what's the panic let's chill a while.

Sarcasm, Suse. No I just thought maybe you might be at Gatwick cos they'd thought of a new twist.

Oh someone thought of a new twist, it just wasn't them.

Anyway, people didn't know about your bad news. Would you like me to, you know, tell people?

No.

I can do it through my agent I'm working with, it would do a lot for your image Suse.

I don't care.

People would know you had a reason for walking out on him like that.

I don't need a fucking reason I don't know him.

In the show you do. You were the only girl he has ever loved and as your car drove away they played a song called 'Shattered Dreams'. Roy must have had it ready.

So you're going to France then. How long's that for?

How do I know, short as possible. Till he's okay.

I don't know if this is the time to mention this, Suse, but maybe when you get back to London we could find like a really nice place to have lunch like away from the crowds? like I don't know, Notting Hill, or somewhere it would be my treat and perhaps my agent could meet you, she's really interested in meeting you and that could be a date for when you get back. You're probably wondering why I've got an agent.

I've got an agent cos it's just, I know at first I wasn't famous like you were, but I was still the star of With Friends Like That, and I did do an interview with Cassidy about knowing Thomas, I say knowing him it was only that one time but we certainly struck up a relationship of some kind, Thomas Bayne and I, and they did screen that interview, and if you don't have an agent then none of that can really go anywhere, it's like it was pointless which is mad. There's no point in doing things there's. No point to. So I hooked up with Caroline Quark from Foster Braney Quark she's really nice, she's getting me a meeting with a lady from the Observer. Are you okay, Suse.

Don't cry Suse, if that's what you're doing. I mean you can, it's okay, but he's going to be just fine your dad.

Everything is.

Mum!

Susan!

Hey you okay Mum you look tired . . .

Oh my lord oh my lord . . .

Can't believe I'm here Mum . . .

Shock to the system eh . . .

I was very resourceful I got a taxi, but I didn't get enough francs so he's still out there.

Euros.

I didn't get enough euros so he's still out there. I mean he's pretty friendly, he's been talking to me for half an hour but I couldn't tell you what about.

Here look I've got some here how much . . .

Give me that fifty that's it. Mum I'm here is he here?

He's asleep, he's fine, he's asleep, he's asleep . . .

He's fine?

Well he's not fine but I'll tell you all about it. Go and pay your taxi.

He's not fine, say how fine, I don't know a thing Mum!

Well he's not at death's door, go and pay your man.

Good, good, to the point Mum, good, thanks.

I couldn't get back to you.

Can't phone a girl on a plane.

It's all been terribly

It doesn't matter I'm here. Can he talk, is he the same

Go and pay your chappie. Of course he's the same.

Okay. Okay,

Don't just stand there!

No, no . . . Great house Mum. Good move.

Cup of tea when you get back.

Yes of course.

You missed lunch.

Forget it!

Au revoir monsieur! Merci beaucoup!

He's still talking and he's driving away. Maybe he has a ghost in his car and he wasn't talking to me at all.

You know it's more like bo-coo, less like boo-coo.

Right . . . By the way what do you mean 'I missed lunch'?

What?

You said I missed lunch, okay, you mean I missed the gong that summoned me to lunch, and I missed the saying of grace, and the butler was just standing there waiting to serve me and was I there was I bollocks.

Susan,

Sorry about that.

Susan. I had some stuff out, I had no idea when you'd make it. If you leave it too long the flies are all over it.

Maybe I could find the stuff and put it out again and pretend to arrive again and take my chance with the flies?

Nothing could be simpler, fridge is full of good things. Ham, salami, cheese, tomatoes, and of course the bread is absurdly good you must absolutely treat this as your own pad.

Well I'll try that. So. He's asleep. And this is your place, after all this time . . . Bright colours, nice table, nice prints, you have a very modern sort of together kitchen Mum.

We like it.

I thought it would be huge and rambling and have enormous great knives on the wall and things made out of wood and pigs wandering in.

No you didn't.

Not the pigs, no. This china's nice Mum where'd you get it.

Do you want to see your room?

Oh God, I do, my room I have a room!

*

Look at all these compartments, I'm going to put one thing in every place.

You can do what you blessed well like, no one's ever slept here.

Well I'll sleep very well here, very deeply, very widely in this deep wide bed.

*

Look there's a toilet you can sit on in France! Instead of the usual shower stall with a shit-hole.

You knew there'd be a toilet, everyone makes that comment.

Hey I'm overtired.

I would think.

But oh you do have the very shallow oval toilet no one understands.

Just for you Susan.

*

This bit's nice.

It's just a sort of landing space, he reads the paper here sometimes as it's always cool. You have to remember. Shutters shut all day, keeps it cool.

They're not shut now, they're open.

Well I was busy, you were coming.

And if they were shut I wouldn't see the sea and I'm happy seeing the sea.

So everyone's happy. Mum busy, Susie seeing the sea, Dad asleep. Universal bonhomie.

Tout le monde est heureux.

Right. What she said.

What's that, is it, what's the name, that headland.

That's Cap Blanchemains. Cape Whitehands, it's supposed to look like two white hands praying.

God look at that rock it looks just like two white hands praying.

I can't see it either. Does have a good fish restaurant.

God, the sea, for once. Is that a really big ship way out there . . .

Cruise liner, vile things, fat Americans.

Still loving ya neighbours Mum.

Oh jolly keen.

I've been suffering fools gladly. Now there's a mug's game.

Well. You said it.

Imagine having that view all day.

Exactly. Drives you loco.

Doesn't it make you peaceful?

Living with your father?

Er, no. I mean the water, the light on the water, that would make me peaceful.

Really.

No I'm just rambling.

Feel free.

Do you get fresh fish from down in the village?

We're getting it tonight.

Will Dad be awake for supper?

This is all new to me Susan, I have to roll with the waves. Maybe, maybe not. When he's awake I'll show you his bedroom, it's the best of course.

Dad's, bedroom?

The bedrooms are all south-facing, apart from the guest of course, but you still get marvellous light in the morning.

So who's in that other guest room?

Well me, obviously, your father's going to need sleep at all sorts of hours, and I can't be disturbing him, can I?

I thought it had a lot of your things in it.

It's got all my things in it, needs must, crisis and all that.

I suppose. Mum I'm suddenly really hungry.

Let's go down and sort you out.

Oh I love these shelves above the stairs.

Mm-hm.

The smell of the old books as you go past.

Actually reading them even.

Let's not go nuts.

*

It's called a transient ischaemic attack. It's like a stroke.

But it's not a stroke? Dad hasn't had a stroke?

It's a warning of a stroke. It's good, isn't it, the bread it's garlic bread but not at all greasy like those awful Italian chains.

Yeah, Italian, greasy etc, what did they do, in the hospital what did they do?

Well they established what it was, which I just told you, then they prescribed some witch-doctor nonsense, and told me he mustn't drink or smoke or eat rubbish or be stressed, and he'll be absolutely tip-top. Twenty more years and so on. Early release for good behaviour.

Okay. I was told he'd had a, well, he doesn't smoke these days. But he drinks and he does eat rubbish.

Not if it's out of his reach.

So you're on it, Mum.

What does that mean, I'm 'on it'?

You know what to do. About it.

Oh yes then, I'm 'on it'.

It was like a wake-up call for him wasn't it.

I can't do it alone. He has to show some willpower.

He really can't drink again ever?

Depends if he wants to die. Maybe he does.

Mum you're so

It's time to face up a little, don't you think?

Okay.

You've not done much of that lately, have you Susan?

Well, no. I've been resting.

Sounds like it.

It's just everyone wanted to watch. Anyway it's over, you won't have to read any more about me.

Oh I know, it's petered out already.

I'm sure it was tough for you, great shame to the dynasty.

The Guardian this morning was saying good riddance to the whole circus: 'A Culture in Bed Forever'.

Right, they'll be sorry it's gone. Now they can talk about economics again, whoopee, Dow Jones has got his FTSE up his, you know

Hang Seng

His Hang Seng.

No they have a special profile of the lady who was running your show.

Cassidy?

'The Queen of Reality'.

A special profile for a special lady.

Have some rillettes. Can't get that at home.

No I'm okay. Actually yeah why not. Duck's guts, whatever, goose-bile, grist to the mill, bring it on.

Goes with this toast. And this compôte.

Compôte.

Use two different knives if you wouldn't mind.

Two different cuillers.

Couteaux. Cuiller is a spoon Susan.

I meant that. I want to use two different spoons. Actually three. No one understands me.

Does he know he has to change his whole life round?

Well he's not stupid, is he.

No, it's just I've,

Well he won't be stupid about this I won't let him. I'm 'on it'.

Just I've been thinking lately he sounds a little stressed and you said that was a factor.

Well that would be your father yes, beautiful house, beautiful sunshine, all this golden light pouring in, lovely food, friendly people, three hundred channels, everything he could want really so yes, very stressful situation.

I mean, I know he liked it at first.

He loves it. And he adapts, Susan, he's a good adapter, and he'll adapt to this.

A good adaptor. Right. I left my phone charger in Mersham.

He even knows to duck his head when approaching a door, now that's progress, you can go to the town tomorrow, there's a hypermarket.

I thought you got the door-frames fixed, I thought some bloke came round.

You can't fix all of them, they're supporting walls, he has to learn, new habits to get into. Anyway he's not walking just now we have to wheel him around.

I can do that too.

You're welcome.

And there's a bloke who helps with DIY, things like that.

There is indeed a 'bloke', and he does indeed help with 'things like that'. You know your father's perfectly useless in practical matters, so it is rather useful. He did offer to collect you from the airport, but we were never informed of your timings.

The bloke offered to collect me?

He does have a name, it's Franck, and he'll take you into town tomorrow.

Monsieur Oliveira.

Well, yes, mm-hm, but it's not formal with him, he's approachable and without him, and without Hélène, and without Mme Chabot, we'd be some miles up le ruisseau de la merde.

If I just tell you what kind of charger it is and give you some francs

Euros

Euros, could he just buy it Mum and I pay him back.

Well you already borrowed fifty.

You know what, why don't I go and spend a nice morning in a French hypermarket with Monsieur Franck Oliveira, who I flew all this way specially to meet.

We need a lot of things, I thought you could help carry. Half an hour at the outside.

Okay. Hypermarket. Hyper fun.

More coffee?

I might try and sleep myself. Busy day tomorrow.

Well, why don't you do that.

I can't believe I left my charger. No one knows this number. Is that good? That's good, no it's good.

You sound tired, Susan.

Will you wake me up if he wakes up?

Susan, you need sleep, you must sleep until you wake, then the dendrites of the brain are at their most receptive.

Mum I don't need my brain to be receptive Mum I want to see my dad I want to see my daddy

Come on now, come on now, hey hey it's all right, it's all right you, come on now, come on you, there there. There there you

You

No you

No you

*

####### JOHN CORMIN. LEAVE A MESSAGE. #

*

####### THIS IS THE ANSWERING SERVICE FOR 0208 6527 2667. EDWARD. HARDHOUSE. IS NOT AVAILABLE TO TAKE YOUR CALL BUT YOU CAN LEAVE A MESSAGE AFTER THE TONE #

Ed. It's Susie Mantle. I don't know why I'm calling you. You said I could. That's not really a reason. My life is still quite strange and I associate you with what sort of makes it that way, but I'll try you again later. Or, conceivably, I won't. Bye.

Mum.

Yes?

Are you in there Mum?

Yes are you all right?

I had a long sleep. It feels like tomorrow. Is Dad awake?

Not yet, but we don't eat till nine or so, I'm sure he'll be up by then.

When I saw it was six I didn't know which six, evening or morning, it was a great weird feeling I was on some sort of dateline . . . I didn't know which way the earth was going to turn and if there'd be anyone to talk to when it did. I had to wait for the light to change.

I'll get you a twenty-four-hour watch.

Good idea. Thanks Mum.

I'll faire a promenade on the beach then.

That's a nice idea. You can manage.

What do you mean I can manage.

I mean do you need directions.

No Mum I thought I'd make a beeline for the sunset and stop when my shoes get wet.

Don't go too far, will you.

What, like Morocco.

I don't want you to get lost.

Okay I won't.

And it can get quite chilly, have you got enough on?

I've got enough on, Mum.

I mean a good three layers.

A good three layers.

Because it's layers that matter, not thickness, layers.

I know, I'll need to remember that when the baby's born.

Thought you'd pick up on that. The ol' baby reference there but hey.

What are you doing in there Mum?

I'm reading.

What are you reading?

What am I reading, I'm reading since you must know and I'm too tired to make something up I'm reading the bloody Da Vinci Code.

Okay Mum.

It's a page turner Susan.

That's good. Do you think, if you never reach the last page then the last page never happens?

Oh well that's just what I need right now, a schoolgirl question about narrative.

If you didn't like the ending you could just stop, couldn't you. All the characters would be in the middle of their secret plans and projects, or about to make tea or do murders and it would suddenly go dark on them all, and they'd stay like that for a while, like when you think it's just a fault on the line, and you wait for normal service to be resumed, then they'd realise the lamps weren't coming back on. They'd sort of relax and get accustomed to the light and say okay whatever and start looking around, noticing other stuff. They'd sit down, or put their shirts back on, or start stacking the plates or something. And in the case of some books, I don't know about the one you're reading, but in the case of some books they'd just all say: thank fuck for that.

Language.

And in the case of all books they'd say: I don't think she's coming back. 'But I've discovered something about Jesus!' I don't think she's coming back. 'But the murderer is Dr Zobolski in the billiard room with a scythe!' I don't think she's coming back. 'But I love you!' I don't think she's coming back.

And so on.

Sometimes I see them all, all the characters sort of marching arm in arm down a hillside to the most fantastic picnic instead.

I'll stop reading then, shall I?

Oh no. Please go on. I wouldn't dream.

*

That's rather splendid, isn't it?

As sunsets go, you'd have to rate that at the top end, do you not think?

Doesn't half save the best till last, the old soleil.

I'm sorry are you talking to me?

Sorry, 'fraid so. Clive Signall. I honestly tend to keep this sort of thing to myself, have no fear I'm not a poet, but sometimes does it not just get to you? Does to this poor soul.

Deep breath.

I'm sorry?

I wasn't really looking at it I was just looking in that direction.

Hard to miss, though.

I was having a quiet walk on the beach.

Sorry I'll shut up. Actually, looking at your expression, perhaps I'll shut the fuck up.

No, it's okay. Just shutting up is good.

I'll try that.

Give it a whirl eh.

Will do.

How am I doing?

Shit.

This any better?

What are you some hired eccentric beachcomber Brit.

That's it

Haunt the bars, bother people . . .

You have it

Dabble in shit watercolours on the side . . .

Bang on

Little import-export . . .

Oh you're good, you're good

Genius at public school, great things expected . . .

Oh great deeds, great renown

Little coke trouble back there . . .

Tell me about it

Now you walk up and down the beach in sandals.

Well.

Well. My little lady died.

Fuck.

That's what I said.

Fuck: sorry.

That's probably what she said. Knowing her.

I'm Susan. I came here to visit my father. He had a transient something stroke. He lives up there above the harbour. He lives on Chemin de Rivalou, he's sleeping, my dad. His name's Alec Mantle, do you know him?

No, sorry. Is he going to be okay?

I don't know. I think so.

Then you'll go home.

I suppose. Yes. I don't live here.

I wish you did.

My. Okay.

That's nice, er, who are you again?

Clive Signall. But you'll be gone in three days, like the Little Mermaid.

Right . . . yes. In the story of that name.

Sun's almost down now, show's over.

Handy you mention things like that. I'd be sorted if I was blind, wouldn't I.

Just think sometimes it needs mentioning.

Go on then.

What do you mean?

I'll close my eyes and you tell me about it.

You'll close your eyes? You're a bit trusting for a girl in this world.

You're not tall and you're not dark.

What's that got to do with the

Price of eggs, nothing.

Tell me about the sunset.

Well, right, I will. Lovely clouds, all sorts of colours, magenta, orange, nice day tomorrow, strips of thin, wispy cloud, can't think of another word for cloud, how am I doing?

Not bad. Bit more.

Great band of glittery light all the way from here to there! It's just like a, like a

No don't do that don't do similes

Jewels I'm thinking jewels

No jewels, do the boats, tell me about the boats and ships.

Er, couple of yachts out there.

Cruise liner?

No, gone now. To Sardinia?

You can't see that, it's speculation.

I suppose. Should I go on?

Unless the sun just stopped.

Right. Well, it all seems a little greyer than before over yonder. Grey seems to be slowly getting its way.

Like in your hair.

You're a tad pissed, aren't you Susan?

I like how you said yonder.

You say I'm not tall, but I'm really not short. I'm an average height, like Jesus.

I beg your pardon?

I'm sorry are you of a religious disposition?

Extremely religious disposisposition. Or I was until The Da Vinci Code now obviously that's all changed I belong to the Order of the Gift and I work in television over yonder.

Very postmodern. Well you're talking to a hopeless agnostic.

You mean you're not good at it? Anyway you brought it up. And Jesus wasn't average height, he was five feet tall exactly and he was the only one. That was just one of the nonsensical things I used to believe before the UK paperback launch of The Da Vinci Code.

Now you're just teasing.

You're old, you'll take it.

You're damn right. But you're pissing off. Too bad we won't have a chance to . . . you know.

What.

Talk more nonsense in the twilight.

Is that what we won't have a chance to.

Well. Yes. Or. We could share a sad burgundy at the bar along the beach.

I sort of did that already. I had my own carafe.

Thought so.

Did you think so.

I did think you were a little, you know, three or four

Sheets to the wind. It's not France for me without a carafe of red wine and talking to yourself.

Maybe another time then.

Keep describing things. More!

Didn't think you thought much of my descriptive skills.

I didn't but go on.

Well, the sun's gone down.

God not again.

It's getting pretty gloomy out here.

Gloomy.

You can hardly make out a couple of Brits-in-exile far off at the water's edge.

Can't see 'em, won't miss 'em.

Thrown together at the fag-end of the day, like two lost

Just describe things.

Well. He: ageing, unhealthy, cynical, wry, disillusioned, dabbles in shit watercolours, but on the plus side –

No you've covered it. She.

She: from nowhere, turns his insides to a river, will be gone in three days.

That's not very physical.

The river bit was physical.

Yes but it's not literally true and if it were it'd be revolting.

Is this, slightly more physical?

Uh-huh that's slightly more physical.

Is this, at all physical?

Again, fairly physical. But too gloomy to tell.

Come here.

What?

Come here.

Okay.

Am I supposed to be describing this?

Uh-huh.

In the fading light, deep feelings that had long lain undisturbed were suddenly

No no keep it physical

Physical

Well vaguely physical.

I think maybe don't do that.

Fair enough.

That's probably what we call slightly on the other side of the line you can't see.

That's; okay.

Fair enough.

Very much fair enough.

Enough, anyway.

Not this?

Yup, okay, so, moving swiftly on,

Amazing who you meet these days.

Mm amazing what the tide brings up.

I could be here tomorrow evening.

I could be dead tomorrow evening. I'm going to the hypermarket with a tall dark stranger and nothing's good about that.

Try not to die tomorrow, old girl.

Yeah that would be naughty.

Naughty to die on me.

And you're sure you're a blond.

Scout's honour I'm a blond.

And you're not going to get any taller.

I'm feeling quite tall right now.

Woah, okay, and cut.

I mean, since you asked about it.

Well. More fool me.

More fool you.

Okay, well that's a wrap.

Tomorrow evening: sunset.

Yeah they're holding it in the evening.

I'll be here or hereabouts.

Okay, well, that's fascinating.

Maybe share a carafe. Or a cocktail with the Little Mermaid.

Turning the green one red.

I'm sorry?

Nothing.

The what?

Nothing.

*

####### ####### ####### *Hello, who's that.*

John?

Sammi, hi, glad you called.

Sammi . . . I'm in France, John.

Is that right, well yeah, excellent, it's good timing, what with the

Wingram people coming in tomorrow. We could probably do this then, I know I have a window from about two-thirty.

I just wanted you to know that I came here because my dad had a stroke, that's why I left the TV show and I'm a little drunk I was just on the beach.

Yeah, right, I'm hearing you Sammi. Glad you called.

Because I just think, John, people ought to know things at the right time and not the wrong time.

Well what we're doing at this point is gathering information from all associated parties, and that will certainly be helpful in the long run Sammi.

It doesn't matter to you but I wanted you to know that all that TV shit is over now and nothing they said to you, if there was anything, nothing is true.

The Wingram people will want that on the agenda, and I can see it from their viewpoint.

Is there always a girl there, John?

That's a negative, Sammi, there will certainly be times we can discuss some of these issues in smaller focus groups.

It's none of my business.

This, however, is not one of those situations, so if we could postpone this for the time being that would be I think the way to proceed. Okay bye.

That is certainly the way to proceed.

That is most certainly the way to proceed.

*

That's certainly the way!

Jesus Christ!

Yes . . .

Dad you gave me a fright!

Dad, there we are . . .

Just sitting there like that I was walking on the beach and why don't you put the light on?

When I sat here I didn't need any limes!

Limes Dad that sounds like you, priorities sorted. God, Dad you're okay

I'll tell you what I'm feeling like,

Go on Dad,

I've trod in something on one side there's no feeling it's great?

Great, Dad?

Grey? Grief.

It'll come back Dad the feeling

One foot's in the ground!

No it isn't

Whole arm in the ground in the grate

Dad it's okay, it comes back, I read about it. I'm putting a light on it's so gloomy right now, look at you! You look well, Dad you look all tropical and healthy, I was walking on the beach I met an Englishman, a right old cad I'm a bit far gone Daddy.

She's getting into scrapes. Did you get what you need?

Um, not really.

Do you have to go again?

Some other time. Where's Mum? She gone out, Dad?

Did Mum go somewhere, Dad?

You're back now. You made it back with supplies.

You gave us a fright Dad.

You were on the telephone.

Not just now I mean, the other day, getting ill. I was doing my show when I heard.

Do you have everything, Marie?

What's, what's that Dad, I was talking about my show.

Yes, what's next on the show.

Oh, I think it's. I think it's done with, sort of, it was a freak show and I was sort of a freak but I'm not any more so, there, done with.

Ramparts-of-the-Geezer.

Yep. Very good village Dad, good choice. Can I get you a – cup of tea?

I like a nice

Cup of tea.

But what I really think we must have is a glass of sandwich on the terrasse!

Well. Sounds good, a glass of, wine but you're still, recovering Dad I don't think you're allowed a glass of anything.

No?

No. No which is a blow. But we could be on the terrace. Is Mum cooking the fish? Look there's, there's nothing in here she must have gone to buy it. Bollocks it'll be hours. I'll put the kettle on.

Everything was very slow.

What's that, Dad? How do you mean?

Everything southerly very slow I couldn't see.

You mean when it happened? It was, suddenly slow?

I couldn't see. Everything southerly very slow. Everyone stopped, like the, when the band plays, you know, songs, tan-ta-ra, songs, what they sing.

Music, Dad?

Music.

Is that what it was like then?

Ramparts-of-the-Geezer.

Here I am I came specially!

Now I don't know what she's up to.

You don't know what who's up to?

She tells me what she's up to. There goes the kettle.

Yes the kettle.

Always tells me what she's up to.

What are you saying? Mum? What Mum's up to?

She's in a show and she's always getting into all

Sorts of scrapes.

All sorts of scrapes.

I know Dad it's me, that's me, in the show.

Now you're here, no one can tell me what she's up to.

Dad; no. I can tell you what she's up to she's here, she's finished the show, she came to see her old dad in Ramparts-of-the-Geezer and maybe they'll steal out for a drink later on the terrace!

She always tells me the news.

Dad, it's, where's the light, here,

Your tasse of thé. Think maybe you've had some pretty strong medication there.

I like a nice

Cup of tea.

But what we really should do is have a glass of sandwich on the terrasse!

I know, we should, but hey, another time.

Something to

Ramparts-of-the-Geezer.

Yeah maybe Dad, maybe when you feel better, you could go back to London for a while, see the old homestead?

Old homestead. She always tells me about it, they had the show in the garden.

No. Dad, look at me Dad.

I always tell you about it, I do.

I think,

You're recovering Dad

I think I've had a few too many!

That's probably what it feels like Dad! You're recovering from a bad attack of the, you had a stroke Dad.

She tells me when the cameras are golden.

No I tell you Dad, it happened to me, the cameras, I told you when the cameras were, going, the cameras, rolling even.

And now you're here. In Ramparts-of-the-Geezer!

Oh Dad I'm right here

Of course you are Sukey

Oh Dad you scared us

Can see you've been walking.

I'm here Dad I'm here

Doing another show!

Just on the beach Dad, no more, no more

And you got into scrapes!

No no, no no

You always do!

Actually, sort of.

Good. You always tell me, don't you.

I tell you lots of things, Dad, the stranger things get, the more I'll tell you. Nothing too strange for Sukey!

I thought she'd have to tell me on the phone!

No, because she's here, in Ramparts-of-the Geezer, with you, drinking a nice cup of tea

A nice

Cup of tea

You know what we should really do is have

A glass of chablis on the terrace, yes, but you're recovering, Dad,

You always tell me. A glass of

Chablis Dad. Not a sandwich. A glass of chablis.

I always tell you. I'll always tell you.

Because,

What, Dad.

Everything was southerly very slow. Everyone had stopped.
Like the music.
Like the music, I said to myself that's queer!
I bet.
I said to myself now, I don't know what's happening any more, because
Sukini
Because Sukini isn't telling me a done thing!

I was in London Dad, I flew here this morning when I heard what happened to you.

And now you're here.
And now I'm here with you. But Mum: she went out to get the supper.
I thought that was you! That's queer, I thought you were the one coming back with the supper! But it was
The medication, Dad.
Marie. She's gone.
Just for the fish, Dad.
She's gone.
Just for a short while.
But he helps us out in these climes.
Who's that Dad, do you mean Franck?
Good pointers for living in these climes, green-fingered Franck.
It sounds like he's a big help.

Hey, someone's coming up the steps.
She's been walking on the beach.
No Dad, that was me, it's Mum who's come from the shop, that'll be Mum with the fish she bought.

Dad: look at me.

Do you think we af everything we need Suzanne?

Since we've been shopping for an hour I would think yes. There's only Mum, Dad and me and we've bought food for seventeen.

We af our supplies!

Now we go and pay for them, yes? Over there.

Your mother is very appy you are here in France, Suzanne.

I'm her daughter, she should be really.

You are both ow you say very strong characters?

She is. Je ne suis pas.

Ah tu parle français très bien.

Don't worry I've stopped.

Est-ce que tu aime bien la France?

It is okay. It is good to get to know you, Suzanne, I af heard many thing about you! It is all good.

Aisle 22 is free look.

*

Your father he is going to be well.

Oh good you're a doctor too.

I know he is, I see it. I see this thing.

Why did we buy these?

These is very very good local delicacy you must taste it.

It looks still alive.

It is ow it is meant to be!

*

Do you think we af enough of wine Suzanne?

It's more SU-san, stress at the beginning.

SU-zanne.

There's never enough wine.

You think we should get more. You wait and I go to get more.

Whatever Franck.

You can call me Franck, it is good. SU-san.

Whatever Franck.

*

It is not far now.

Whatever.

It is traffic. I af fed up with the traffic.

Whatever.

You are a famous celebrity in London, Suzanne! But I think you are appy to be away from this circus, yes?

It is not good, that life, it is drinks and drogues and it is better to . . . take? To take, an alternating road. Like that road to l'Espagne! We do not take this road or we are in the Spain, yes? We do not want to bullfight! My little, my jeste, my little, qu'est-ce que c'est, joke.

Are we there yet.

Your mother and father loave you very much.

It is okay to cry.

It is. It is okay to cry.

It is okay, it is okay, it is okay, it is okay.

*

Salut Pascal, une pichet please, my usual.

####### HELLO. THIS IS MIRANDA KAYE. I AM NOT AVAILABLE TO TAKE YOUR CALL RIGHT NOW. IF YOUR CALL IS CONCERNING 'THE BABE IN BED FOREVER' OR 'WITH FRIENDS LIKE THAT' PLEASE LEAVE A MESSAGE, IF IT'S ABOUT SOMETHING ELSE, CALL BACK ANOTHER TIME. THANK YOU #

Min it's Suse. I need to talk to you. There's a tall dark stranger and he's getting quite familiar. I've gone to a bar to get away from him. I know you told that bitch Cassidy you didn't believe in my fortune, but I know you do, or I hope you do, which is different. But I know no one else does and oh Jesus my mum just walked in –

No prizes for finding you here, taking care of business.

Well I did le hypermarket, now I'm doing le neighbourhood brasserie, tomorrow I'll play pétanque or maybe go to a concert of Johnny Aliday.

(Et voilà.)

Pascal un whisky.

Blimey Mum.

Since we're all boozing ourselves silly at lunchtime.

It's like I say, I did the hypermarket with a total stranger and now I'm relaxing with myself.

Franck isn't a total stranger, he was there at breakfast and you seemed to have a perfectly polite conversation. A little one-sided. He says you hit it off very well on your expedition.

He's got a low threshold.

You can be very, you know, bitchy sometimes.

You calling me a bitch Mum. Outside.

He's just trying to help.

Okay. Maybe. Who's at home?

Hélène is cleaning the kitchen, Franck is trying to fix the cable box. So your father can watch the rugby. And your father will sleep through all the noise.

I know he will, it's just not much fun if he wakes up and the only people there are the girl-who-does and the handyman.

Your father knows Hélène, he likes her, he probably fancies her, he probably has French-maid fantasies about her and look: Franck's a friend of ours, he just happens to be a handyman. You're such a snob.

Snob and a bitch, I'd be good TV.

Which pretty much says it all.

And why exactly should my life here not include dropping into the local bar for a drink when I feel like one?

No reason. What did I say?

Look there's nothing funny going on, Susan, this isn't some cruddy art-house movie.

Okay.

Merci Pascal.

(Et voilà.)

Okay I believe you Mum you're my mum you wouldn't lie.

Good. So then you might make more effort with him.

I am making an effort with him.

Yes an effort to dislike him.

At least it takes effort.

Always a comeback, isn't there? It's so like you.

It is me. I'm finding it hard with strangers Mum, it got very weird in London.

Seems to me you rather asked for it.

It was the fortune teller, the old woman, it wasn't good, and it started affecting how I looked at things. You used to be interested in that, we had tarot cards once.

Well, one grows up.

Is that what yours said, your fortune?

It's what they should all say, all the cards, all the lines on your palm, all the star charts. I saw a cartoon once, Susan. There were hundreds of shrivelled little African children dying of starvation in a desert. And then there were arrows pointing at three of them, marked 'Virgo', 'Libra', and 'Aquarius'.

Okay.

The water carrier.

I get it Mum. Astrology's shit.

Pascal l'addition s'il vous plaît.

Look, she said these things could happen, in a certain order, and the last one was I'd die.

We know, we've heard.

And okay, we all get there in the end, but she made it sound pretty imminent.

It's cheap theatre, Susan, drop it.

Then some of the things did happen.

I don't believe that at all, I think you've misremembered what she said and started fulfilling it yourself, it's a common phenomenon.

Possible. Maybe. Okay, but . . . I suppose I was wondering, because you used to know a bit about it, if what she, might have seen was: someone else's death. Or, near-death, it's all about what forms she could make out in this sort of mist.

What a piece of work.

She was looking in a crystal ball.

Oh Susan that sounds like complete shit. See what Scotch does to me I'm something out of Hogarth.

I'm glad we're having this talk.

Don't look like that, I meant that. I did!

You should report her to whatever it is, the Magic Box or something. Did you ever go back to the woman?

One thing led to another. I asked Miranda to take a look.

The dim one from school.

She's not dim now Mum, she's lit up like a cake.

Well what did she say, was the old lady there?

She said there was no one home.

Sounds like Miranda.

Ho ho.

What a class operation. And it's this that's messed with your mind.

Well, indirectly, yes. It's a long story.

We have to get back.

We do, okay.

Dad's memory, right,

Yes?

Is that the medication he's on?

No.

Okay.

He's on warfarin.

It's not a side-effect of that then.

No. That's against it happening again.

So, you're saying, as I understand it, without you saying much at all, that his mind is a bit damaged and the damaged bit can't be healed.

No I'm not saying that. He's had a minor stroke, and he's recovering from it.

So the memory will come back, and he'll get words right again and so on.

I don't know. He lost some blood to the brain if you want to get technical. Bit of a break in service.

Okay.

Okay.

We might just have to adapt, you know, slow down for him. I'd been rather doing that anyway.

Really.

Lately, yes.

Will you be able to manage here on your own Mum? I don't mean on your own, but with him a bit, slightly, slower?

I'm not on my own Susan, I have Hélène, I have Mme Chabot, there's Franck, I have the girls from the magasin, I have Pascal here for emergency rations I'm doing absolutely fine and I think I'm going to knock this off in one.

But are you not, Mum,

I mean, are you not,

Bloody devastated, yep. Cheers you.

Cheers Mum.

*

Dad.

Dad can I come in?

Dad it's me it's Sukey.

The girl said you'd woken up.

Hélène.

That's right, Hélène said you'd woken up.

There's a

What's that Dad.

Soldier in the window.

A soldier in the window?

Hm.

I can't see that Dad. Do you mean that window there, there's nothing there. There's just this wonderful view I'm about to show you. It's Sukey, Dad, Sukini, your courgette, I'm going to tie back these curtains, except they make it impossible, there, that goes round there, that goes round there; and, no. What's this. Oh I get it.

And now the shutters, and I'm the little lady in the doll's house, out you go, et voilà. Look at that. As we say. No soldier Dad. No soldier in the window. No sailors on the sea.

Hey you're not even looking! Sun going down, Dad, very nice.

Ah yes.

Any ships Marie?

It's Sukey, Dad.

Any ships?

Oed und leer das Meer. Not! Yachts, three, four yachts, and some guy doing what's that, paragliding, parasailing? Parashowing off, dunno. Lot of kids down on the beach. What day is it is it Sunday? Go to church ya hooligans.

Susan!

Yep! hi! You okay there?

Good, to see you.

God, pretty bloody blinding to see you too Dad!

Hey! Big hug or what.

Pretty bloody blinding . . .

She tell me everything.

Ah well no Dad, I tell you everything.

Yes. Didn't I say thing?

It's okay, words come out how they want sometimes.

I can see you quite lately, I'm a little black to one side, I feel not, on one side, that side.

Little blind? or blurred that's just the shock, Dad, it'll wear off in a while, you know, why don't you have some of this water Dad.

Ah-ha!

There you go. I think you're meant to have a bath now Dad, sounds good to me. Hélène? Hélène!

Now. Sukey.

Yes it's me your Sukey.

What's next in your show?

I was <u>in</u> a show Dad, but I'm not in a show any more.

Tell me all about it.

I will Dad, yes.

Tell me or I don't know.

Yes Dad of course.

Don't know a done thing!

I'll tell you Dad, you'll always know about her, me, you'll always know about me and the, you know, scrapes I get into.

That's the, that's the

The ticket.

That's the done ticket!

That's it Dad, that's the, that's the done ticket.

*

I can see him. Franck. He's very far away, this beach goes on for ages. It's early so it's deserted. I think of the south of France being sunny round the clock and gorgeous people on the sand in shades reading big useless books it's sort of always going on.

Yeah right.

But it's November. It's grey, with litter blowing about. It's Britain. All the places I ever went as a child. People remember childhood being sunny on these crowded beaches, but when I think about mine everyone's scarpered and it's pissing down like this.

It's really sunny here now but it's really cold. I wore my fleece today, the green one? Maggie Trove in Logistics said I looked like a Christmas tree. It's not like I had tinsel the cow I needed it I was cold.

Talking about the weather.

Famous people can talk about the weather!

Famous people can fuck themselves up the arse.

Wow. You're saying that because of one bad experience.

Would you say you're moving on from all that then.

This is a chat on the phone Min, not an interview.

I know that! Just asking. I can ask in a chat on the phone!

Right. True. You can ask in a chat on the phone.

I mean really, we go back. I know we've had our troubles when you were more like the famous one, but I think we've put it all behind us.

It's definitely him.

Can he see you?

Don't think so. Mum knows I like coming here, she must have sent him to come and sweet-talk the sulky daughter. I think he knows I've seen him but he's pretending he doesn't, he's just going to stroll this way and then Oo-la-la, quelle surprise, it ees ze beautifool Suzanne all alone, so like ay beautifool mermedd . . .

Did he say that Suse?

No. It's me, imagining him, saying it.

Doing his voice, I knew that.

He has not to my knowledge called me ay beautifool mermedd. The guy on the beach did that. Franck just thinks it, I can tell. But I am sitting on this black rock that juts out to sea and my hair is a godawful straggly mess and I am keeping my legs together so yes, in the grey light of morning, who knows?

Sounds like you look a bit like a mermaid!

Er . . . right.

With your hair.

I need a cigarette.

I've never seen you smoke! You know it's bad for you.

Oh no I didn't, have they stumbled on something?

Of course you know, you just don't care any more.

I care a lot, I sat there smoking and drinking and I cared a lot. My dad's turned into an old man, my mum's turned into a moody teenager and there's a tall dark stranger hanging round their house all the time smoothing his hair. I smoked my little heart out.

Wow. Can you still see him?

Mm-hm. Following some sort of script. Walk slowly down to water's edge, toss hair back, look out to horizon soulfully as if waiting for white sail. Maybe he thinks he's being videoed.

He's being videoed?

No. In his head.

I just know he's the tall dark stranger. Don't say no to him, will you.

That was all I was going to say.

Well you can, as long as you never say yes.

That won't be quite as hard.

Because he'll try to make you say it. He's the One foretold.

Min, he doesn't know about it, does he. Why would he be trying to make me say yes or no? He doesn't know he's the tall dark stranger. He knows he's the tall floppy-haired poseur but how would he know the witch saw him coming?

Oh yeah.

Min. You're the only person I can talk about it with.

I know I am, Suse. I'm the only one. I hold a special place. Only me and you know these things. Stay away from Franck!

It's not that easy. He's all over my mum. I went to the hypermarket with him in his sports car.

So you do like him?

I went to the hypermarket to help him lug the shopping it's not fucking Romeo and Juliet.

Suse!

Sorry.

I didn't say you loved him! I can hear you smoking.

That's actually my breathing Min.

What's he doing now? Is he walking towards you?

Ever since I saw him he looks at me with this grave look of sympathy, which we both pretend is sympathy that Dad's not well, but I know is sympathy that he keeps showing up. It's like he's saying Ooo-la-la, I make sadness for tout le monde, but it is simply my, ow do you say, destiny, what can I do? Je suis comme je suis.

Suse, when you do the French bits can you slow down slightly. Remember I dropped French at school.

Are you writing things down, Min?

Not all of it.

When I called you from Gatwick you said you had a meeting with someone from a newspaper.

That's right, I've done it already, my agent got me that, Caroline Quark from Foster Braney Quark, she's my agent she's on speed dial, I don't even know her number! And I've already had that meeting. With a journalist from the Observer.

Which is something to do with you writing down things I say.

She's this really important journalist and she's very beautiful and she only does celebrities. And she did me!

How did she do you Min.

She'd just done a film star and she was about to do a stand-up but she couldn't say the names. She drank white wine spritzer and she bought me a Tequila Sunrise which was amazing colours.

And what did she want from you.

She made me shake hands on it, that everything was secret.

Whatever. Hey look he stopped again.

Franck stopped?

I think he might have seen me, but then he pretended not to and got interested in something in the sand. Maybe a mirror or something. So you're writing an article about me.

God! God! You are so full of yourself Suse! I know you've had a, not a bereavement but a family event kind of thing so you're probably under pressure but Suse! It's an article about me!

Minni, sorry but, respect and that, why would a journalist want to write about you?

Why? Because! No reason! Only because I met Thomas Bayne, <u>*the*</u> *Thomas Bayne, in incredible circumstances and if it hadn't been for a certain slightly screwed-up person things might have gone just a little bit further okay? You know like there was chemistry? And, because although the programme was about you and your weird behaviour, I was often asked my opinions in interviews by Ed and by Cass, and so people have started to google me apparently and ask questions and no it's not just 'Susan Mantle's friend' nowadays, it's 'Minni Kaye, the girl at the heart of the drama!' was how she said it. I was the one you told about the fortune teller that day, I was the one you told about Thomas, I was the one, and, other things, other things I was the only one of, so: yes, in a way, she, the journalist, thinks we should* <u>*start*</u> *there in the book,* <u>*start*</u> *with like how I met you and how it all started, but*

Book what book

No, it was only a meeting, with the Observer, there'll be a piece on Sunday, but, also, she thinks we might collaborate on a book written by me? my first book, about the whole story!

Congratulations Min.

Thanks Suse, because you could be writing your own book, and the journalist said 'she probably is', so we had to act quickly. She's going to be the 'ghost-writer' which means she helps with it.

It means she writes what she wants and there's a picture of you on the back.

Yes it's a collaboration.

Min, the show's over, I got out of bed and left, I behaved like a normal person and no one's interested any more.

This is, well, this is something we discussed at our meeting. It's like, it's important more things happen. Or the whole thing's dead she was very clear on that. She called it a deal-breaker, she went to get more drinks, it was 'on account'. The Observer was paying for my drinks!

Nice Observer, what else is supposed to happen?

Well you know, just you being in sort of famous situations. I don't mean famous I mean exciting, glamorous, I mean turning up to things, for example openings, shows, parties, having relationships. Those aren't terrible things! When was the last time you were in love, for example.

She told you to ask that, didn't she.

It's just a standard possible question but I don't have to ask it, in fact I'm not, it's not that sort of book.

What are you asking.

We're old friends, Suse, we mustn't allow our professional relationship to affect our, you know,

Our amateur relationship.

Our friendship. Me and her agreed that you'd been under a lot of pressure and you might behave strangely.

Oh d'ya think? And you want to know what I'm up to.

You keep coming back to you, Suse, it's really a book about me.

Uh-huh. You got a title?

'I Know The Babe Who Was In Bed Forever'.

A working title.

Yeah a working one. But you're still a part of my story.

Well let's see. I'm sitting on the rocks at the far end of France and my dad sort of survived but he's not in great shape and this creepy guy's on his way across the beach to ask a lot of questions I'll say no to and then yes to and then you'd better tell your white wine spritzer chum it's curtains tomorrow.

So, you still believe in the Dawn Sage prophecy?

Do you still believe in the Dawn Sage prophecy?

No. I've never believed in it.

What? You've always believed in it!

I don't believe a word of it.

We were just talking about it, you said you'd been practising not saying yes or no!

No. Yes.

Those two words could kill you!

It's make-believe.

I'm not going to write that down.

Hey you're a natural.

Because it's a total lie: you're just doing opposites again. You totally believe it, it all started coming true! The fame, the money coming in, the money going out, the journey, the tall dark stranger, he's just standing there, he might kill you at any moment!

Hey, way to ruin the ending.

It may not all come true.

Just the bits we like eh.

As long as you don't say yes to who you say no to.

I'm getting surrounded by seagulls here. I have a feeling they're full of shit.

So, moving on: I was wondering if you'd been in contact with any of the following people . . .

Miss Observer do you a list there Min.

Nigel Pilman.

No.

Because he was the One, remember, just before this all happened, you had an affair with him, right?

I wouldn't go that far.

He's saying you did go that far.

He's saying? He's saying to who?

Well. On his blog.

He's got a blog? Who the fuck reads his blog?

Well it's sort of the Guardian's blog this week, like a special, people want to know how Nigel feels about your actions.

I think I'm going to be sick.

'The Guy Who Came In From The Cold', it's called.

Just selecting the right rockpool here.

He sees himself as kind of your boyfriend like in waiting? He feels you and him have a deep bond.

Then he's got a worse memory than my dad. Could you tell your agent to tell your journalist the sex with Nigel was over before I'd finished saying the Jack section of Jack Robinson.

Slow down slow down, I think they'd want the sex bit at the start like a headline.

Oh d'ya think? Who else.

'Jack . . . Robinson . . .' Next point . . . umm: obviously you didn't like Arthur, or 'Points', that came over pretty loud and clear!

I think Points is taken, by the sound.

Well no, because he said in the Mirror today that you were still The One.

He said that in the mirror today? Oh the Mirror today.

But I need to confirm: you have no interest in reviving that relationship?

I'm taking that as confirmed. It's just, I mean the thing is, well you know it would be, like,

Great for your book if I shagged someone who's already in the story.

But I'm not in the business of fiction here.

Good phrase Min. You know these seagulls are getting closer and closer to my rock. Maybe they're vultures in plain clothes.

What about Ed Hardhouse?

As we're not in the business of fiction here, I can tell you I actually dialled Ed's private number the day I got here. I don't know why. I think it was just things were so absurd I thought he might understand, he sort of always did. He wasn't in.

Well with Ed we're in a pretty bad situation since he did the, you know, when he,

Said cunt on live TV.

Suse! well yes he melted down, yes, he's very much in the wilderness, so if you were with him it would be more like kind of

Outlaws, oh I'm suddenly excited, get me Ed on the line!

It wouldn't be the best way to get you back in the public eye.

Minni, how can I put this . . .

Klaus is a no-go, he's in The Glade.

What, rehab?

No The Glade, it's a kind of supergroup, I'll burn you some tracks. I'm assuming I can forget any of the figures from your past.

What figures.

Stuart Gable.

Never heard of him.

Me neither and then John, the main man, I know he's real!

Nah, sorry. Memory runs in our family, it runs away.

I like that Suse, I <u>am</u> actually writing that down. I'm also going to learn shorthand. What about Franck?

He's just standing there, no hang on, he's on his mobile.

I don't mean what's he doing, I mean maybe he's The One?

He's the tall dark stranger. The one I say no to.

The One you say yes to!

If I want to die the next day.

So you do believe it!

I don't believe it. I just think Death believes it.

Suse!

You wore the T-shirt.

Well yes, we all did, but that was you know, at the height of you know . . .

That was at the height of that.

Yeah, the, the craze.

Maybe no one's The One.

That's, Suse! Everyone's got one somewhere in the world, one who's The One. Some people actually think it may be Thomas Bayne with me, can you imagine? I mean people who heard us having a laugh together that time, like Steve from the crew? he said it was possible. But you know, how am I supposed to just bump into the world's biggest film star?

I dunno, check out the kitchen.

You all make jokes about him and apparently he's now got a bit of a reclusive lifestyle, which means he only sees very close people round the pool for meetings and there's always like bodyguards? He just flies from one stunning location to the next in his own jet he pilots. He's got all that money, but it hasn't brought him happiness. Just thought you ought to know.

Well thanks for that update Min. I think we can safely say that's one tall dark stranger I won't be saying anything at all to ever again.

That's terrible, though, saying 'never again' about anything. To know that Thomas Bayne knows you, and you'll never again, I'm shivering Suse.

Everything's never again Min.

Don't say that!

Nothing comes again.

Just stop it!

Okay.

There's someone out there for everyone and it might be anyone!

I'd go the whole wide world.

What?

It's a song about it. Old punk song. About there being this one someone in the world for you.

You'd go the whole wide world?

Probably not, personally, but the guy in the song would.

I was going to say, cos you wouldn't even get out of bed.

Fair point.

I think Franck's The One.

Well. I think he's the one shagging my mother, but I've been under a lot of pressure haven't I.

Yes. You have. And I'm not writing that down. I'm your friend. That's your private life. What's Franck doing now?

He's still on his mobile. He's about a hundred metres away.

Right . . . Suse, what's a hundred metres I mean I know what a hundred metres is but, like, how far is it?

Like the running track at school, the short race, the sprint, you know the hundred metres race, same concept.

I didn't do running, you were the runner, I played rounders in the B group.

He's still talking. He's probably got no one on his mobile at all, just thinks I'm watching, just thinks it looks good. The waves keep coming in and just missing his black suede shoes. Go waves, one more push.

And you know for a fact you haven't said no to him or yes to him.

I do. I believe I do know that for a fact.

And there's no one else you've said that to, the Y word or the N word.

There was this older guy I met on the beach, I was a bit pissed but he was sort of faded blond and the same height as Jesus. Anyway what do you care, he's not on television. For the record I went to meet him on the beach and he wasn't there. I guess he thought what's the point, they all die.

Wow. And there's no other men you've talked to.

I talked to the guy in the café. That was all in my bad French and he isn't tall.

And that's all the men.

Well there's Dad.

How is your dad?

Oh I don't know Miranda.

But you've seen him, you said.

He sleeps a lot, I've seen him twice. There's some problem with memory, getting words wrong and stuff.

That's like me. But I'm not ill though. But that's terrible!

It is, actually. It is actually, a bit terrible.

Mm, how's your mum?

I dunno. Like you'd think. Dry, busy. Sort of snapped inside, he keeps mistaking me for her. I had to keep saying no Dad it's me.

Bloody hell Suse.

I know. He had to sort it out in his head. But he got there. But . . . when he doesn't think it's me there, it sort of feels like, it isn't me there. It's like, who the fuck is it then.

Wow. That's incredible.

And he's someone else. Some of the time he's. He's someone else.

Like you mean a stranger.

I suppose it's more he's, his own dad? No that's not it.

Not a tall dark stranger anyway.

Suse.

Wait.

Suse, he's not tall, is he, your dad?

Stop.

And I know he's not dark.

He's, actually he's very tanned, he's very brown, I suppose that's. He is tall. He was tall. I just haven't seen him standing up. I haven't seen him standing up for about . . . a year.

But he's not a stranger really, he's your dad!

He's . . . he's, my dad, Min.

That can't be right.

But he, he feels like a stranger but you're right, he's my dad.

Well . . . okay . . . if, I'm only saying if.

If . . .

I'm only saying if, if you did say no to him.

He was calling me Marie. I thought I ought to say no to that, to help him, to help me

Did you say yes to him?

I . . .

Did you?

He, he asked me to tell him things, to keep him up with anything I was doing, scrapes I got into and yes, I, I said yes to that.

So you said no to him Suse, until the day you said yes.

Stop.

'And on the next day' . . . when was it you said that? what day did you say yes to him?

Yesterday.

You said yes. Yesterday.

Yesterday at sunset in his room Franck's seen me now he's coming this way –

Suse, just like, you know, just like, in case? maybe you should like –

'On the next day'

Suse.

Suse get away from there.

*

'And death shall have no dominion.
Dead men naked they shall be one
With the man in the wind and the west moon;
When their bones are picked clean and the clean bones gone,
They shall have stars at elbow and foot;
Though they go mad they shall be sane,
Though they sink through the sea they shall rise again;
Though lovers be lost love shall not;
And death shall have no dominion.'

Suzanne!

Franck I have to get away from you!

Pardon? Come back Suzanne!

I have to talk with you!

Franck please stop following me, arretez, arretez!

I am stopped, okay! Stop running Suzanne!

*

'And death shall have no dominion.
Under the windings of the sea
They lying long shall not die windily;
Twisting on racks when sinews give way,
Strapped to a wheel, yet they shall not break;
Faith in their hands shall snap in two
And the unicorn evils run them through;
Split all ends up they shan't crack;
And death shall have no dominion.'

Please just stay that far away. Please Franck.

It's okay Suzanne, it is me your friend.

So; I might walk a bit further along the beach, and you could maybe, for me, walk back that way towards Mum's house?

Suzanne.

It's nothing against you, Franck, okay, it really isn't, it's just been hard for me, you know with Dad, and I need to stand a long way from everyone just now, I mean physically. Thirty feet is good, beaucoup de metres.

Suzanne.

It's, a day for me to be all toute seule.

Suzanne, I need you to come back with me to the home.

That's not possible Franck.

This is not right.

What's not right.

(C'est fou je téléphone c'est absolument fou)

Don't come any closer, Franck.

Who are you calling, Franck.

Franck. I'm going to walk further away right now.

Non non non, attends, wait wait

I don't think I can do that Franck. Who are you talking to?

Your mother, Suzanne. You must speak with her, il faut.

Mum's on your phone? What's that about?

Come on now Suzanne talk to your mother.

Look. Look. I know this is ridiculous, c'est ridicule and so on, but could you put the phone on the sand and walk away as far as that sort of post?
I, – oh mon dieu. Okay, I do that.

Voilà. Post, okay. I do it.
Thank you. Franck. I'm very sorry about this behaviour.
It is okay Suzanne, c'est dur, it is hard times.

Mum?

(Susan . . .)
Mum, Franck's running after me, Mum, why?

Mum?

Mum are you

No

No

No

Oh no no please God Mum no

*

'And death shall have no dominion.
No more may gulls cry at their ears
Or waves break loud on the seashores;
Where blew a flower may a flower no more
Lift its head to the blows of the rain;
Though they be mad and dead as nails,
Heads of the character hammer through daisies;
Break in the sun till the sun breaks down,
And death shall have no dominion.'

*

Mademoiselle

Mademoiselle. Ça, c'est saumon, ça c'est poulet, est ça c'est, c'est quoi, c'est aubergine

Saumon, poulet, aubergine

Celui-la? Saumon. Voilà

Je vous empris

*

That was just such a lovely idea
Did brilliantly in the circs
Marvellous lilt to that piece I think it's a Welsh thing that lilt
Played a blinder there ma cousine
Someone get this girl a drink

*

The daughter was fantastic
Had that thing off by heart
And to do that. I mean
Hush Bill she's right there
I'm saying how good she was I don't care if she hears
Sshh I know but still
She was a credit Pam she was, she was a credit

*

We're so very, I know you know, I just did want to say

She read wonderfully, you did you know

You know when I last saw you you were what fifteen? you were deep in some book or other

Toujours la poésie, Suzanne

Couldn't get a word out of her not the TV star of today!

Bill

You have a most beautiful speaking voice Susie

Very stylish, you looked up three times it was nicely judged

You have a drink do you dear look you're empty

Let me get this babe a drink, rouge or blank, rouge it is!

*

'Do Not Go Gentle Into That Good Night' is a villanelle mate

It's a sestina

It's a villanelle mate

Fifty euros

Angel come and pass judgement on these two fools

*

Did you not ask her for the poem

I'm not asking her for that you can get it in a bookshop

We were thinking you might sign it dear

God you're inappropriate

Would you sign it so we remember your lovely recital

*

Mademoiselle, saucissons?

Saucissons

Moutarde?

Moutarde

Dijon? or Cole-Mans?

Both

Tous le deux

*

You okay there

I wouldn't eat that
Come here

Susan
Look at me

Look at me
You're my star you
You know that

*

Can you take the Renault

He also wrote Under Milk Wood
That's a play though not a poem mate
She's taking the Renault

What, why are you looking at me like that
Shit you can't drive can you
Doubt it
I'm so out of it, can you go with Jean-Pierre and the Lavalles is there room
There is always room!
Sure it's a dramatic piece but it's poetic in style

*

Look someone left their umbrella

Anyone leave their umbrella

Is this anyone's
Last time of asking

Going, going, gone

Won't need it for a while

Another bright one tomorrow

I'm having an interval right now, I've paused it I'm telling you sweetheart, I'm in the middle of let's see, Act Three, and it's all kicking off, there's these noblemen and they get into a quarrel, but you know this.

Nope. It's not a good line Ed.

Well you may have forgotten the details, but I'm way up on it now, so some bloke plucks a white rose like just there's a hedge right there, then this other geezer plucks a red one and it proceeds like that: I'll have a white one, I'll have a red one, white, you're a bastard, red, you're an arse, fuck you then, outside, let's do it and it's actually, historically, the beginning of the Wars of the Roses. Or, obviously, reflected through the prism of the bardic mind.

You get that rose imagery to this day. You still there Mantle?

You keep cutting out. Someone picked a rose, someone was an arse.

I'm pacing about my cottage, you see, in the general surge of excitement at hearing the Mantle tones. That's all, it has a chemical explanation, sshh, anyway . . . yeah, so Wars of the Roses and I feel I'm present at the dawn of it, down through the magic of literature, I got it all set up in my study, got the lights dimmed down, got the fire going, got the Beeb's Collected DVDs.

You're watching all of Shakespeare Ed.

In the order of its compositions.

Pretty good.

I mean, there's a lively dispute about which of the texts was first, but I thought the Harry Sixes was a decent place to launch it, you know, historical grounding and all that it's a weakness in my game, you know that well, and I'll probably bring Andronicus and maybe

Errors into the mix at some point, get a blend of the genres. Is that your flight being called?

Nope. Security announcement. Incomprehensible.

You know the terminal you're coming into?

Wait wait it's in English now.

No it's nothing. Still shit. Nothing into Gatwick. Security scare.

Well that squares with the website, poor wand'ring one.

Age of air travel, eh.

My flight departs 15.15, that's six hours ago. Arrives 16.15, that's five hours ago, or four, or six, there's some missing hour somewhere fell in the Channel. I should be home in about two hours ago.

Got it. You got a book to read there Mantle?

Yeah I got a book, my mum lent me this book about how Jesus marries a sex worker and has a kid and obviously that kid has descendants and one of them ends up being a gendarme.

You what?

Give it a moment Ed.

Jesus . . . sex . . . gendarme . . . ah, very good. You're reading Brown. Bit of a page turner.

I'm going to write a novel, Ed, and my pseudonym will be Paige Turner and maybe people will see that on the cover and, sort of,

Subliminally, right,

Etc.

You know the extraordinary thing, going back to the Bard for a second, is: you know anything about this bloke Robert Greene?

Tell me, Ed, keep going.

Right, this bloke, this critic and this is early on, when the youngster's maybe done Adonis, Lucrece, few sonnets maybe One to Ten, the Rose series, but not much of what we now know, so: Greene calls him, I wrote this down: 'an upstart crow'

'In borrowed feathers' Ed, it's famous.

Oh . . . Not to me it's not, I'm like, I'm a little shocked to tell you the truth, a little put out on behalf of the young Bard.

I'm sure he got over it and you will too.

Shake-scene, he calls him. Greene.

Yep.

Talk about missing the mark eh?

Mm.

You okay there chicken.

Got my book. Twelve shit magazines. Patch of floor.

You know, there will be, angel, people at Gatwick, I mean, when you finally make it.

Mm there'll be people.

But you know what I mean.

Yep.

When the news came through I think it caught 'em on the hop, it was like, haven't we moved on from that lady? Like it's all about this Kiss of Life chap, you know,

Points

All Points Bulletin yeah and whatever babes they can get from Hollywood to fish him out of a pond. Also, you know, it was said by some, let her have her privacy at this sad time.

That's nice.

I know, I'm just quoting from the nonsense.

I know Ed.

Been no one else on my mind since the hour I knew.

I know.

No one but you Mantle night and day.

Stop, Ed, I know, it's fine.

But what you got now is

Ed you're cutting out again.

Sorry I was in my fridge, I'm getting a snack here I'm like Pooh Bear or Paddington or one o' them hungry bears, you know, Yogi there in Yellowstone, an astounding place, here, I'll go back where I was I'll, I'll perch on the stairs that's best, got a big ham baguette here, so; yeah, someone saw it this way: we're all pieces of shit, to put it mildly, we're the worst people out, what in the name of Christ have we done, all sorts started coming out, about how Plume behaved, how the network behaved and De Coex, De Coex my protégée I'm proud to say was instrumental in this change of angle, and soon we have a total, you know 360-degree change of perspective on the whole thing.

Ed, I really hate myself for doing this, but a 360-degree change of perspective isn't a change of perspective. It's, I'm sorry.

Oh yeah.

180-degree.

180, right, so: Plume got the boot is the big news.

Cassidy was fired?

She took the heat for it. 'Cassidy De Ville' they had in the Express as in one-oh-one Dalmatians, and they photo-shopped her all dressed in the dog-skins of her victims.

Is she in the wilderness too? She reading Milton?

Behave, the Beeb snapped her up within the hour, girl's fronting The Zoo Game. But vis-à-vis young Mantle, well, now it's all, got the papers here, woah, it's a bit major really.

Go on.

Can you take it babe?

Take anything me.

Well here goes. SAD SUZIE: ENGLISH ROSE WE THREW AWAY *. . . that's fairly typical of the genre . . .* WHEN TRAGEDY TOLLED, WE TURNED OUR BACKS *. . . well tell us something we don't know . . .* MORE TEARS FOR SLEEPING BEAUTY . . . DEATH AND THE ICE-MAIDEN . . . SORROW OF SNOOZIE MENTAL, *that's the Sun of course but they're trying to do the decent thing, they got the old original picture from 20/10 . . .*

So I'm crying about my dad a month ago when he's fine.

They're okay with that. Oh this one's a little out there: DEATH – THE EMPIRE STRIKES BACK, *don't want to go there, that's all in the news sections, then there's stuff further in, a tad more considered . . .* DREAM GIRL WHO DARED TO BE DIFFERENT, *that's the Economist. And there's a big swing back to the whole Thomas Bayne Revelation hoo-ha, how you lifted the nation in the dark days. Here's another one, this is a Telegraph leader about this whole moral decline they're seeing, it's the final ringing phrase: 'The babe in bed forever? We'll remember you forever.'*

Oh Jesus

Nice headshot too, ya radiance, and they got Knightley on the facing page and it's close girl, it's even-stevens, sshh, anyway . . . bit of a turn-around, right, bit of a lurch on the ol' swingometer.

I don't want any more of that, Ed.

I know babe I know.

I don't want any more of it. How come everyone knows when my flight is, the only person I told is

Oh.

Right.

How is ol' Mini-girl.

Said she'd come to meet me. I thought,

I wasn't thinking straight.

How could you be love, how could you be.

Little bitch.

Yeah well I saw her piece.

Her piece in the Observer?

Never made it, got spiked, I got a sneak at it. Just got her angles wrong, that's all, no one wants to read about your old boyfriends, or that you're two-faced or you stabbed her in the back, sod it, water under, we've had it with the bad times, you're England's Rose now, Mark II if you will, you're bereaved, people want to make amends.

She's doing a book about me Ed.

Think she just lost that gig. Look I can meet you if you like, I can bring you through the crowd Costner and Houston-style.

I don't know when I'm flying. I don't know if I'm flying. This is all just, awful.

Hang on in there doll.

Everything awful waiting to meet me at the gate, all holding up signs saying HELLO I'M RUBBISH and HI I'M SHIT.

I'll come and meet you doll, and my sign will say WELCOME HOME YOU STAR.

Hey now.

Hey girl don't cry.

Mantle, love, go back, get a taxi back to your ma's. Leave another day.

I can't Ed, I just

I know, I know,

I wanted to come alone, so no one would be nice to me at the airport, it's people being nice to me I've been dealing with all week, I don't even know how long. Uncles, aunts, cousins, friends, I don't know them, they just showed up and everyone started partying.

Old-style send-off, eh.

Excuse for a winter break

It's Celtic-style, you know?

One-eighth Irish Ed, that's all

No but it's the bit you want at times like this.

Is it. Maybe.

It's where I am y'know chick.

You're in Ireland?

The old hideaway. Got O'Leary's down the road, always music playing, someone's always shouting about something or other. Cheers me up anyroad. Not like your voice, but, y'know.

Loud noise is good.

Loud noise is good.

Drink's been good too. Drink's been a real mate.

You got a bar there in the lounge?

Lounge. Ha.

In the terminal?

It's just packed out Ed it's horrible I'm too hung-over to cope. My aunt gave me some miniatures and I can't even touch them.

Wish I could descend from above, sweep you off to your little home. Or mine! Got the fire going here.

Sounds nice Ed.

Raining outside, chucking it down. Fire blazin away.

Lovely.

It's just my little hidey-hole from the old ill-gotten gains.

Well I'm stuck in an airport.

Be home soon.

I'm just, I feel empty sort of.

I know.

Like something's over. I mean . . .

What's that?

I mean all that stuff that witch saw. She saw this, she saw him, Dad, but she was useless at her work. Thought she was seeing me.

You're going to be just fine Mantle.

And now there's also . . .

Also what?

There's, a little man, a little bald man in a brown suit, a little bald man in a brown suit with glasses just looking at me from over by Gate 10.

Thought you were in disguise babe.

I am. Short hair, dyed red, big shades, cap with some team logo on it.

Right, every star anywhere.

It's my new look. I'm Paige Turner, I'm researching a new novel about being stuck in an airport forever.

Good on yer Turner.

Just making some notes here.

Bloke still eyeballing you?

Pretends he isn't, then does it again. He's checking me against something like some document he has.

Chill out, princess, he's a fan of the show.

No way he can tell it's me. I can't tell it's me. He's looking right at me.

Ignore it chicken, you're tired here.

He's approaching.

Come on . . .

He's smiling, he thinks I know him . . .

Mantle you there? Turner?

I'll call you back in a minute okay?

Don't hang up.
It's okay Ed.
Hold your horses babe.
Just wait.
Mantle!
Okay, just stay on the line while I do this.
I'm right here babe, don't hang up.

(Afternoon, Susan, I'm delighted to meet you. George Ball. I'm from the network. We heard about the delays and we just find it intolerable that you would be in this situation.)

I'm sorry are you talking to me.

(I know your work, I'm something of an admirer, and we find this intolerable, after what you've been through, so; if you like, if you don't mind, we have you on a flight to City Airport which leaves in twenty minutes.)

I think you've made a mistake. What work.

(Here's my card, I'm from the network, George Ball, no, direct flight, private jet belonging to the network, usually reserved for the bigwigs, but there's pressure on your behalf, you know, with one thing and another.)

I, no.

(Look, tête-à-tête, in confidence. You gave; we took. Understand me? Now we'd rather like to give back a little. First-class, look, here's the ticket, if you come with me we'll check you in, fast-track, Susan, no? come on there look sharp! Oh and I need your passport. Susan?)

Look, I'm not

(In all of sixty seconds you can be out of this hellhole and sipping Veuve Clicquot in the VIP lounge.)

I think you broke me.
(That's the spirit.)

Ed?
You okay love?
It's fine, I'll call you from London.
You sure babe?

It's fine, they got me on first-class.

Who got you on first-class?

Bye, I'll call you.

Mantle?

Okay where do I sign.

(Just follow me Susan and you'll be spirited out of all this! Try to think of me as your fairy godfather.)

Okay.

(Many have. And it's Ball, that's how we remember!)

What?

(Cinderella <u>will</u> go to the Ball. Or in this case the Ball will come to Cinderella! George Ball will come to Cinderella!)

I get it. Thanks anyway.

(Don't thank me, thank the network!)

Thanks network.

(It's our delight. On a Saturday night.)

*

Just sit yourself down there, Susan.

It's a chair. It's soft, it has arms. I don't think I'll ever get out of this chair. Can you carry me on to the plane in this chair?

I'm going to ask you what you'd like from that little bar.

I'm going to call this chair Bonner, like my cat, until I see my cat again.

We are so very sorry you had to go through this.

What, this?

All a bit of a mix-up at HQ. What can I get you, Susan?

Yes, things, a Bloody Mary, spicy, a selection of those tiny posh sandwiches anything but tuna.

And here's your passport back, that's all done and dusted, and I'll hang on to this which is your boarding card, so you have one less thing to worry about. Right, snacks, back in a mo.

Good little man. Good little man in a brown suit.

*

How's that going down, Susan?

It's going down very well thank you.

George Ball. Not too spicy?

It's excellent, George Ball.

We have five minutes or so.

Yup.

Now you understand, don't you Susan, we are asking for absolutely nothing in return?

Well this sounded so good I didn't give a monkey's for a while back there, but now you say so, good, I appreciate that.

Our treat!

Don't do the limelight any more.

What a jolly good idea that is!

We think so.

There's another plane taking off. Up, up and away.

Right. Forgot about that. Have to get on one of those. Fuck.

Safest way to travel, Susan.

Yeah right.

Well. Have you ever flown on a private jet, Susan?

Funnily enough no.

I think you'll find this not only the safest way to travel but also the most stylish.

Okay. How many, um, private jets you got then.

Just the one.

And, er, no one else wants it tonight.

No one else can have it tonight. Would you like another cocktail?

What do you reckon.

I'm going to plump for the affirmative!

Go for it.

As soon as you call me George!

George.

*

And here there's just this one very last beastly security check.

And this is going to City, right.

It says so on your ticket, must be true! Closest airport to your home I do believe.

I can see all those people still waiting in the lounge.

Yes. Good, isn't it.

Kind of. Feel I'm still sitting there. Poor old patch of floor.

Here, sir, this is Susan Mantle.

(Evening Susan.)

Evening mate.

(Enjoy your flight Susan.)

Thanks mate.

And there we are.

Abracadabra.

And this passage takes us straight into the cabin . . .

Hey presto. Jack Robinson. Zbigniew Jackson.

*

Oh. My. God.

You did say you'd never flown in a private jet.

It's,

It's amazing.

It's a bit small.

It's a bit private!

It's a bit empty.

As I say, it's private. We don't take just anyone! This gentleman is the steward for the flight and his name is Mr Gary Lord.

(Good evening and welcome to Flight Delta-Charlie-Five-O to London's City Airport, Miss Susan Mantle!)

Thank you.

(Gary Lord!)

Gary Lord.

(Please feel free to choose from any one of these luxury seats!)

I'll, I shall choose Luxury Seat . . . Number . . . Two, Gary.

(Gary Lord, that's a good choice. You know who sat there last week?)

I don't. Who did.

(Well, I'm not at liberty to tell you, but seeing as you are a Very Important Guest I shall write his or her initials on the window in my own breath.)

Oh, him. I think he was playing football in my garden at one point. Everyone else was. Where's George?

I believe George Ball has deplaned.

He has? Blimey. Puff of smoke.

And I believe you should make yourself as comfortable as possible.

Um, Gary,

Ms Mantle.

I'm not the world's most frequent flyer, Gary, and I find it a little grim and so, perhaps you could sort of keep the drinks coming a little?

I'm on my way to do that right now.

This is a bit good Gary.

The pilot will be out to say hello once we've reached our cruising altitude.

Um. Okay. Who'll be flying the plane at that point?

When the pilot's in here with me I mean.

Oh my word. Lord in Heaven I hadn't thought of that!

Okay it's a stupid question

I'm joking with you! It is so not a stupid question and I'm kind of a bit of a joker, Ms Mantle, I'm known for that, and for which I apologise, and also for my language just now, but I have this kind of need to put people at their ease?

Okay.

No of course there are two pilots, like on any regular commercial flight.

Whatever can I have my drink.

You only have to think of what you want and I'll be in the galley getting it ready for you. I'm your genie, Ms Mantle. You need to think of me as the lamp guy. Now we just need to get your seatbelt fastened, good, and let's put your handbag right down here all nice and comfy, and we're pretty much ready to rumble. Would you like the blind up or down? There's a pretty impressive view Susan as we rise up over the bay.

Down.

Down, and without further ado, I shall strap myself in back here, well out of your way, and let's get ready to take to the skies!

####### HELLO. THIS IS MIRANDA KAYE. I AM NOT AVAILABLE TO TAKE YOUR CALL RIGHT NOW. IF YOUR CALL IS CONCERNING 'THE BABE IN BED FOREVER' OR 'WITH FRIENDS LIKE THAT' PLEASE LEAVE A MESSAGE, IF IT'S ABOUT SOMETHING ELSE, CALL BACK ANOTHER TIME. THANK YOU. #

No offence but it actually is the babe in bed forever, so, just to say, I should be at Gatwick about twenty-three hundred what's that, eleven, Min. Thanks for meeting me, you're a pal.

Telling a little fib there, are we!

Yeah Gary.

Gary Lord. Our destination is of course City Airport.

I don't care if she's waiting in fucking Basra.

Mmm, matters of the heart . . .

Hey feel free to comment.

Now at this point I do have to tell you to switch off your cellphone and any other electronic items on your person.

Is this the safety demonstration?

My intention is to begin the full safety demonstration in approximately: sixteen seconds.

Would it be okay if I didn't watch it.

I'm sorry?

Would it be okay if I didn't watch the safety demonstration.

It would be most irresponsible, I would have to report you to the relevant Aviation Authority. The consequences could include a custodial sentence.

That's you putting me at my ease again, isn't it.

Of course you don't have to watch it! Joke, hello-o! I assume you're familiar with all the major elements. Of course legally I'm obliged to recommend you watch it, but I don't get offended when people turn their heads away I'm way past that.

Okay, it's just it makes me nervous. I know an oxygen mask drops from the sky but I know I'll freeze when it does, I'll look for some child to tie it on to, and when it comes to needing to blow that whistle to attract attention I always think, don't you think if our plane has crashed near some people who might help us, they might have noticed that happening and if it'd somehow escaped their attention a whistle wouldn't make a huge impact on them,

Do you know, Miss Susan Mantle, what the odds are against a catastrophic real-world event happening in an aeroplane?

Could you say a really big number that takes ages.

For a catastrophic real-world event in an aeroplane to be statistically likely, you would have to take a flight every day for twenty-seven thousand years.

Bastard commute.

Let's do the demonstration, shall we.

*

We have now reached our cruising altitude. The captain has turned off the seatbelt sign, so please feel free to walk about the cabin. However we would recommend that you keep your seatbelt fastened at all times in case we encounter unexpected turbulence. There, that's the script out of the way.

Did well.

We can relax now.

Can I get another drink please?

Hey, maybe I should do the safety demonstration concerning alcohol!

No. Be the lamp guy.

While you're doing that I might just feel free to walk about the cabin.

Sounds good to me, Miss Mantle.

How exciting . . . Here goes nothing. There. I'm over here now. Hello! I might try out Luxury Seat Number Three for a short while. There. Very nice. Leg room. Woah what was that –

Little bump, that's all, maybe a good idea to fasten your seatbelt, like it says in the script!

Okay, maybe. That's enough walking about the cabin. I felt a bit, free there for a second, now I'm – shit!

Hey hey, it's nothing, little air pocket

I know I know. It's just, I'm in a posh hotel room I don't want it bumping around on me – shit –

Hey now it's just air Miss Mantle, think of us rolling over it like a little boat on the water, sometimes it gets a little choppy is all.

I think it's smoothing out –

Take a look at the view, take your mind off it, I can raise the blind,

No that would remind me I'm millions of feet in the air, wouldn't it Gary.

Oh but the beauty of the coast at night.

No. I'm happy like this, I'm just waiting for the – fuck – sorry, for the bumps to stop, okay

FUCK –

Hey hey, little boat, over the waves,

I like that keep saying that keep saying that

Little boat, over the water,

Okay,

Hey hey, just hold on, no worries Miss Mantle look I'm still fixing your drink, how bad can it be?

Okay okay okay okay you're right, tomato juice, vodka, lots of vodka,

You're the customer.

Worcester sauce, pepper

Lots of spice.

Stick of celery

May have to pass on the celery. Not my fault.

Okay okay we talked it down, we're, oh that's good, it's bliss, it's gone, we're good, we're very very level, we, I can't even feel it, in my hotel room we're, room service we're okay

I think the Captain was using the toilet facility.

What?

So the Second Officer took control and he's kind of a rookie!

What?

And here's your cocktail, Susan Mantle, and it's about time for me to take your dinner order!

You cannot be serious! You finished that drink already?

★

Well hi there!

Uh?

Second Officer Miles Field!

What?

I'm your co-pilot today. Thought I'd come and keep you company while Gary Lord's fixing dinner!

I'm really not I mean I won't be much company, Miles

Miles Field!

I won't be much company Mr Field

Miles Field!

I – I'm tired, Miles . . . Field.

That's it you got it! Miles Field.

I'm tired Miles Field and I think I'll probably just snooze all the way home.

Fantastic.

I'm Snoozie Mental, you see, that's my name.

I know that it is NOT!

No, er, right, it's a nickname, it was, doesn't matter. So, you're the co-pilot.

It's a huge day for me, man.

It is?

First time on this run.

First time on this, okay, right.

But you're pretty experienced, right?

Well, there's nothing like experience, and every moment I fly with the Captain I get just that little bit more!

Right. But you must have thousands of air miles, Miles. Sorry, miles-miles you must get that a lot.

I'm sorry?

You must, get that a lot, Miles Field.

I have many air miles under my belt.

Thousands, right?

Certainly a couple of thou.

That's,

Just working it out here, that's not all that many, is it.

When I fly with the Captain it's like it really doesn't matter, it's like I've flown all my life, he gives you that feeling, when in fact I'm only, how old do you think I am?

Um, okay, little sip here . . . if you weren't in that uniform I'd hazard that you're, um, sixteen. Miles Field.

Man. Man I like that! I'm twenty-one. A youthful twenty-one!

Very impressive.

You're a very elegant lady, Miss Susan Mantle.

Well, thank you. Miles. You're a very gauche young man.

Miles Field. Thank you.

Miles Field could I just ask, what is it with the names, it sounds a bit weird to me to keep calling you all by both names, is that wrong of me I don't want to offend you.

You do not, my friend, and people do sometimes find that unusual, but we feel it shows respect both to the person and to the person's parents.

I, suppose it does, um, Miles Field, I suppose it, right.

Who's we?

The Captain and I, Miles Field, also the steward Gary Lord, hard at work over there, the navigator Chip Cloy – he's off today – and of course our associate George Ball.

Why's the, you say the navigator's off?

Chip Cloy's off, that's right. He's off doing his wild thing the Chipmeister!

Okay but you, Miles, Miles Field, and the Captain, the Captain has skills in navigation, does he?

Hell yes! Man!

The Captain does.

The Captain can find his way anywhere, like, darkness, fog, storms God forbid we hit a storm! No he's a superb flyer the Captain. Me, I'm not quite at that level. I was never great with maps, Susan Mantle, now my brother, Lucas Field, he's in a different class.

He's not on the plane, is he.

No. He's no longer with us.

Could Gary Lord make me another drink do you think.

I know that man can! And you know I think I could do with a smoothie!

(Hey I heard that, I'm the man who can! you two guys just need to keep each other company and you'll have your heart's desire in a couple minutes!)

That's all good.

(And soon the Captain may come and join you for dinner.)

I'm sorry?

(We have a tradition that the Captain comes to join our special guests for dinner.)

That's, nice, um: He doesn't need to, um, Gary Lord, he, he probably would rather carry on flying, right, like it's not the sort of plane that can fly itself, is it?

(Hey, pretty much!)

Pretty much!

Ha ha, right, no, right. So, okay. So you, Miles Field, you'll be flying the plane if the Captain joins me for dinner.

I sure will! It's a huge night for me!

You know what, um, Miles Field, I am just so tired now that it would be really, truly, awful for him, I mean deadly boring for the Captain if he sat with me, I'd really spoil the whole flight for him by how anti-social I'd be, you know, falling asleep in mid-conversation, that sort of thing.

The Captain is ultra sympathetic and he would not mind that at all.

Well, okay, good on him, but. Well, one other thing, and I think you all know this, is that I've had a, I'd had a loss in the family, and in many ways I need to be, I mean I sort of crave, alone, ness, being alone.

We are all extremely sympathetic to your needs at this sad time.

Thank you, Miles Field.

(Here comes dinner!)

Thank you too, Gary Lord, and if I might now

(It's swordfish steak!)

Right. Okay. Thanks. Thanks Gary Lord.

(Kind of a nice surprise, right? A little birdie told us this was your favourite!)

Mm-hm. Cheers.

Susan Mantle, it's been an absolute pleasure speaking with you on what's genuinely a major night for me.

Right. Right Miles Field.

And I now return to my cockpit duties!

Yep. Good luck. I mean, not good luck you don't need luck you're a trained pilot.

I'm getting' there, my friend, I am most definitely gettin' there!

Fucking hell.

(You know . . .)

What. Gary Lord, what.

(I have absolutely no problem with that kind of language.)

Well. That's fucking handy.

(Hey right! And now I do believe the Captain's coming!)

He really shouldn't trouble.

(I believe it's his pleasure!)

You'd be right to believe that. Everything to do with Susie Mantle is my pleasure.

What the fuck –

We are points of light, Susie Mantle, where can we be but together?

No wait, no. No, no, you're on this plane

Check.

No no, you're, you're the Captain, you're flying the plane

Check.

No you're, can you stop saying check

I think I can safely say I am not flying the plane right now, that's in the hands of Second Officer Miles Field.

Wait, stop, wait. This plane belongs to the network?

Negative.

This is your plane. This is your plane.

I have a very good relationship with the network, Susie, and I have nine hundred thousand miles of flying experience, it's really what I do best, and if I happen to want to give one of my favourite people in the world a ride home to England in my jet

at a difficult time in her life, well there are enough good people on the pathway ahead to facilitate that gesture. Gary Lord would you get me a soda.

Thomas, Thomas Bayne, it's

(Soda coming right up Captain!)

I'm grateful for that, that gesture, Thomas. I really, I, I really needed someone to help me get home, because you're right, it's a sad time for me and I really am, glad you've helped, so, thank you.

It's such a beautiful thing to do a good deed by a friend.

It is and you know what, Thomas, Thomas Bayne, I wonder if you could help me a little more.

What do you think?

What what do you mean what do I think.

Hey Gary Lord. She wants to know if I'll help her, this extraordinary young lady, what do you think my answer's going to be?

(That's an easy one Captain, your answer is going to be Yes.)

Gary Lord you're a winner and you just won again. When someone is in need, Thomas Bayne's answer is always Yes.

Thank you, great, could I tell you now how you can help me?

You don't need to say it Susie, you know what the answer's going to be, it's going to be Yes!

Look I just want to go home, and, also, I want you to fly the plane because you have millions of hours and not that other guy because he looks about ten and he seems nervous, so, well, okay, that's what I need you to agree to.

You know what, that is funny.

Can you do that then, I was telling the others, I'm quite a nervous flyer, Thomas, but you don't make me nervous, it's smooth when you're in there in the cockpit area I feel safer that's all so yeah: you, not him, in there, that would be great.

Susie, Susie Mantle, Miles Field may be a boy, but he's a boy wonder, he is just a supremely gifted flyer, he's an absolute natural and he's going to be a top pilot one day. Sure he makes mistakes: don't you make mistakes? You do make mistakes. I should know!

You think I'd have him up there if I doubted him? I know I'm kind of crazy, but hey my life's in his hands!

Mine is, yep

You could not be safer Susie, you make me laugh! Tell me you believe me!

Deep breath, I believe you

Look me in the eye and tell me: I am safe with Miles Field at the controls!

I am safe with Miles Field

At the controls

At the controls

Don't you feel safe now, woah!

FUCK!

FUCK I hate that oh my God

(I am so okay with that language.)

That's cool, Gary Lord. You got your seatbelt on here Susie?

I do, I told him, I hate turbulence, that's all, and you said I could feel safe

I command you to feel safe! Obey! OBEY!

Jesus Christ, can he fucking fly or not?

(I hear the suffering in that language.)

Hey, Susie, look at me my friend, we call that mild turbulence, low-level, a little wrinkle in the air,

(Very much what I said, Captain.)

Hey, hey, Gary Lord. Who's talking here.

(You are, Captain.)

Who's talking here?

Susie doesn't need two voices here, do you think?

You think she needs two voices?

(I told her about the boat on the water Captain.)

Then that's good, Gary Lord, you did a good thing. Now it's my turn to do a good thing. Do you think I'll do a good thing, Gary Lord?

(Captain you will do a beautiful thing I know it.)

A good thing?

(A truly good thing Captain.)

Please, Thomas, Thomas, please fly the aeroplane

I would love to fly the aeroplane, Susie

FUCK!

Hey that was a wild one!

Oh God

Hey Thunder Mountain style! Pitch'n'roll, pitch'n'roll, just go with it Susie, it's like Gary Lord said, little boat on the waves

Little boat on the waves

Little boat on the waves

Little boat on the waves

Sshh . . .

Sshh . . .

And you know there's nothing Miles Field can do about the little air pockets, that's just part of the fun Susie!

Can he fly higher or lower and get away from it please

Well he could but it's a pretty general picture.

What do you mean, shit, what's a pretty what did you say?

It's a pretty widespread system.

System, what, what?

It's just a little storm system, you Brits and your weather! It's kind of a long way round and you know what, Miles Field could kind of do with the practice.

What?

Now don't go saying I said that.

I don't want him to – ***SHIT***!

Woah, up we go!

FUCK! FUCK!

And down we go!

I'm fucking begging you fly the fucking plane

(Little boat on the waves)

Shut up you CUNT!

(Oh line crossed, line crossed)

Oh no no no no no no make it stop someone, make it stop Thomas

Hey hey there Susie, hey now, we're getting you home here, sshh, we'll be through it soon . . .

I want to go home I want to go home

Hey you want to see Bonner, right!

I want to see Bonner again I want to see my room again and the garden again I want to see Ed again he's been kind to me he's my friend we can watch Shakespeare by the fire I want to see my daddy again oh God help me

Hey, hey, and you will, you know he's in a place of brightness

I know okay he is he is he is

You will meet him again, you know that, he's waiting

I know he is, thank you Thomas thank you.

We're good, we're good, we are in the capable hands of Second Officer Miles Field. I think we can all agree he's handling this pretty darn well. Pretty darn well. How we all doin'

We can't be far, how far are we, can you just go and take over the controls now

Hey there Susie, what just happened, were we not just guided through the valley by that young man? What would it do to his confidence if I bust into there and said Hey Second Officer Miles Field, I think maybe you should hand control over to Thomas Bayne now?

(That wouldn't be fair at all!)

Did I ask you, Gary Lord?

(You did not, Captain.)

Look Thomas it's me, the passenger, the only one and I just really really want you to be in control of the plane he's done a great job, heroic, but he's not very experienced and we're flying through a fucking storm

Oh I think we're past it.

You do? Really?

Sure, don't you think?

It's, it seems a bit better.

Could Gary Lord maybe get you a soda?

Vodka, vodka.

(Afraid of a few bumps, not afraid of cirrhosis.)

Gary Lord: attitude.

(Another shot coming up Captain.)

People don't like their confidence to be taken away from them Susie.

Nope.

When we think we've done a little good in the world, and we have a certain respect that goes with that, and you know one day that can just go away, you could just meet someone who does not respect the good you've done in the world, someone who decides to take that away.

Look, Thomas,

So that it becomes more difficult for that person to do good in the world or give that pleasure, and you know that's okay, perhaps the person who takes away your pride or your sense of achievement has his or her own reasons for doing that, human souls are complex, we do not know the harm we do,

Thomas you don't understand what I was

Thomas Bayne understands this: on his journey through the forest he met a soul in distress, a wild animal, a she-leopard, and she did him wrong, but Thomas Bayne was not as other men, because he had been given a Gift, and because he had been given this Gift, instead of turning upon the she-leopard with violence and intemperance,

(Here's the lady's liquor Captain.)

Gary Lord, are you involved in telling the story?

(No Captain. I am not.)

Suddenly, out of nowhere, Thomas Bayne looked up and saw a brightly coloured pink parakeet bringing a drink. He knew he would have to stop telling the story for a moment. Pass the drink to the lady, Gary Lord. Good. Then away flew the brightly coloured pink parakeet and the story resumed . . .

Instead of turning on the she-leopard with violence and intemperance, he

WHAT THE FUCK IS THAT???

Now that shouldn't be happening. Gary Lord, go and ask the pilot why the siren's going.

WHY IS THE FUCKING SIREN GOING????

It tells us we've gotten a little too close to some other celestial object, probably another plane but not necessarily.

I DON'T WANT TO DIE

What we can do is take a little look out the window, well, I don't see anything, I guess we're in a cloud, Gary Lord what does he say?

THERE'S NO TIME TO SAY BOTH HIS FUCKING NAMES

(He's not sure what it was, nothing on the radar.)

WHY IS IT STILL FUCKING GOING

Did you ask him to switch it off?

TELL HIM TO SWITCH IT OFF YOU WANKER

Ask him to switch it off. You know, Susie, it's not the simplest thing in the world to master the controls of a jet hey there we go, he's in control.

Oh my god oh my god oh my god

Is he okay Gary Lord, how's he doing up there?

(He's feeling good, Captain.)

Would you tell him from Thomas Bayne he's a star-child of the skies?

(I'll do that Captain.)

Hey Susie, what's wrong, don't get upset, he's got his confidence back, I've got mine, Gary Lord's kinda slowly getting his, so now we better see about you, right?

Hey there.

Hey now.

And I will wipe those tears from the world.

I will wipe away those tears.

You know what, I feel closer to you now than I've ever felt.
Fly the plane. Please fly the plane
I want to do something for you, Susie.
Fly the plane. Please fly the plane
I still believe Susie Mantle and Thomas Bayne have this convergence of destiny. I think we may be, woah
SHIT!!!
Hey,

Hey I thought I told you all about it, nothing poor Miles Field can do about air pockets!
Yes he can do better, fly the – OH FUCK, FUCK!

Easy now, easy, ride it through,
OH MY GOD OH MY GOD –

Easy now, be home soon
HELP ME, YOU CAN HELP ME, YOU'RE DOING THIS, HELP ME YOU BASTARD –
Now that's irrational Susie, I've been called a lot of things, but a master of the weather? I think I've some way to go on that journey!
You have a mother you have a father you have a child stop doing this
Doing what Susie? You know what, I think you should possibly lay off the liquor a while, it really has no benefits at all and you know it's also a depressant – woah, here we go!
JESUS CHRIST, oh, oh, Our Father who art in Heaven, hallowed be thy name, thy kingdom come, thy will be done,

on earth OH SHIT

Now that's got to be an error, I'm not quite so pleased with Miles Field now. Gary Lord would you go and investigate why that keeps happening? Susie I'm thinking it might be time I went up there to see for myself!

JUST GO –

You know Miles Field might benefit from a little guidance

JUST GO –

Will you wait for me here?

I'M IN A FUCKING AEROPLANE OF COURSE I'LL WAIT –

Will you trust in me, will you trust in the Gift?

WHATEVER JUST FLY THE PLANE –

Will you travel towards the light with me?

WHAT?

Will you be my companion through the world?

I CAN'T AGREE TO THAT –

Why not Susie?

I CAN'T SAY YES TO IT –

Why not Susie do you hate me that much

FLY THE FUCKING PLANE –

Now my confidence is gone again, it's just, woah

OH GOD HELP US –

Oh God help me –

Yes! Yes, whatever, I'll travel with you, yes, I'll be your fucking yes, I'll fuck you, I'll marry you what d'you want from me, yes, yes, yes, yes YES YES YES

Hey I'm on it Susie!

Oh my god oh my god

oh my god oh my god oh my god oh my god oh my god oh my god

Oh

Oh my god oh my god oh my god

That's better it's better it's better it's better it's better

Hey there Susie Mantle.

Uh –
Miles Field.
Miles –
Miles Field.

Miles –

Field –
Be landing soon. You can see London if you look out the window.

See? There it is. No place like home. Sorry about that siren back there, I think I pressed something. Like an asshole! The Captain's not too happy with me. But you know, I got more experience, I'll do better, I'll get there. I just love to fly. Can't help it. You're looking a little pale, my friend. Hey Gary, I think Miss Susan Mantle is in a little trouble here, you got some water back there? Maybe some water?

(Still or sparkling for the lady.)

Hey I don't know. Still I guess

*

She's okay, Susie, you okay, little smile there, we're just getting you through Security here
No, she's fine
Yeah, European Community, happy community of, little Europeans, little smile there? We're working on it
We're working on the smile
I can tell you it's special when it comes

*

She's fine, give her the cushion. No, that one
Hey there Susie you can use my topcoat for a pillow
Taking you home, Susie

Her eyes are open Joel
You hearing us Susie, we're in London England Susie
Sleep all the way you got your own personal chauffeurs
Go left here
You can't, it says
Goddamn, let me look at the . . . okay. You gotta go right round the terminal again
This is a bad system Kenny
Hey look this makes sense, you need A-ten-twenty
This is A-ten-twenty
But south this is north
Shit Kenny this is crazy

The lady awake?
Don't think so
Okay okay this is right, Greenwitch
Greenwitch do I take it
Yeah take it
I take it
Take it
Greenwitch it is
Not Cambridge? that sounds kind of more classy
Greenwitch I'm telling you

Greenwitch it is for better or worse
Richer for poorer
Sickness and in health

Greenwitch it is

You know I think it's like, 'Grennitch', kinda like the Village
Okay, right, as in, Greenwich Mean Time I gotcha
I think it is Joel

So this is what, this is where they make time
I guess!

I like that, where they make time . . .
This is where they thought of it . . .

No, you know what, this is where they make <u>*mean*</u> *time, they make mean time here Kenny!*
Not nice time,
Mean time,
Mean time, I like that

In the Green Witch Factory

Where do they make nice time Joel

I don't know that Kenny. I don't know where they make nice time

On the next day you will die

. . . a grid system, you know. This is kind of hard to follow like in the dark. This is Pondford Road we're on?

Kind of a name is Pondford

Little streetlighting here'd be kinda helpful

Man it's so empty here

It's night-time Joel, people have jobs

Sunday tomorrow Kenny, they don't have jobs on Sunday

Okay now this is what this is Lensmere, that was Pondford

Lensmere, that's good, you see it?

It's right on the goddamn join, I can't read this thing

If it's Lensmere you've gone too far

Hey, Susie!

Susie, you okay!

Gettin some shut-eye back there?

She says we gone too far

There's a rotary, what about the rotary Susie?

Go round come back

Go round and come back

You know this map sucks Joel

We don't need a map, we're taking this lady home and the lady knows the way

You know the way home Susie?

Was that a yes back there? She nodded

She nodded?

She nodded in the rear-view

That's good enough I'll take that

You got it

*

We are a door-to-door service, Susie: our Mission is complete.

Not quite Kenny.

What time is it

That's, not our service we're not a time service Susie.

Kenny we can be what we want to be. It's 1.20 a.m. Susie, we got you home in good time.

In nice time Joel.

Nice time, not mean time. Going back to that earlier crack.

Where's Thomas

Say what?

Thomas Bayne, where is he

We were engaged to return you to your home by the Client but there's no real call for discussion of the Client's identity, which he has asked to be kept confidential.

He or she has asked that, Joel.

He or she has asked that.

So you're not going to kill me

Say what?

Not going to kill me

Hey. This is one exhausted lady.

Susie we're a driving service. We're not a killing service though there are such things I believe no our Mission is complete.

Not quite Kenny. This girl is tired, the flight was late in, wasn't it Susie?

There was a storm system

There was?

We flew through a storm

You did? I guess it passed. I didn't hear of a storm.

Miles Field was the pilot

She's so exhausted. But there's still time for the gift.

What gift

It's in the car and Kenny will wait with you while I fetch it.

What gift

You're still waking up, aren't you Susie?

This is the day

Say again there?

This is Joel here now, he comes bearing the gift.

Susie, the Client asked that you be given this at the door. He was most insistent.

Joel, he or she was most insistent.

He or she was most insistent.

What is it

Looks like a box.

Could be a box.

A special box.

With a special gift inside. He or she asked that we make sure you open it.

I'm not going to open it

He or she really did ask that.

Then he or she can come and fucking open it himself

Or herself.

Shut up Kenny.

Look. Can we open it?

I don't think we should open it Joel.

I'm kinda curious now and I would kinda like to open it.

Well I have issues around your opening it, so I'm going back to the car because in my opinion our Mission is complete.

Susie. Kenny is going back to the car, but I'm going to step back here and open the gift from the Client to you. I'm now opening the gift.

Well:

Joel, have you opened it? Have you opened the gift?

Susie. Do you happen to own a cat? Because if you don't, you could probably use one, as there's a whole ton of catfood in here. That's kinda unexpected. Now I can confirm that our Mission is indeed accomplished. Good day Susie. Start the car Kenny.

We're going to have to inform the Client that Susie opened the gift, Joel, and that's an untruth.

It's a limited untruth.

There is no such thing as a limited untruth Joel.
Curiosity got the better of me, Kenny.
You know what curiosity killed?
No.
You have a think about that Joel.
Okay.
Everything connects.
I'm aware of that, Kenny.

*

ALLO ALLO. NOUS SOMMES PAS CHEZ NOUS. LAISSEZ-VOUS UNE MESSAGE, S'IL VOUS PLAIT. HELLO HELLO. WE ARE NOT AT THE HOUSE OF US! LEAVE YOU A MESSAGE IF IT PLEASES YOU!

Mum. I got home. You still haven't changed the answer message. You need to have your voice on it. Not his or people who don't know, might think, you know . . . It's, you know I, I told you about the witch and what she said. Well: I had a really bad flight, and I did the thing she said I would do. Mummy I did. Then she said I'd, everything would end on the next day and it is the next day Mum and I'm home now Mum but it's two in the morning there's twenty-two hours of that day to go, today, and could you, call me, to help me, as I don't know what to do or where to go to stay alive because I believe it, I believe it, it's Sunday and I believe in it as if it would happen and, I'm . . . Okay. I'm okay, I*really there goes the fucking noise Mum call the house, call the mobile, Mum, please think of me and call.

*

####### ####### ####### ###### *Yes . . . Yes . . . Mantle?*

It's me I'm home are you there
Mantle you made it, you're home
I'm alone in my house Ed I'm scared
Hey slow down slow down let me get the light on

We flew through a storm

Slow down babe

Thomas Bayne was there they drugged me Ed

They what?

Thomas Bayne, it was his plane, his jet it was Thomas Bayne's jet, he flies jets only he didn't fly it this terrible kid flew it and we flew through a storm but it passed and I'll never fly again Ed but I'm home my God but I said it to him Ed I said it to him

Mantle, Mantle, Mantle

No and no and no and then yes and yes and yes

Mantle Mantle they called me, said there's this media scrum at Gatwick but you never showed, I thought you'd gone back to your ma's but you said you had a first-class ticket

To City, Ed, City Airport, on Thomas's private jet I didn't know it was his it was a surprise but it's not that it's not that

Hey you're home now it's okay, and they all went to the wrong place and that's good, so tell me, tell me

He made me I said yes and it's all come true and there's only one thing left and it's the next day Ed on the next day I'll be gone Ed, it's today, I've got twenty-two hours to go

Hey hush you're in mourning babe, just hold on, hold on . . .

I don't want to die Ed

Hey now sshh, sshh . . . you think they spiked you?

It was only, like it was one moment then it was much later but time didn't pass it just jumped it jerked onwards to now

They spiked you, friend. You feel ill?

I no, no I'm tired, but they'll all come here Ed, when they see I'm not on the plane I was on they'll all come here looking and one of them will get me

No one's going to get you, Susan, deep breaths, come on now.

Deep, breaths I can't stay here

It's the middle of the night, chicken, stay indoors till morning

I know where I know a place, it's not far it's my lookout, I can curl up I can see things from there, I won't sleep I'll just watch and I won't eat or drink, because something will be poisonous he gave me catfood Ed, Thomas gave me catfood he's trying to destroy Bonner!

Mantle, listen now, sit down, you sitting down?

I'm sitting down, I can still feel the plane, I can feel the jolting and the bumping and the engines Ed it's

Ssshhh . . . Now just listen and we'll think of what to do

One minute's passed Ed and that's all, one fucking minute it's too slow Ed there's too many to make it through them

Sshh, hey, be quiet, be quiet,

Little boat over the waves

Be quiet. Can you be that?

Help me

Friends, Mantle, come on, where are your friends

I don't know Ed, I don't know where they go

Do you have a doctor, Mantle, like a family doctor,

No, I don't know, yes. He doesn't like me he doesn't mind if I die I asked him for the morning-after he folded his arms he despises me he'll give me stuff to take I'll sleep forever

Mantle! Oi! Bit o'hush

Hush little boat, little boat

What about the police? You can say there's an intruder, then they'll come round, hey, you can play it like you've lost it, then they'll get some nice police-girl type to sit with you

No no not the police Ed I'd have to be in a car and if I'm in a car it'll crash, the violent people will come, the nice people will turn violent I have to get out of this house I have to get out now! Oh I can feel the engines turning

Hush up and listen girl: have you got your mobile.

It's, it's out of batteries this is a landline in the living room the living room I can live here I should stay here in the living room!

Mantle, charge the mobile. Do it now. What did I say?

The mobile, charge the mobile, good that's good that's good

So then we can stay in touch, right?

That's good, that's very good I'm doing that right now it's gone blank! Oh no it's okay it says it's charging, it's going to take forever I don't have forever I have twenty-two hours

Leave the house while it's charging. Go where you feel safe. Then go back in and get it when it's charged. The vultures can't be there that soon. I'm going to get you a hotel, somewhere peaceful they know me, Susan, a place you can rest all day, it'll be easy, we'll be laughing about this soon! What will be doing? Laughing!

Laughing

All week about your troubles!

All week

About this, good girl. Go to your safe place, try and sleep, call me when you wake. Okay love?

Okay Ed

Stuff doesn't come true like that, you know, like a movie, stuff comes true in such a mess you don't recognise it

All of it's coming true

Never the way you think

There's a million ways to die!

And one of them is dozing off at a hundred and one with your great-grandchildren reading you stories, and that's the one you picked from the catalogue right? In heaven you did, waiting to be called, queueing up love, cast your mind back, can you see it?

Okay Ed okay

Now I want you to count the months and years all the way to that moment, can you do that, can you do that?

Okay Ed

Good girl. Strong girl.

*

####### ALLO ALLO. NOUS SOMMES PAS CHEZ NOUS. LAISSEZ-VOUS UNE MESSAGE, S'IL VOUS PLAIT. HELLO HELLO. WE ARE NOT AT THE HOUSE OF US! LEAVE YOU A MESSAGE IF IT PLEASES YOU! #

Mum. I'm going into the garden now to Sukey's Lookout. You can't call me there. I'm not going to sleep. I'll try you again every hour in the house on the hour every hour because no one's going to sleep except except you I suppose and Franck, il dorme, il dorme and

and

and Mum could you maybe

Morning miss. Ahoy!

Morning miss. Are you without accommodation?

Oh Jesus Christ it's sunny did you say ahoy?

Are you without accommodation miss?

What, oh my God, what?

You're a bit dirty miss.

Yes, I am, sorry, I, I'm in this this

Hedge!

Yep. Ahoy.

You must have needed that sleep miss.

I did, I, I'm from there, that house, I live there . . .

I'm delivering papers miss. I spotted you from the road.

You, spotted, okay, I didn't mean to be rude, can I have a paper, I'm number 52.

Oh. Are you Snoozie Mental?

No. I'm, her friend.

She had different colour hair. Tell her I'm sorry, will you miss, our whole school is.

What? Yes. Can I have a paper?

Number 52? Your paper's on the mat inside your front door.

You've . . . been delivering papers. But, I didn't see any.

Probably they get tidied miss.

By?

The cleaners.

O-kay. I've finished being here now, what time is it?

9:01. I'll be free by 9:15. Yippee. Wargame Club. You should probably have a bath. You could have it in Tropical Tones, miss. Tropical Tones was her favourite bath gel. You might like it too.

*

####### *Mantle?*

Ed.

Where are you, did you sleep?

Outside, I didn't mean to, I'm having a bath.

Good, that's good, Susan, soak away your troubles . . .

In Tropical Tones.

You soak away them troubles.

I'm in my parents' bedroom, I'm checking the ingredients. I think I'm going to stay here. I feel safe here. People will come, but they'll all come, and then none of them will do it.

Do what, love?

Kill me. None of them will have the nerve Ed because they'll be witnesses.

Susan, listen,

And I'll be hiding in the attic.

No Susan, you have to listen

Ed! Ssshh!

What?

Jesus help me

What?

The front door just opened

No.

They've come

Look it's going to be some neighbour, Susan, you're overwrought, poor girl

Ssshh! oh Jesus help me someone

Mantle, Mantle

He's standing in the hall

You are the death of me Mantle

He's coming up the stairs, the front door opened again, there's two of them Ed!

(Hello who's that?)

Oh I say! Who said that?

(Up here.)

Oh. Oh, right. I'm just, um . . .

(What.)

Well I might ask you, also, I'm not sure who you are, I come here every morning for the moggie. See? Bob from next door.

(Gotcha.)

Jingling my spare key here.

(Snap.)

Jingle jangle.

(Jangle jingle. Gotta lotta keys m'self mate.)

And you are?

(Pilman. Nigel Pilman. Friend.)

All right. Nigel. What's your, er, role in the whole Susan Mantle support system?

(Unclear.)

Oh. All right.

(Put it this way. We're close.)

Well, I've known her for twenty years, but I hardly know her.

(She needs someone here when she gets back. Someone on her side. See anyone else volunteering? I don't.)

All right. And that's today, we believe, the return of the lady?

(You tell me, Bob.)

Right . . .

(Supposed to be in late last night. Pulled a no-show at Gatwick. Figure she done a number on us all, she's sly that way, thought I'd get here, beat the crowd.)

Jolly good. Well. I don't suppose you know anything about all these tins of catfood strewn on the garden path?

(That's your area Bob.)

Right . . . yes so you're what, getting the house all smart?

(That's right.)

I see you've ventured into the upper floors!

(You know. Whole place to look after here. Clean sheets. Towels. Stuff people like when they've been in hell.)

Ri-ight . . . I wonder, this is probably a bit mad, but is that room at the top of the stairs <u>*the*</u> *room?*

(What d'you mean <u>*the*</u> *room. You said you known her for twenty years.)*

Well, you know, yes, but not as a, not up there. The room where she did The Show . . .

(It's that one down the landing. I tend to keep the door shut.)

I say. Makes me feel a little giddy, being so close to the, I mean, that's a piece of minor British televisual history right there a few yards away, like a living archive.

(Minor? Maybe. Could see it that way. I was in that room, just me and her, night Thomas Bayne came by. Totally threw our relationship that whole fucking shebang. Talk about bad timing.)

Hmm. Well, it must have been a testing time for a, a boyfriend, is that what we should call you Neil?

(Nigel. If the cap fits.)

But I don't suppose it's permitted to go in now.

(It's not a crime scene Bob.)

No. So you keep everything shipshape.

(See anyone else stepping up to the plate?)

No. You have that woman's touch then.

(Maybe. Want to look inside?)

I say, that would be a bit nuts on our account, wouldn't it!

(Be crazy, Bob, be edgy.)

Edgy, well.

(Who's going to know? Who's going to care? In the long run. Life and death I don't think so. Why don't you come up those stairs Bob, I'll give you the guided tour.)

Well. Right, indeed, in the long run.

(I'm telling you, come up.)

Would it not be very wrong?

(Depends, Bob. You want to look through the drawers?)

I, no. Of course not.

(Nothing much to see.)

Well, so what. I just want to see the, the,

(You want to see the bed.)

That happens to be where the action was, I mean in terms of the show, in terms of popular culture.

(Action? I've seen some action, Bob. Susie and me have seen some frontline.)

All right, well, that's rather your business, isn't it, Nigel.

(Not exactly a secret. Five times, three ways.)

I haven't read the literature.

(Literature mate, where you been, these are daily updates on the blogosphere.)

Well it's not a crime to look. I help out with the moggie on Mother's orders, and I just happen to think I'd rather like to take a look at the room where, I mean it's a famous site now, it has a niche in the culture!

(Hold it right there Bob.)

What, shall we not go in?

(No sense of occasion, mate.)

Oh come on don't be silly!

(It's not silly Bob, show respect.)

All right. I'm not paying, you know.

(Joshing with you mate! Let's have a butcher's.)

Now I have to switch this over . . .

(Gonna phone a friend Bob? Is that your final answer?)

No I'm setting it to Camera. You wouldn't snap me, would you, just standing by the bed?

(You crazy motherfucker.)

I'm a crazy what did you say?

(Let's close the door on these proceedings.)

*

Ed.

Christ babe where are you?

They're in my room I can't hear them any more

Angel, listen to me, no one's going to kill you

They are

Mantle, think, think

Sh they're coming out

*

You have your work cut out there Nigel.

(What do you mean I have my work cut out.)

I thought you were rather getting the place nice for Susie.

(Meaning.)

Well it's like nobody's touched anything, the bed's not made, stuff everywhere, dirty knickers and what have you.

(That's how they left it, the TV people. Animals.)

I thought you were getting it nice.

(I said I's getting the house nice. She'd like her own bedroom to look familiar I would think. You keep forgetting I know this girl.)

All right. You're the boss Nigel. Boss of the upper realms!

(I'm just close, that's all, can't help it.)

Well, I'll um, I'll feed the cat on my way out. I don't know why there's extra catfood, it's not as if we're short.

(That's interesting Bob.)

Yes. Well. I think this little jaunt should stay strictly between us, don't you think Nigel?

(Why. What did we do wrong. Just stood there, took the air.)

All the same. Top secret eh?

(Capiche.)

Er. What?

(Granted.)

Yes let's keep it English if we could.

(Private.)

Oh I think so.

(What d'you take pictures for then.)

Well, the snaps, that's just

(Just for you eh, Bob. Bob's private collection.)

This may be my last time here.

(Souvenir, Bob.)

Sort of thing. Silly! I'll. Be off then. Cat can't wait all day.

(It isn't your mobile, then.)

I'm sorry?

(If that's your mobile in your hand.)

Not with you, Nigel, sorry.

(There's a mobile charging down there in the living room and I don't remember clocking it.)

Keeping an inventory are you?

(Don't see anyone else stepping up.)

Can't help you. I'm off.

(I just don't think it was there.)

(I'm dead certain it wasn't.)

*

####### *Babe what's going on.*

I'm still alive Ed, sshh.

Course you are ya headcase, what's going on?

He's downstairs. He's watching TV.

Who is?

Nigel Pilman. He's watching our videos. Over and over.

Help me out. Nigel Pilman.

An ex, a why, a zed. He was there the Thomas Bayne night. He got a key somehow, he comes and goes as he pleases.

Keep him there, we'll kill him, we'll do it together, we'll chuckle over his mangled remains.

Ed,

Trying to keep you sane, love. You know this bloke well?

I don't know him at all.

Can you get out?

I don't think so. Not if he's sitting there. You can see the stairs from where he's sitting. Also, my mobile's in there. And I can't get out the front anyway, there's two vans parked there, people inside. Satellite dish. They've come.

Like clockwork.

I'm scared Ed. I'll never make it to lunchtime.

Hey. Hundred and one. Great-grandchildren.

Yep. That's a lot of great-grandchildren.

Hey, that's the spirit. Look. Susan. I'm meant to fly in to London tomorrow, meetings and stuff, see what's left of my career. I could make that earlier.

No Ed.

I could, I could get a car to Shannon, be in London mid-afternoon.

It'll be over by then.

Come on. You told me, I'm an absurd soul for an absurd situation eh? I'm the man for this.

It would expect you to come.

It?

It's after me.

Well, who knows, but 'it' doesn't know me, eh?

You said cunt on TV. Everyone knows you. Even it. It doesn't care what you said. It knows you.

Mantle come on . . .

It will be on the plane with you, reading travel magazines.

Hush now . . .

It will order a tomato juice and pick up one white case from the carousel.

Okay okay okay old girl, what's the fellow doing downstairs?

Him. When he moves I'm going to run for it. I'm going to go out the back door and off through the gardens.

To where, babe, to where?

Somewhere quiet, somewhere nobody goes.

Keep your phone on, I'll keep calling you.

I can't get at my mobile, Ed, I said, he's right there. If I go I won't have a phone, I'll have to use phone boxes. And there's no such things as phone boxes.

Red ones, love, everywhere. You just don't notice.

It'll look there first.

It? Come on!

It'll look through the glass with its eyes.

Jesus and Mary there's no such being

Then tell me how to survive this day. I'm interested to know.

Right, given you . . . believe what you believe, and I believe you do, so, I'm with you all the way . . . let's think about: the Titanic.

That's a bad start Ed.

Thinking about survival, thinking about the lifeboats. Who gets to go in the lifeboats?

Where we going with this.

Women. Children. Old folks. Go where they are. Women, children, old folks, and stay off the main roads. Go where crowds are, but stay off the main roads.

I'm not getting on trains, they derail. Tubes get blown up and stop in the dark. Not getting on any buses.

Go where people are. Shopping centres, babe.

Hoodies, stalkers.

I'm thinking I'm thinking: parks!

Drug dealers, perverts.

Concerts? Plays? School plays!

It's Sunday morning Ed.

Jesus Mantle talk about the bleedin obvious: church!

Church . . .

Get yourself into that big echoey lifeboat. Is there one, where is it?

How the hell would I know. Any church would do.

Any church would have a phone somewhere. Call me when you're there. Stay in groups of people. Stay away from young men.

Old men, men,

Away from roads and look around you babe, 180 degrees.

You mean 360.

400, 500, 1000 sodding degrees, just keep out of trouble because I'm coming to get you, Mantle.

Sshh!

Mantle? Sweetheart?

Sshh. He switched off the TV.

Talk to me talk to me talk to me

He's,

He's going out the door Ed I'm going to the bedroom window

Keep your head down babe

He's going, he's on the path, he kicked a tin of catfood

Keep your head low!

Now he's – my mobile –

What?

He's got my fucking mobile, he's walking up the road examining my mobile that's it, I'm running for it Ed, I'm going out the back

Susan!

Okay

A church, find a church!

Pray for me Ed

I will, I do, I have

Okay okay here goes

*

Hey, excuse me!

Excuse me, what are you doing up there, you can't come in here it's a private garden!

Oh it is?

Well yes it is, what's it look like?

What's it, look like. Well it looks like heaven.

I beg your pardon?

It looks like heaven, you know, paradise. It's very well kept.

I, I say, you can't come in here, you know.

I mistook it for a place I could.

What did you say?

I mistook it for,

This is private property.

I'll go then, I'll climb down into this next one and you'll never see me again. There. Gone.

That's another private garden. These are all private gardens.

Are they all your private gardens?

No they're not my private gardens, but they're private gardens!

It's none of your business then.

I'm afraid the law is everyone's business.

You can't even see me.

I said the law is everyone's business!

You can't even hear me.

Did you hear I said the law is everyone's business!

*

####### *Police, how may I help you.*

There's an intruder. 52 Hazeldene Avenue, Mersham.

Is that your residence?

No.

Are you inside the house?

No.

Are you a friend of the occupant?

Yes. I'm her friend, and there's a strange man in the house. He's tall and dark also.

Is anyone else inside the house?

No. Just the intruder. Please hurry! I think he's armed.

Where are you, miss?

Um. Nearby. Please come. 52 Hazeldene Avenue, Mersham.

Can you see the intruder?

No I'm fleeing him I'm out of breath I'm fleeing him!

Miss? Calm down. Where are you calling from?

Phone box! Fleeing him! Took a break from fleeing him for this call.

Can you see the intruder, miss?

Look forget it

Miss?

Forget it

Madam?

*

Miss!

Miss! Hi there miss!
Hi there.
Are you a new girl in our class?
Yep.
Mrs Bind is looking at you.

Okay.
You're a bit too big for our class!
She's a bit too big for our class!
You're a bit too big for our class!
Too big! She's too big!
Come on I'm not enormous.
Too! Big! Too! Big!

Excuse me can I help you.
Yes.
We're just on our walk here on this lovely day, how can I be of assistance.
I'm, I'm looking for the church.
Oh? Which church.
Well. Any church.

Are you, are you all right?
I'm just, trying to get to a church.
Let's, step over here a moment. Children, stop, tell those two to stop, we're stopping.
We're stopping!

Robbo! Jacka! Stop!

They're not stopping, miss!

They're mad them two!

No they are stopping!

They are stopping!

They are stopping, miss, look.

Thank you Glen. Are you all right? You seem a little

No it's okay, I just need to get to a church.

Well look. If you loop around with us, we're really just going in a grand loop, if you loop around with us we'll eventually fish up at St Jude's on Plymstock Lane.

That's just, that's great. Is there, a service then.

Well, the eleven o'clock is on now, and I've taken the children out as it's so nice, and they're not in anyone's hair, we'll be looping back for about noon to sing the last hymn with the choir.

I'll um, I'll, loop with you then if it's okay.

Do you, well, would you like to tell me, are you in some kind of trouble?

No. I just, need to be, where people are.

Right. Well you're in luck. We're people. Little people!

It's good, that's good, I'll walk with you if I may. Thank you.

It's absolutely fine, and if you want to tell me anything that's fine too. I'm Janet Bind. This is Sunday Club. And you are?

I'm, Sally Carpenter.

Wonderful. Children, we've made a new friend: Sally, and we're going to carry on our nature walk with Sally in our midst!

Thank you Mrs Bind.

Oh come on now call me Janet. On we go, children!

Miss . . .

Hello.

Miss . . .

You can call me Sally.

Sally.

And what's your name.

Robson.

Robson.

Can I ask you a question miss?

Yep.

Are you famous miss?

You can call me Sally.

Are you famous?

No Robson. Are you?

Nah. Not yet.

Are you going to be?

Yeah.

Okay. In, do you know in, in what field?

Eh?

What area.

Wot?

All right now children, I want us to move on to Number Four. Number Four: The Great Mulberry Tree. Are you all on Number Four? Fatima, Number Four I said. Nala, Number Four. Good. No, you're sharing with Kylene. Now, hands up who can see a tree anywhere that looks like the one in the picture?

That one.

Hands up I said Antony.

Yes Antony.

That one.

No. Vamilla.

That one.

No. It's big, obviously, but that's one of the oaks we were talking about earlier. Can you remember how they were damaged?

Tornado miss.

Hurricane miss.

Yes the hurricane of 1987 what Derryl.

Miss, can I wear sunglasses?

No, we don't have sunglasses at Club.

But it's really bright miss and that lady's got sunglasses.

Yes, well, she's not a member of Club, Derryl, she's our guest. She can wear sunglasses.

You know I can take them off.

No no of course not, keep them on.

Okay.

If you must.

Is it that one, miss?

Very good Britany, very good, now see where Britany is pointing, that's the Great Mulberry Tree, now don't all, well, all right, you can run towards it but don't fall over and don't push!

Just another Sunday morning in paradise.

Yep. Good tree.

You look at those children all running around it, they couldn't be happier could they, and the papers say it's all video games all day and all night. I don't think we're quite finished yet.

No Mrs Bind, not yet.

Right: better sort them out!

(You go girl.)

Miss . . .

Robson.

Have you got a boyfriend?

No.

Why not, miss?

I don't know Robson, have you got a girlfriend.

No way!

Okay, well, same thing.

Are you married?

No Robson.

Have you been on TV?

Well, yes, in the background.

Wot?

Um. I was just, where I was, and someone started filming.

Were you like in the nude?

No Robson.

Have you ever been in the nude?

Yes Robson.

What for like sex and stuff.

Sort of thing.

This is the Great Mulberry Tree, Number Four on your worksheets.

Quiet! The Great Mulberry Tree is supposed to have been planted by James the First, who was the King of England! Now how long ago was that, do you suppose . . . Vamilla.

Twelve, hundred years.

Actually a little closer than that. Tanith.

Umm . . . Fifty.

Bit further, bit longer. Robson? Robson are you with us? How long ago do you think James the First was the King of England?

Twelve, years.

Well no a tree wouldn't manage that in twelve years Robson.

We're talking James the First, period of the Gunpowder Plot, think Guy Fawkes, when was that.

Two weeks ago we got taters-in-their-jackets.

No Robson, not when was Bonfire Night, when was the reign of James the First? Shall we see if Sally knows!

Oh no, please

Shall we ask our guest!

SAL-LY! SAL-LY! SAL-LY!

Okay, okay, okay. Um . . . four hundred. Ish.

Very good that's very close indeed I ought to let you have a work-sheet to tick off!

Well actually now you say that

Now what's interesting about the Great Mulberry Tree is that King James introduced it into England so that it would attract silk moth caterpillars. Now: why would he want to attract silk moth caterpillars?

Why do you think he might wish to attract silk moth caterpillars?

Glen.

Cos . . . they're . . . beautiful miss.

Well you know I'm sure they are Glen, but there was a more practical reason. Robson.

To squash 'em miss!

Why would the King of England want to waste his time squashing worms?

Dunno. 'Swot I'd do.

Good answer.

Wrong, though. Scarlett?

Cos they . . . make silk.

Good and why might he need silk.

For like . . . I dunno. Gowns and things like, cloaks.

Excellent, they'd help him to start a silk industry, here in England, four hundred years ago. Only, what James did not know was that silk moth caterpillars only feed on the white mulberry tree, and the King had been sold a black mulberry tree! Wrong tree! So it was absolutely hopeless! I think there's a moral in there somewhere.

(Sounds like some of my shit.)

What d'you say miss?

Can I share your worksheet, Robson?

Yeah miss! Can you hold it miss?

Sure Robson.

Cos then I can have my Mars.

On we go, everyone, on we go.

Miss . . .

And what's your name.

Tone.

Hi Tone.

Are you in our church?

Well I'm going to visit your church.

Is your hair really that colour?

No.

Did you dye it?

Yeah.

Why.

So no one would know who I was.

Why.

Because no one likes me.

Why.

Because I'm a witch.

There's no such thing as witches.

Is that right Tone.

Yeah.

Do you think it's possible to see into the future, Tone?

Um . . .

Take your time.

Um . . . yeah.

How do you think that's done?

Sort of, like, magic powers.

Do you think they exist?

Yeah.

Okay, well. Who has them?

Well . . . Queen Zygorax.

Queen Zygorax has them?

Yeah. She uses them for evil. Like: against the Akolytes it says it on this card look.

Okay. Well, that's one way of using them. Look Tone you haven't filled in any of your worksheet.

Nah.

Why's that Tone?

It's boring.

You'd rather be in the future, wouldn't you Tone.

Yeah. I am. In the future.

You are?

Yeah. I know what's gonna happen to everyone.

Is that your superpower?

Nah. I just do. I don't have a superpower yet.

Really. Okay. So, is Robson going to be famous?

Yeah. He's going to be on TV. In The Zoo Game. But later, when he's really really famous, he gets killed in a crash.

So sort of good news bad news.

Yeah. It's not his fault, it's just

Never mind, stuff happens, what about Mrs Bind.

Well, dunno, just . . . carries on being old. Till she like dies and gets buried in a grave. Probly a ghost after that.

How about me, Tone, what happens to me.

Um . . . you, you, um, I dunno.

You're in the future Tone, you can see everything, can't you see what happens to me?

I think, yeah, you become a princess.

I do? Hey.

But. Bad news. You get killed in a crash.

That's okay, it goes with the territory.

Eh?

Can you see what happens to my father, Tone?

He's. Bad news. He dies.

Blimey Tone.

Yeah in a crash.

As we walk towards Number Five, which is a sweet chestnut tree. What tree is it, Derryl?

Wot?

Jackson, what tree are we looking for now?

Er . . . a sweets . . . nuts tree.

Nice idea Jackson but it's a sweet chestnut tree, you have a picture on your worksheet and we should come across it in the next five minutes or so. As we're walking towards it, I shall read to you from the guidebook: 'Shinglewell Heath is the home or feeding place for many birds and an interesting variety can be observed in the woodland and ornamental gardens. These include all three British species of woodpecker; green, greater spotted and lesser spotted. The unmistakable laughing call of the green woodpecker and its habit of foraging for insects on the lawns ensure it is the most noticeable of the three.' So I want you all to listen out for that laughing call, you get extra points if you hear it.

How many, miss?

Well, hm, let's see. Eighty.

Oh wicked!

'Jays, magpies, collared doves, blackbirds, song thrushes, robins, wrens and several members of the tit family are regularly seen and all live within the woodland.'

Tit family!

The tit family!

Tit family!

Jacka's in the tit family!
You're in the tit family!
No you're in the tit family!
No you're in the tit family!
You're a tit!
You're a great tit!
You're a great big tit!
No you are!

Well I suppose I asked for that.

That's what's written down Mrs Bind, can't fight it.

Do call me Janet. Quieten down everyone! 'More usual visitors include kestrels, pheasants and ring-necked parakeets and the graceful tawny owl is also known to frequent this beautiful woodland! The woodland ponds attract Canada geese, and mallards, and both occasionally nest there!' Losing my voice here, 'A less frequent visitor to the ponds is the grey heron.' Phew!

Now, has anyone found that sweet chestnut tree?

*

It has to be here somewhere!

Sally's helping us miss, she's on our team! We're the Acorn Squad.

That's nice Vamilla. It's somewhere near the base of the tree.

Oi it's somewhere near the base of the tree! Sally where's the base of the tree?

Near the roots, I can't find it, you go round the other side, Vamilla.

Will do! Is this it?
Is this it, Mrs Bind?
No, no, you'll know it when you see it, it's quite striking.

Oh. Oh my God.

Sally would you mind rephrasing that.
Has she found it?
Sally's found it!
Miss, Sally's found it!

No, actually Sasha, the whole Acorn Squad found it together.

It's horrible!

It's not it's beautiful isn't it miss?

Well, Glen, to quote from the guidebook, 'This sweet chestnut has a face at the base of the trunk that is said to look like the face of a dryad.'

Miss, what's a dryad?

Well it's a kind of spirit of nature.

Don't look like that at all what a swiz.

Look: there's its eyes, there's its nose, there's its mouth miss!

Very good Antony.

Miss, miss, I think it's looking at Sally!

*

Would you please all now kindly rise . . .

(Here, you can share my hymn book.)

Don't think I know the tune

(Of course you do, they sing it at Wembley Stadium, they sing it at the Cup!)

I'm sorry?

(The vicar's football mad, he always chooses this one!)

Abide with me, fast falls the eventide;
The darkness deepens; lord, with me abide!
When other helpers fail and comforts flee,
Help of the helpless, oh,
Abide with me.

(Do you recognise it now?)

(Does she know it Eleanor? Why does she have those silly sunglasses on?)

(Perhaps her eyes are tired Marion, from the sunshine.)

Swift to its close ebbs out life's little day;
Earth's joys grow dim, its glories pass away;
Change and decay in all around I see;
O Thou who changest not,
Abide with me.

(Everyone knows this one, you can just hum along if you like.)
(Who is she, Eleanor?)
(She came in with Janet and the Sunday Club, and I'm looking after her.)
(Hold the book so she can see.)
(She can see perfectly well, Marion.)
(But she's got those sunglasses on, she can't see a blessed thing.)

Come not in terrors, as the King of Kings;
But kind and good, with healing in thy wings;
Tears for all woes, a heart for every plea;
Come, friend of sinners, thus
Abide with me.

(Eleanor.)
(Marion I'm trying to sing.)
(She's in a real state Eleanor, there there, dear, it's all right, it's all right . . .)
(I'm dealing with it Marion.)
(We're dealing with it together.)

I need thy presence every passing hour;
What but Thy grace can foil the tempter's power?
Who like Thyself my guide and stay can be?
Through cloud and sunshine, oh,
Abide with me.

(I do always like it when they get the weather just right in a hymn, then it's as if it was written for today.)
(It was written for today Marion, today and every day.)
Where are the children where are they where are they
(Sshh it's all right they're all singing at the back look)
(One of the little boys is waving at you, dear)

I fear no foe, with Thee at hand to bless;
Ills have no weight, and tears no bitterness;
Where is death's sting? Where, grave, thy victory?
I triumph still, if Thou
Abide with me.

Will you please now kindly all be seated.
(There we go dear, let's tiptoe out to the side . . .)
(She needs a nice cup of tea, Eleanor.)
(That's just what I have in mind.)

*

######## ### *Yes: Mantle? Susan?*

Ed I'm still alive, I did what we said, I can't talk long.

You got to a church?

St Jude's. It's east of Shinglewell Heath and west of Thamesgate and sort of inbetween, it doesn't matter where.

You sound better, love.

St Jude is the patron saint of hopeless causes. When the vicar told me that I laughed so much I spilt my tea, Ed, I'm at a vicar's tea party! Oh also a little boy told me my future and it was just the same as before.

Focus, angel, focus. You're with the vicar now?

He's next door. They've let me use this phone in the office. God works in mysterious ways right here, I'm writing Him a note.

What I want you to do now, Susan, is stay there.

I'm confessing I took six pounds from the collection plate Ed.

You renegade, stay there!

For the red phone boxes Ed, I'm telling Him I'll pay it back, who's the angry woman with you?

I'm at Shannon, I'm about to take off, I've gotta switch you off babe, stewardess is killing me here, you gotta wait for me at that church.

You're flying back? For me?

My girl's in trouble you bet I am. You stay there.

Oh. Well . . . these old ladies asked me for Sunday roast, Ed, I think it's the safest way to go but I won't eat I'll just sit there.

Perfect. Call my phone and leave a message with the address, I'll come straight from Gatwick in a cab and get you.

Get me . . . okay, okay . . . what then?

Sorry babe?

What will you do then?

Now I gotta go, they're unhappy with me, bye babe, stay with those old 'uns, stay with it I'll be there.

*

Hello again.

We were trying to think of a pop star!

I'm sorry?

The ladies and I, I was saying how interesting it was that you always wore your sunglasses, and then I was trying to remember there's a pop star who always wears sunglasses, even indoors, and I was trying to think who it was and it's Marion here who pipes up with 'Bono!' and of course she's right! Bit of a dark horse Marion.

(Well you see him in magazines.)

(Is it Bob Dylan?)

(He was thinking of Bono, Marion, Bono was the answer.)

(Bob Dylan. He's one. And there's another one.)

Where's Mrs Bind? er, vicar.

Roger.

Roger.

Ah now Janet wanted to say goodbye but you were still on the old phone call there in the corridor, though it's nice to meet someone who doesn't have one of those blummin mobiles! I was once as you! Then I fell for the sleek Motorola.

Janet's gone.

There were the children to see to, she did want to say ta-ta.

She's not coming to lunch.

You off to lunch with the ladies? Marvellous.

(No Sally it's just Marion and I, I'm sure we'll be a little dull for you.)

(Speak for yourself Ellie.)

You won't be dull! Do we walk to where we're going?

(Well I think it's an absolute duty on a day like this, don't you Marion?)

(You don't have a car, Ellie, you don't have a choice.)

(It's ten minutes at the most. Now I insist that poor redhead girl has a biscuit.)

I'm okay, thank you.

(She's sticking to her guns, Eleanor.)

It was a beautiful service, vicar. Roger.

Roger yes, oh well, thank'ee kindly, usual fare, you know, the ladies will tell you, if I'd known we were having a special guest I'd have laid on something a bit different for you!

Well, it was, something a bit different, for me.

Can't beat the old favourites!

(I was telling her that they sing 'Abide With Me' at the Cup Final game, Roger.)

They most certainly do! I've heard it twice in the flesh, and the Gunners won on both occasions, 2–0 over Southampton, and rather fortuitously on penalties over United, I think the Force was with us that day! Is it clouding over slightly there?

(It was lovely this morning wasn't it Sally?)

I was on the Heath with the children, I saw the mulberry tree the king planted. And the face of the dryad, in the chestnut tree.

Actually 1–0 over Southampton. Now the thing about 'Abide With Me' is that we all know William Monk wrote the tune, but rather more interesting is the story of Henry Lyte, who wrote the text. You realise the poor guy was dying of TB?

(As a matter of fact, Sally, it was Mr Lyte's farewell sermon to the parish where he had served for many years.)

Spot on, or rather, it was the day of his farewell sermon, and he wrote those words that morning, just in time for the service! Talk about a deadline! He left for Italia the next day, in the hope of taking the healing waters or what-have-you, however,

He didn't make it, did he, vicar.

Roger well no, sad to say, he did not, I suppose my ending is in my beginning so to speak, he died at Nice, three weeks later. Not so 'nice'.

He died in Nice. Huh. There's a. There's a,

There's a story eh. And a monument of words he left behind.

('They urged Him strongly: stay with us, for it is nearly evening; the day is almost over.')

That's right, Marion. Luke 24:28.

(24:29 Roger you need to be replaced.)

Let's not bewilder the poor girl! Now. Ladies. I wonder . . .

(Yes, Roger, we're going to leave you in peace . . .)

(We'll be right outside the door . . .)

Where are you going, don't go!

(Oh it's just that the vicar wants a word, that's all!)

No!

It's really nothing, Sally, just

Everyone stay here. Please!

(Of course, dear, if you like.)

Well, I suppose there's nothing terribly private about it, it's not confession! I don't think anyone would find my confession anything to write home about! No . . . no do all sit down while I, actually, am, going to go, for my third biscuit no, it's simply, just to say, that Sally, we have a group Sally, and they'll be meeting this afternoon, together and it's really, it's very, very broad, very open-minded, absolutely non-judgemental and non-faith-based and it's right here, right here in this room, and it's not, I mean, it's both, it has elements of both, both AA and NA so really it's anything relating to, to addiction and they are some of the nicest people they could be just anyone, from, I don't know, from the local library, or the police, we have schoolteachers, we have youngsters like yourself we have or they could be bus drivers, absolutely all sorts. We had an actor here once, he sat right there. Did not give his name. Did not have to. Though we all knew it. But you would not have to, either. You would not have to say a word. And I'm not saying you need anything of the sort. What I do say is: you seem a little bit alone today, a shade down in the dumps and I thought you could do with the company. You would find many like-minded souls.

Well. That's er, kind. It's just I, I do have one friend, and he's going to pick me up from Mrs Wendiforth's.

(Eleanor, please.)

From Eleanor's when I call him, his name's Edward, he's just a friend who looks after me and then I'll be okay.

You are absolutely welcome in this place at any time, Sally, and I hope you will do us all the honour of bursting through our doors again! You were a bit of a hit with the children.

I was?

I hear you're a life member of the Acorn Squad and no, I won't ask! but there is one thing I ask of you and one thing only.

What's that? Roger.

That you open your hand.

What? I mean: pardon?

(Do as the vicar says, Sally, no harm will come to you!)

Open your hand, Sally.

O-kay.

And take this. No no don't look at it just take it.

I can't.

(She looked at it, Marion!)

(Has she spoiled the surprise?)

Roger, I'm, it's kind but I can't take money from you.

It's not much, Sally, but I absolutely insist, you have to get home, don't you?

Yes.

And as it happens I'm in charge here! So you close that pretty little hand up and forget about it till later. And now you have a proper reason to return here to our Home of Hopeless Causes!

I –

Go! Go! Go placidly amid the noise and haste!

*

Chantilly Road, is this your road?

It's the last road but one.

And we're in, where are we, Shinglewell?

Oh heavens no, would we be, we're further east than that, we're just about in Thamesgate now, I have a Thamesgate postcode, we're really quite near the river, and you have a friend coming to collect you, dear?

That's right, if I could just call him from your house, I'd be very grateful, I have the money from Roger

Now don't be ludicrous.

(You're not taking her money now, Ellie.)

Of course I'm not, I wouldn't dream of it. She's my guest at Sunday roast.

(She's probably very hungry. Are you not hungry?)

I'm, I am, but I'm on a kind of a diet, Marion, I can't really eat anything.

Well, now, you know there are many support groups organised by Roger and Sheila at the church, and there are certainly groups who can help you.

I don't have an eating disorder Eleanor I don't, I'm not that thin am I, it's just some days I try not to eat anything at all, just to sort of cleanse my system.

To cleanse the system?

(You must give her the green grapes, Eleanor.)

I think that sounds a little bit silly, Sally, you have to eat something. Even if it's just a little fruit. You could have an apple. I won't hear of you eating nothing at all!

I really, I really just wanted to come for the company. I mean if that's okay. And the phone. I mean –

(She will be unable to resist the grapes, Eleanor.)

I'm allergic to fruit Marion.

(Oh you big fat liar, Sally.)

I'm sorry?

(I said, you're a big fat liar, Sally, whatever, Cavendish.)

Carpenter.

(Whoever you are.)

Don't mind her, she gets like that, feels very free, don't you Marion, you feel very free and easy in what you say on a Sunday.

That's fine with me as it goes.

A typical Sunday with Marion. No one agrees with you saying that Sally is a big fat liar Marion and happily we're home.

Not fat anyway. Nice garden.

*

####### THIS IS THE ANSWERING SERVICE FOR 0208 6527 2667. EDWARD. HARDHOUSE. IS NOT AVAILABLE TO TAKE YOUR CALL BUT YOU CAN LEAVE A MESSAGE AFTER THE TONE.

Ed it's me. 12 Hillary Avenue, Thamesgate SE27.

*

####### ALLO ALLO. NOUS SOMMES PAS CHEZ NOUS. LAISSEZ-

Mum. Change the message.

*

Everything all right there, Sally-on-the-telephone?

Yes, Marion. But it's Susan on the telephone.

Not Sally?

Oh God yes: Sally. Sorry. And I swore. Sorry.

You did.

Just one more call.

Take as long as you like, Stephanie.

It's Sally.

Whatever. It will keep.

*

####### JOHN CORMIN. LEAVE A MESSAGE. #

John, it's me, it's, I have to whisper, it's Sue. I'm in a difficult situation and I just wondered if . . . but you can't really call me back, so

Sue.

John! Oh,

What's up?

I'm. It's sort of ridiculous. I'm in Thamesgate in a house.

Mm-hm. Nice.

Um: I'm in trouble.

You are? How was France? How's your dad?

He: passed away John are you alone there?

Oh man. I'm really sorry Sue.

No no

I am alone, as it goes. If there's, you know, with your dad, anything I can do. I met your dad, didn't I. Great bloke. We watched England.

I can't talk for long, it's not my phone. Can you meet me?

I, could. You mean, today could I?

Yes.

Er, well. Where?

Somewhere here.

What in Thamesgate?

No. But near. I can't get very far. I'm on foot.

You're on foot.

You're really free to do this, John?

I'm: well, calls for a bit of a reshuffle. But you sound –

I am.

Well I played cricket down there once, so I only know one place it's a pub, it's in Biltham. That's one stop east of Thamesgate you can walk it.

What pub, John, where you played.

Well. Okay. One that plays cricket. Which involves me looking through the old fixture lists and they're filed away I think I know where, can I call you back?

Yes. 0208 7621 3998.

Okay. Won't take a minute. Getting to you's a good hour and a half though Sue, you gone a bit east on me there.

It's okay, I can wait in this house of this lady.

Fair enough. Let me sort this out.

Thanks John.

S'okay. For an old, you know . . .

*

####### THIS IS THE ANSWERING SERVICE FOR 0208 6527 2667. Edward. Hardhouse. IS NOT AVAILABLE TO TAKE YOUR CALL BUT YOU CAN LEAVE A MESSAGE AFTER THE TONE. #

Ed it's me. This is, going to sound really strange after the things I've been saying, but I think I'm going to be okay now, I've found a friend, sort of an old friend, who can look after me sort of, until the madness passes I know it's madness, until it passes, but he's someone I know from before, so it's maybe better to, to go with this. I am so terribly sorry you've changed your plans and got on the plane, Ed, and I promise I'll make it up to you somehow when I see you. Maybe this week? For the first time I think there'll be a this week! I've been out of my mind and maybe I'm not now, and it's all worked out for the best. So we can meet next week and I can say thank you for how you've always listened to me, especially at the airport when I was stuck, that time, you were great, Mr Hardhouse, and I don't think you're a piece of what I used to think you were at all*and there goes your bleep mate, so bye for now.

*

Was that the last of your calls, Sally?

Yes, Eleanor, it is, and I'm really sorry, and please please please take some money from me

Oh do stop Sally, they're all local calls aren't they?

Yes. Yes!

Have you found a friend to help you?

Yes!

Well, good, I'm very pleased but I'm also a little bit disappointed as I was rather hoping you'd stay for tea.

(She's not permitted tea Ellie it is against her religion.)

Oh Marion hush if you can't be friendly. No, the Brown boys are coming round.

The brown boys.

My grandchildren I call them boys but they're great strong young men now and they're always in and out of trouble!

(She means prison.)

Marion! Silly old bird.

(Where are you off to, 'Sal'?)

I'm, I'm going out for a smoke.

You can smoke on the patio, dear.

No! Because: I left my cigarettes outside, I dropped them.

(What a load of tripe she talks)

I was quitting, I changed my mind

I insist you stay for tea.

(We demand you stay for tea! In God's name we command it!)

The boys would love to meet you.

(Exterminate! Exterminate! God help you if you go!)

Shut your cakehole Marion, you always go too far.

*

####### ####### ####### ### *Hello?*

John it's me.

You still in that house?

No, I'm, I had to leave, people were coming, I found a telephone box in this street it's, Watchpole Road, there's no one, I'm going east towards Biltham you said Biltham, right, and you'd tell me the name of the pub I can meet you?

I did, yeah, okay. You might have, you might have to wait a little while there Sue.

I can wait, John.

Just, a few things at this end.

Yep.

Can you tell me anything more about, you know, what's up?

I don't have long.

You said that before. Someone told your fortune?

No I don't have long on the phone. I have seven pound coins and I'm trying to save them. Can I tell you when I see you? John?

Well, okay. In for a, Christ I have to go

What's the name of the pub?

The Royal Oak in Biltham call me from there

I will, Royal Oak I'll be there I'll be outside, John, I can't eat or drink today you see so I'll wait for you out of sight, okay? John?

*

Do you know the way to the Royal Oak?
No.

*

Do you know the Royal Oak?

Hee hee.

*

Royal Oak in Biltham?
You're in Biltham.

Royal Oak pub, in Biltham?
You're in Biltham.

*

Keep going past them lights. Turn left, keep going past them lights. They've got Cranhams on tap you know. It's shut mind.

What?

3:30 on a Sunday it's shut. I know where you can get a drink.

I have to meet someone.

I know where you can meet people.

I already know someone! Goodbye.

I know Biltham like the back of my hand I do.

*

####### JOHN CORMIN. LEAVE A MESSAGE #

John. I'm by the Royal Oak. It doesn't open till six. You must be on your way. I'm across the road in a phone box, but when you come I'll be in the bushes to the left of the pub, between the pub and the Esso garage there's some bushes, I'll be there please hurry John. People go by sometimes and they keep looking at me in here.

*

####### ###*Yes who's that?*

Ed it's me! It's Mantle!

Christ where are you baby?

I'm okay Ed, I'm in Biltham

Biltham? Jesus why?

It's okay it doesn't matter, I'm alive, I'm playing the game, like we said, children, old folks I've been moving among them Ed and keeping myself safe, and now

Biltham where, where?

Someone's coming to meet me, Ed, and he'll look after me till midnight, that's all I needed isn't it, to be looked after till midnight, that's why I called you, just to say I didn't need you

Mantle, stop

And I know you came all this way Ed, and I do thank you but it's okay

It's not okay, calm down girl

I'm calm, Ed, I'm calm I have five coins left. It doesn't know where I am

You're in Biltham, where in Biltham?

I'm in the Royal Oak, or nearby, he's meeting me there

Who is?

Just, a friend from before.

I'm getting a cab right now, 'friend from before' are you nuts?

No!

You don't want to see me?

I, want to see you, Ed, it's just

I'm the man you turned to, Mantle, Susan, am I not? I'm the first port of call.

I know, it made sense, to call you, I was hysterical

You still are, that's clear enough

I'm going to be rescued Ed, I can start my life again now, and I'll never ask what's coming I'll just stare out in the fog like now

You're making no sense to me, angel, who's it you're meeting?

It's from a time before you Ed don't be angry, I'm your friend

You want to be my friend, ahh, that's sweet I'm calling a cab.

I'd always want to be, Ed, you've been so good to me

I have, sweetheart, you know I noticed that myself

But there's just no need to come now, I've got help and I can't talk more I need to save my coins Ed I only have five

I'll call you straight back, what's the number.

Ed. No.

Royal Oak in Biltham. On my way.

Ed, I'm not

Look, Mantle. I think it's understood, my feelings, I think, these last weeks I think it's understood where I come from, where you take me, where we go to. Inconvenient yes but that's the big L excuse me my heartbeat, so, Royal Oak at Biltham, what's the number, 0208 and?

Ed no no no no no

Only I know what you've gone through Susan, I have been constant and I don't believe that's deniable, so you are going to stay right where you are and I will find you by hook or by crook.

That's just what It would say.

What?

It's just what It would say: I will find you by hook or by crook.

No, no, it's a saying, it's

Ed you always called me, then I always called you, but now I think about it things just kept happening, the fame and the money, my flight back

That wasn't me!

It was your world, Ed, it's your world this is happening in it's not mine, I curled up in my chair and read books and told lies to tourists in the sunshine but the world came right up to me like a dog on its hind legs

Susan, Susan

Like it suddenly got hungry

Come on now

It was with you all along

I only happen to adore you

That's something It would say

Oh well excuse me for caring

Then It would say that

Give me your number Mantle, I am going to save you

I have to hang up now

Give me your number NOW!

I have four coins

I love you

It said that

I'm coming to get you

It said that

*

Hi who's that? 'UNKNOWN' – 'UNKNOWN'?

Hi Min.

Omigod it's you where are you? Why are you UNKNOWN?

I'm in the east.

East of what.

Eden.

Where's that, you sound far away! You disappeared! How did you get back?

Broomstick.

You said you were on that flight! I went to Gatwick for nothing it's in Surrey Suse it's miles! People wanted to just hug you and we waited while all these ordinary people came off and people kept saying There she is! and we'd all move quickly in a gang to hug that person and then it would be like, someone else from like regular life and we'd be like false alarm sorry not you (loser) and then the crew and this woman said That's the whole flight! I said impossible at her desk and she confirmed it on her list, there was no Susan Mantle, she cancelled! You cancelled! You have got to meet me! I've been talking to the Sunday Telegraph Suse, I was taken to an actual private club with like butlers you are so, just, loved, Suse, people want to be near you.

I have three coins, I'm safe, I'm going to be with John.

John? John Cormin? Oh MY GOD!

I won't be back till tomorrow, if there's anyone left to tell.

Wow. I'm just, WOW. Are you guys an item?

I was afraid, Min, something happened, about the prophecy. It made me think today was a dangerous day,

Omigod who was the guy? The tall dark stranger! You're still alive! Who was it in the end? Who did you say yes to?

It doesn't matter now it's not John, he's not a stranger, he's

The police were round your house they arrested Nigel Pilman! He threw paint on every wall! You know what he did in your bedroom Suse?

I have to go. I've three coins left and I need them for John

It needs industrial cleaners!

⁎

####### ####### ####### ####### ####### ####### ####### ####### ####### ## *Hello.*

Hello, who's there.

Can I speak to John. John Cormin, please.

Who is it.

This is his girlfriend who is it.

Barbara.

Can I ask what's it concerning.

Of course, yes. This, Wingram business.

(Ubiquitous Barbara and her fucking Wingram. On a Sunday.)

Yeah really, typical, hmm . . . Barbara what's up with Wingram.

It's me.

Yeah, thanks for calling, sorry to bring this up on a Sunday Barbara, my fault. (It was my fault I called her about Wingram.)

It's okay. Aren't you coming, John?

We can talk about that at tomorrow's meeting. It'll all be

Hello? John? Are you there?

Look Sue, don't call me here, give me a number I'll call you.

I'm in the phone box by the Royal Oak in Biltham, the number is 0208 7330 9353.

I can't get there, things didn't work out, I can get to you later.

When? Where? I don't know anywhere John I only know this pub and it's shut and it's getting dark and it's foggy now

Hey hey, come on, you've been on the box you're fine

No I'm cold, John, I thought you were coming, I've two coins stills but she said I would die, I'm cold, John, it opens at six, it's 0208 7330 9

Look. Sue, look.

It's the only day in the world that'll ever be like this but I need you John I need someone to help me

Look, all right, I'm thinking, there's somewhere,

Where? When?

I'm trying to think, I'm trying to think, I know Dartford, I've played there, are you near the Dartford Crossing?

It's cold and dark I don't know, I can wait, just say you'll meet me somewhere

You know, the big road bridge over the river, the toll bridge.

I know, am I near there? I can't be, I don't know, I've been walking, I've been walking so many miles John

I played a tournament near there once and I know for a fact there's a decent pub. It's got a fire. It has all these Belgian beers.

I'm going there, what's it called John?

Hang on, I think it's on the other side though, the north side.

What's it called, John, with the Belgian beers? Can we sit there in a corner? Can we wait till it shuts? Can we wait in there till midnight comes and it's Monday John?

Unbelievable I know. Who on earth do those Wingram people think they are, Barbara?

No! No! I'm not Barbara I'm Sue, I'm Susan, I'm Susie!

And we've got the restructuring panel, I know, I know . . .

You have to help me!

It's just a shame Wingram's come up at this point in time, Barbara, we may have to shift the RSP and delegate Brinkley to the southern team.

Get rid of her John get rid of her

I know, we've had that discussion, I said the same to Tim Palley but it's been that kind of quarter Barbara, tell me about it.

I have two more coins that's all

So, good, I think we're sitting pretty on that one Barbara, and let's try and close on Chadwick in the meantime

Please
And have a catch-up in midweek. Ciao.
John?

John.

John

*

You all right lovey?

You all right?

Yep.
You're not a bit cold out here?
Yep.
You lost? Why you sitting out here?
I, I needed to find a phone box. A red phone box. I couldn't find one anywhere, so I sat on this bench and I, well I'm waiting for one. I've got two coins I can use. Here in my hand I stole them.

Never mind. Shouldn't be out here with no coat and no gloves it's getting dark, lovey.

I needed to find a phone box, but there never was one.
Is that so, you daft thing, look where I'm pointing.

Look where I'm pointing lovey.
I don't see a phone box.
No, you daft thing, you're not looking where I'm pointing. Up them steps.
Oh. Yes. Yes!
You look so miserable there.
I don't know where I am.
You're in Dagnall, lovey.
Dagnall.
That's Dagnall High Road.
Dagnall High Road.
You're in Dagnall now.

*

This phone does not work. Hello?

Hello. Do you work? No. You do not. Red phone box. You took my coin though. You took half of what I had. You're quite like that saint who cut his coat in half for the beggar, but instead you cut <u>my</u> coat in half and just stood there grinning. One coin left. Well I think that's the fee for hell so perhaps thanks are in order.

Hello. Hello. We are not at the house of us. Leave you a message if it pleases you!

Dad. Are you there? Yes. Sukey . . . How's my, how's my fille de la paparazzi . . . are you, getting into scrapes. Yes, Dad, yes, Dad. I'm in one, in a scrape. I was famous, Dad, I was rich for a time. I travelled over earth and water to see you Dad and I did, didn't I, we had a cup of tea there.

Then what . . . Sukey . . . then what. I met a tall dark stranger who I always did say no to, then I changed my tune on a jet plane, Dad, you always said avoid them, take the train, see the countryside, see the landscape rolling by! I said yes to him and then, then the day passed and it was yesterday and now it's today and it's still today but it's getting dark and cold. The sun went cold before it went down and when it all comes true I'll never see the sun again. I saw it for us both, for a week I did, I saw it. It was nothing to write home about Dad and it doesn't let you look. I told you I'd tell you everything and I've not been very good at that, I've been busy all day, Dad, with church of course it's Sunday, and before that Sunday school, and a nature trail with the children, on old Shinglewell Heath. Where we had picnics you and me Sukey, you read me your new story.

Well I'll tell you what I can Dad, but don't look at me now, it won't make you smile at all. And I know you're somewhere happy, so just listen out sometimes and I'll see you when I see you.

Yes Sukey I'll see you

When I see you

Because right now at this time I'm going to sit down here in the broken glass at the bottom of the world.

*

Look at her

Fuckin hell

Is this her home or what

Oi

Oi ginga!

What you doin down there ginga

What you think she's doin you twat she came to make a call and some cunt's trashed it

Yeah like Loxy

I never

It was Nogo

I got bigger fish to fry than fuckin phone boxes

Shall we

What

Shall we do her

Listen to him fuckin gangsta shall we do her. Twat

I don't mean do her I mean her pounds sterling

Yeah right

Don't look like she got much in the way of pounds sterling

Let's do her then fucking ginga bitch

Who asked you ya lowlife

No one

Oi

Look at us will ya

Look at us ginga

Don't ignore us

Is this phone box your new home ginga

We done that gag shut up Maggot

You cryin ginga?

She's cryin

Like you care

Didn't say I care, said she's cryin. Fucking observation

You, you, are you . . . are you . . . 'right there, ginga?
Course she ain't right she's fuckin sobbin
I'm just saying what you say for fuck's sake in a situation
Ha! You love her! She's a tart and you love her!
Let's do the bitch she's hot
Who asked you ya lowlife
No one

It's okay . . . look, it's broken, that's all, don't cry
Get a mobile, bitch
Leave her alone
Didn't touch her, just giving free consultation
Fucking hell she's bleedin
She is, this tart's head's bleedin
Someone done her

Hey. Hold my arm ginga let's stand you up
Fuck me this is emotional I might cry
I got a fiver gizza blowjob
Eat me ya lowlife
It's her profession is the point
Terry's comin
Oi Terry

What you toe-rags doin here, piss off
Found this girl in here, someone done her Tel
Someone done her, she's bleedin
Blimey. You all right, love?
Blimey says Tel
You all right? Give her some room you lot, you hurt yourself love?
No, I,
Ugh look it's all over like her time-of-the-month!
Yeah right, on her face you twat
Got the painters in eh?
Shut it you two
Sorry Tel
I needed to phone, it was broken, I fell down

My name's Terry
Like she gives a shit what his name is
Shut it. Do you happen to know you're bleeding, love?

What?
Down your, no, do you mind if I
Don't touch me
Sorry. Down your cheek love, look, and there.
Oh my God
Is that blood in fact,
No it's, it's, hair dye
It is oh yeah look it's everywhere

God, God my hands
It's okay . . .
Bitch ain't a ginga at all fucking pretending is what
Just piss off you lot the pubs are open
He's right an' all
Yeah we piss off and he gets to do what he likes with ginga
She's not a ginga as it happens she's a fake
Fake ginga tart she's hot
Someone shut that little toe-rag up. I'm taking her to Coldway, let her get washed, I'm on shift right now
Yeah right
Yeah right
You lot have filthy minds and it's nearly half past six. Lads at the George'll think you died or something
Catch ya later y'old perv
I'll see you lot
Not if we
See you first blah blah. Jesus H fucking schools these days, what's your name love?
Sue
You in a spot of bother Sue?
No
Look, I dunno, but d'you wanna get sorta cleaned up a bit? Cos between you and me love you look a bit of a sight. What with that

red stuff streamin down you look like something out of Alien or Dr Who or something.

I'm okay I'm not meeting anyone

Billie Piper in a spot of bother eh

Sue

Cos I'm just heading over there to Coldway, and you could use the facilities. Unless you got your own Tardis eh?

There's lights over there

Coldway Sports, I work there love I only popped out for some Red Bull had a late one last night I'm all over the shop. Least I don't look like the flaming creature from the deeps.

Are there, are there people there

Eh? The Flyers are in, the girls, booked a court till eight then they got pizza coming in till nine odd, but I know 'em they're cool kids I usually let 'em run over, ten or so, depends, later sometimes.

What have they – booked a court for.

The Flyers? Footie, love. Ladies' game these days. Sunday evenings anyway and they're pretty much top dogs. Them and Dartford I should say, they'll settle it sudden death. Look, that's the nearest spot you're going to find a towel, know what I mean, and running water and a cup of tea love. You up for that? What's your name again?

Susan.

I'm Terry, Terry Vine

Thanks, Terry

They're not bad kids. Well. They're not great neither. Anyway I showed up. And you come with me to Coldway, get a hot shower love. You go home looking like that you're gonna give your old man a fuckin seizure mind my French.

*

######## *Hardhouse.*

Ed. It's me.

Fire.

Yes. Fire. I made a mistake. I have no help. I'm in a sports centre in Dagnall in East London. Someone has lent me his phone but I've not got very long. I think It tricked me, Ed, the thing that's looking for me, and I'm sorry I said I didn't need you I do, Ed are you there?

You know what. Call my PA.
What?
Nothing she can't handle.
NO!

ED!

*

####### ALLO ALLO. NOUS SOMMES PAS CHEZ NOUS. LAISSEZ-VOUS UNE MESSAGE, S'IL VOUS PLAIT. HELLO HELLO. WE ARE NOT AT THE HOUSE OF US! LEAVE YOU A MESSAGE IF IT PLEASES YOU! #

Mum. I don't know where you are. I thought in a moment of madness you might stay in in case I called you today, as you knew I was terrified. But everything is lovely, don't worry, I'm in a filthy toilet in a girls' changing room in a sports hall in Dagnall, talking on a borrowed mobile that's low on batteries. I'm starving and tired and dirty and I've got no money to get home and no one to take care of me, oh and the house got vandalised so all in all it's gone okay today. Well. I'm going to have a shower and a cup of tea now, that'll make everything better. I can't*tell you what I'm going to do now well two reasons I can't tell you, one the tape's run out and two I have no idea what I'm going to do now. I'm going to watch the Dagnall Flyers playing indoor football Mum, then I'll try and make friends forever with them so they make a magic ring around me till midnight. It says on the wall DAGNALL FLYERS RULE and I*believe that Mum. This is where I'll be till the witch is right or wrong. Now no one's listening, not even me. I've never heard of Dagnall and I walked here, can you imagine? I walked the opposite way of everything I wanted, and this is where I ended, Mum. I saw these weird lights in the air, like there were towers where there couldn't be. Could that be Canary Wharf? It's Sunday I don't know anyone. I'm really not sure where I am. I'm not sure where you are, and I wanted to tell you something.

Because Dad's here, did I say? Yeah Dad's here, he's left you. He's got a little tired of life down in Ramparts-of-the-Geezer and he got up out of his armchair and he fucking flew away did you know?

You didn't even notice, you were down there in the café with Franck with your heads together and he flapped right by the window, he swooped away, he did a turn in the sky over la mer for le last time and then he set his sights on England and was whistling his white cliffs melody as he swerved this way and that towards me and he made it Mum.

He's got his breath back now, he's outside, he's waiting. This is a girls' changing room so he has to wait outside and go all red and beaming as he does. He's then, he's then, he's then going to escort me to the football game, he's told me all about it Mum, if only he'd had a boy, he's going to buy me a programme and get us both Bovril and a hot dog with two types of mustard and we're going to watch the game. When we get home we'll tell you all about it Mum, what the score was, who won, and you'll be making supper, doing a recipe from a book.

The sky outside the kitchen will be dark dark dark blue, and Dad will draw the curtain over it, with a frown like that's his big contribution, that's his labour for the day. Then he'll sit down and wait for our supper, he'll still be leafing through his programme finding items of interest.

*

You all right?

You all right?

Sorry. Miles away. I'm fine.

You a friend? Of one of the girls?

No just, checking out the game. Good play.

They're all over the place. You tell them, you show them, you put it on the white-board, you plan, you strategise, you – SQUARE IT KAYLA SQUARE IT – but when it comes to it they're out on their own and you know how much you can do.

Yes. Very little.

Nothing. This much. Talking in my sleep might as well be.
Might as well be. It was, good play by Tyra though. Just then.
Tyra's class, but you can't beat the Crossers with one kid.
Yes. No.
Plus there's no way she's a hundred per cent.
I was thinking that.
Did her ankle in the summer COME ON, COME ON, LOOK UP KERRY! Didn't look up dozy cow.
Looked down if anything.
KAYLA MOVE UP YOU'RE TOO DEEP she's too deep.
Too deep. She should give it.
Yeah, GIVE IT!
Give it.
GIVE IT, JESS, HOLD IT
Also hold it.
HOLD IT, YOU GOT TYRA USE TYRA
Yes she should.
USE TYRA, YESSS! GOAL! GREAT WORK JESSIE ABDUL, GREAT FINISH TYRA POVEY! GREENS YOU GOTTA WORK FOR EACH OTHER, SHELLEY WHERE YOU MEANT TO BE PLAYING? PARDON? OKAY PULL BACK THEN! 5–3, GREENS COME ON NOW, SHOW FOR IT, MAKE THE PLAY! Come on, you dozy cows . . . You, you in the league then?
Yes. I am.
Who you with. Who d'you play for.
I don't play. I mean any more.
Injury? What, Achilles?
No. Spinal.
Bummer.
Well, yes, but it's okay I can, I can do things I can run in the park I just can't play at this level. I can't, you know, give it.
You a coach.
Well. No.
TYRA USE FRAN, USE FRAN, SHE'S SHOWING FOR IT!

She didn't use her.

Nah Tyra never passes anyway.

Fran was showing for it

She's hopeless I'm just trying to bring her on, needs time on the ball. She'll probably feature Sunday, late sub maybe God help us. So. So I'm trying to figure out what your role is here.

I just, I, thought I'd come and watch the Flyers tonight.

What, in training?

Yes. Really see them up close.

Okay, okay . . . Okay I get it . . . (SQUARE IT SHELL SQUARE IT! GOOD. MORE OF THAT, GREENS!) You're watching Tyra.

Sorry?

You're watching Tyra, I'm right, aren't I? You can tell me, I won't tell her it'll freak her out.

I'm, well, better not to.

That's brilliant. Yesss! No it'd freak her out though, she's like everywhere on the pitch but she's shy in herself, doesn't like any fuss, totally different character off it.

Yes. I've heard that.

What d'you think so far, shouldn't ask you, tryin to do your job here. Secret's safe with me. You know she did her ankle in the summer, no way she's hundred per cent, you'll factor that in yeah? Cool. Cos Tyra's class. COME ON YELLOWS HANG BACK! Thought you'd like have a clipboard, always a total giveaway. Then I noticed you were talking into a hands-free.

Yep, kind of dictaphone system, just if I have, thoughts.

Freeze up if she knew, she's a shy one.

I hear you.

TYRA POVEY, SPREAD IT OUT MORE BABE, SPREAD IT! Paula Greshey.

Sue Carpenter.

Good to meet you Sue. I'll leave you alone in a minute. USE SHELLEY USE SHELLEY USE SHELLEY, COME ON, LOOK UP! Always the, blue in the face, Jesus. You know I got to ask, and there's no way you have to answer this, but obviously I'm curious,

I understand that.

Are you attached?

I'm going to pass on that one, Paula.

Totally understood. Cos I only ask cos, it's just a private thing between me and Tina Sumpter over at Dartford, she's saying she had Millwall in last week, and before it was like Barnet, and I'm saying, can anyone actually prove that's not in some old fantasy of hers? I don't think so. Just thought I might be able to tell that dozy cow I had Arsenal in to watch us bloody training! Personal thing. No it's next week you should watch Tyra, she's a big game player, and they don't come bigger than Crossers.

That's, Dartford, right?

Uh-huh. Dagnall-Dartford. The crunch.

Dartford Crossers, Dartford Crossing, right, get it.

Bit corny.

Are we, are we near there?

Eh?

Dartford Crossing.

Yeah.

Lights in the air, like towers

Eh? You came over the Crossing?

No, No sorry I'm, I came up from Mersham.

Mersham, okay, my geography, that's Woolwich way so I'm thinking you're I'm thinking you're Charlton, else you're Palace? No I know, discreet, mum's you know, cool, I'll probably tell Tina you're Arsenal anyhow just to see her big gob hanging open. YES!!! NICE ONE JANEY, LET'S SEE YA WORKING GREENS YOU'RE NOT OUT OF THIS! Well I'll leave you to your work, Sue. This is probably a shade out of order, but we got pizza coming in after, we're having a little party cos it's Kayla's 21st, have a bite with us if you want, they're sweet girls.

Thanks Paula I'd really like that.

Wouldn't want you to think I was trying to bribe you there!

*

No I hate them cos I gotta pay a quid just to even like play them cos I gotta go over the stupid toll bridge

That's not why I hate them I hate them cos they're dirty bastards Shelley that Donna Blight she kicks you seen my shin

I seen it we all seen it

Look at this Miss Carpenter

Oh yes that's bad

Bad she goes. Janey cut me some of that pepperoni

That's pepperoni Kel you don't want that you want plain

I said pepperoni I want pepperoni, duh

We're out of the other one. You know who she looks like, she looks like that girl in the bed on that show?

Yeah you do an' all

She was always sayin no to like amazing stuff?

I get that a lot actually

It was shit

It was awesome you mean

It was so shit Kel

She had like she could be a model, and she was like she was gonna meet Klaus outta Vermin Jones and she just like lay there

Oh I know who you mean

Yeah she told Thomas Bayne to fuck off or somethin

You go girl!

Weirdo you mean

Yeah like the best actor of his generation an all

Complete crackhead I read

Yeah and he's gay I read

I read that's a total lie

She was just like a total nobody no offence but you do look a bit like her Miss Carpenter

No you don't

She so does

No you're okay you don't at all, she looked sort of posh, what happened is that still on

Nah, she quit the show, couldn't take the pressure

It was cos her mum died

Nah it's cos it tanked in the ratings

Nah they sacked the guy who done it

I coulda done that show, just laid there

You could so never, like, just lay there when someone's offering you five hundred grand modelling contract yeah right

Zoo Game's on tonight with that Cassidy Plume

I love that show

It's shit

I saw an interview with a friend who said she was a bit of a bitch in real life

Who Cassidy Plume yeah

Nah the girl in bed

I thought she was well classy

She was a total slut

She was the best Hales

It was shit Kel

It was awesome

Why we talkin bout that?

Cos of her

Oh yeah

D'you ever see it?

Me? No.

Girls if I could muscle in here I just, Tyra has to go in a minute and I want her to meet Sue, Sue, this is Tyra Povey.

Hi

Tyra, Sue was watching tonight

Uh-huh

Hello, earth to Tyra, Sue was watching you tonight babe

Oh

You played really well Tyra

Cool

She's a bit of a star, ain't cha?

Well coach

You gonna take it to Dartford?

Yeah coach

You gonna give it to Dartford?

Yeah coach

FLYERS WE GONNA GIVE IT TO DARTFORD?

FLYERS ROCK!

Hey, gimme five ones, yo. Sue I'm gonna leave you with Tyra for a minute, I've got to pack up the stuff.

Okay.

Tyra's gotta go in a minute but you can stay as long as you like Sue, Terry lets us hang here till midnight sometimes.

Midnight? He does?

It's his call, he's our mate. Tyra, talk to Sue, back in a minute.

Okay. Well, as I said, you played well. You, particularly, you spread it well.

Thing is, right, Megan's not supporting me first half, I'm havin to go deep, right, and it's not my position, but I can do it, but I need some width, right, which, are Kayla and Lucy givin me? No, so I'm like in sort of no-man's-land first half, but second half, right,

Second half was better, yep,

Second half Megan pushes up, right, cos Tracey drops back and Tracey's class in the air, right, so I can press up sort of thing and then we just spread it a bit.

You did, I saw that.

Game over.

7–4 in the end.

We sucked at the back, though, them four goals it's pafetic, right, we was more like some kind of 3-5-1 situation when we needed 4-3-2.

Yes. That's nine, nine players all spreading it it's good.

Dartford's what matters.

Dartford's what matters. You'll waste them.

We better!

Tyra you gotta go babe

I gotta babysit my kid sister, Miss Carpenter!

It's okay Tyra.

Yeah, bye, maybe see you at Dartford!

Will do. Good luck.

Sue would you step over here a minute I just want a quick word away from the girls.

Okay Paula.

Look. I don't really know what your game is.

Sorry?

Maybe I don't need to know.

Well we talked about being discreet and so on.

Look I just had a word with Terry who works here. He says when he found you were you slumped at the bottom of a smashed-up phone box crying your eyes out. He says your face was streaming with cheap hair dye and you were totally incoherent. He thought you were probably drunk. So maybe I'm thinking you don't look to me much like an Arsenal scout.

I never said I was from Arsenal you did

You don't look like anyone's friggin scout.

Well. Paula,

Yeah what.

Well, I try to keep my private life private.

Do you.

I can still do my job, and my job,

Yeah and your job probably involves you using a mobile to contact the major club you work for, right?

It does. Oh, and . . . you've just found out I don't have a mobile.

So, what, you're just talking to yourself.

I use a dictaphone. Old technology. Never been bettered.

How about you show me your old dictaphone.

No.

Yes.

No I can't.

Yes you can.

No, I can't, because: I don't have one. At all, so you can't.

You better tell me who you are girl.

I'll go.

Spy is it, come here from Dartford, from the Crossers, you watching us? and there's me chatting away.

I said I'll go. I'm not well.

Not well. Right. Not well are we? All right go. Since you look totally screwed in the head to me I'll let you off with a warning. If I see you anywhere round here again ever, I won't just stomp your head in, I'll tell the whole friggin squad they can help me stomp your head in. Okay there Miss Carpenter? Red card. Out you go.

*

What you doin'.

I've said: What you doin'.

I'm going Terry. She asked me to and I am.

You was touching my phone. I let you make calls on it and now you're looking to swipe it, I leave it there for a second, and

No.

No? What then?

I, I mistook it for mine.

Bollocks. You lost yours, you said. I let you make calls on mine, didn't I? Done so out of kindness. Am I right or am I wrong?

You are. I'm, confused.

We stood there, and you was cryin', and I got you out of bother with them scumbags, and you needed to make a call and out of kindness I allowed that. And I let you come in, clean up, cup of tea, and the girls let you watch them, talking tactics and that, and you hang out with them after, and it seems to me you're just a nasty piece of work intcha. Way you repay them kindnesses.

I'm not a nasty piece of work Terry. I'm not well.

Who is. I want you to step outside with me, you know why?

No.

I don't want Paula to know what's going on here. I don't want Kelly or any of them athletes to know what's going on here because if you cross them they'll fucking have ya. Rip ya to shreds them girls. And you may not be well but do I want to see that happen? No. Cos I could just walk in there and say guess what, know what this clown's up to now? Swiping my phone, that's what she's up to. But I want to have a private word with you, so I think we should step outside.

Going to hit me are you.

I said a word. Let's go.

*

Watch that step there.
Thanks Terry.

*

Yeah, yeah you're a nasty piece of work Sue.
I'm not, I'm just lost I'm just,
Who was you calling?
What?
Who was you calling on the phone, or what, you're just swiping it to flog it eh.
I was, I was trying to call my mum.
All right Sue. Mum. Nice idea. Why don't you try again?
It's okay, it's okay,
No I insist, I insist, and I'll just stay right here this time.
No really I don't need to
I don't believe a fucking word you say Sue. You call your mum this minute or I'm calling the old bill.
Don't do that
The police, right. And I don't think you want that, do you.
No I'm not well
G'on then, do the number. G'on then.

####### ALLO ALLO. NOUS SOMMES PAS CHEZ NOUS. LAISSEZ-VOUS UNE MESSAGE, S'IL VOUS PLAIT. HELLO HELLO. WE ARE NOT AT THE HOUSE OF US! LEAVE YOU A MESSAGE IF IT PLEASES YOU! #
– See no one's there.
That ain't a woman's voice
It's a fucking answer machine it's my dad
Put me on to him I want to speak to him
I said it's a fucking answer machine so fuck off
You fuck off you dirty tart, give me my fucking phone
Don't touch me

Touch you, what you gonna make me, you think I can't have you cos you're a bird is that what you think, is that what you think

Let go of me

You think I can't do pretty much what I choose in this particular grip

Fucking let go of me, no!

I do know what to do with birds in this particular grip you know I do know, I do, I might let it all slide by, you know, I might turn a blind eye, I might say hey, bygones be bygones, why don't you and me start all over again Sue, boy meets girl, boy kisses girl

No! No! No! get the fuck off me

Cos it's in my power to choose what happens in this particular grip of mine, you could leave without

No! No!

Ssshh a stain on your character, where were we, boy meets girl . . . sshh . . . sshh . . .

Boy likes girl . . . mmm . . .

What girl where's there a girl

I mean of course man likes woman, man likes woman on a lonely Sunday night in hell, I do have a place to go

Where's there a woman, Terry where's there a female, Terry I'm not a female Terry I'm just not one.

Eh?

I'm sorry. I thought you knew.

Some people like it.

No. No. No fucking way.

You want your saliva back? You want a little rewind? Or were you aware. I know the tits are a little disappointing but how d'you think I feel? I paid for these.

You're fucking winding me up.

Want a peep in my knickers Terry? Shall we measure our knobs Terry this is a sports hall.

Don't touch me. Don't come any nearer.

All right Terry? you're looking a little pale there, seem to have cooled on me a bit there.

You . . . you . . . you let me do that.

I just wanted it so bad Terry

I shoulda let them do you, you filthy little freak

All God's children Terry

Fuck me. Fuck me. Yeah well yeah I mean, fuck me I'm, fucking, speechless. Heard of it but like. Course I can see it now. See it plain as daylight.

It's pretty fucking like, well, I can tell better than anyone, you know I'm a, they say I'm like a good judge of character and that and I *couldn't tell at first, me, I can now, so that's pretty fucking incredible work that is you got done. My, opinion is it's disgusting but you know that's pretty fucking professional work you got done and I respect that in this day and age. And what I said or did, back there, just then, that was totally out of order now, knowing that, and I never would, cos I don't have a bone in my body of that chemical type, you know, they say it's chemical, people who feel that way and, do them like, acts it's okay, like you say, God's sort of, all right, but I'm not, among, I do not condone that, I do not respect that, them acts but I do, at the same time, tolerate it in this day and age.*

Okay

What I said, and or did back there, it's like, a reaction is all it is, words, I am not, Sue, such a thing, as you might think. I am sad for you in your condition, in your type of chosen 'lifestyle', I pity you, I do, but: I accept you. I am open to the, acts you do. It disgusts me, as I say, but I accept its, I accept its, place in, modern lifestyle. I am sure it makes for a very, for people of that way inclined, very strange different acts which I stress I totally oppose.

Okay Terry

Though I would defend your right, in a free country, to, in a private place, in a room sealed off for that purpose maybe, if the gentleman is prepared to pay to make himself available to it, I would still, to the death, defend your, you can do that, if needs must be, in a free world.

Thank you Terry

I will not I repeat inform the Flyers of what you've told me.

Better that way Terry

Hang on you went in the ladies

You led me there Terry, you showed me the towels

Jesus . . . You knew what I was thinking, you knew,
Everyone knows what you're thinking
You stitched me up you little freak
Oh I didn't touch their stuff. They won't catch anything.

What.
I said they won't catch anything Terry.

Look I can live with this illness Terry, we all know a lot more about it, there's new medicines I can take I've got a chance of a normal lifespan. Anyway that isn't how it's spread. They know that now. It's more things like intimate contact. Can I call my mum again?
Phwa – phwa – angels fucking preserve us –
Or do you want your phone back?
DON'T COME ANY FUCKING CLOSER!
Are you off then Terry Vine.
Phwa – phwa – phwa –
Bye then. I'll just look after your phone then.

Until it develops symptoms.

####### ####### ####### #######

Allo? Hello? Susan?

Mum

Susan, are you there?

I'm alive Mum

Where are you, where are you, what on earth are you doing?

I don't know Mum, I was running I can't breathe I've just been running I'm on a running track so I'm running I've no choice

Susan slow down, I heard your message are you drinking?

I won't be poisoned, Mum, I have two hours to go then it's not the day any more and that means nothing will come true

Good lord you can't believe that shit can you?

It's the only thing that stays Mum

What do you mean it's the only thing that stays?

Everything runs away from me Mum everything always runs away but it stays and it keeps coming

Susan you're overtired, you need help, do you have a pen?

It keeps coming like It cares

Oh good lord

It cares Mum It has no other interests

Look don't worry about the house, I have things under control, now where are you, where are you?

I have two hours to go Mum and this phone is dying, I stole it

You stole it? Susan.

I stole money from a church Mum, I lied to the old ladies, I'm dirty, I'm a male, I'm an Arsenal scout did you know that are you aware I'm an Arsenal scout?

Susan

Is Franck there? I want to talk to Franck

Oh Susan (Franck elle veut parler)

I wasn't serious Mum oh no oh no

Suzanne? Ça va my poet friend?

Franck, please put my mother back on

We are missing you Suzanne.

Please Franck my phone won't last forever its immune system is right down and I need to say goodbye

You must go to the hospital Suzanne.

People die there people die

Or to the police, no?

Where is my mother?

What have you done with her Franck?

Sshh, sshh . . . she is very upset with you on the terrasse I must be the strong man now for the two!

I'm cold, Franck

Go home Suzanne, you are beautiful and kind, she is coming back to the kitchen, here –

Susan, you, you, look: there is no such thing as clairvoyance.

I'm so cold, Mum, I'm nowhere, I'm walking through this marshland, I'm near the Dartford Crossing, I feel like it's the future Mum something brought me here

You are suffering some kind of delusion: forget that fucking woman. I want you to come back out here, I want you to

Get on a plane, you are out of your mind

(Franck c'est impossible) Look, Suzanne I mean Susan

I'm looking for a pub Mum

Susan

With Belgian beers and a roaring fire do you know it?

Susan!

On the north side of the river

Susan

####### ####### ####### #######
####### ####### ####### #######
####### ####### ### *Hello, the Mantle Residence!*

This is the Mantle Residence.

Hello.

To whom am I speaking?

Susan Jane Mantle.

Good Lord! At last! The prodigal!

'To whom am I speaking' . . . to whom am I speaking.

Robert Christopher Trellis! I'm in your house! What sort of a time do you call this you dirty stop-out! I jest! I jest, I jest . . .

Bob Trellis.

I'd completely dropped off, you know, what the hell is the blinking time . . .

It's twenty to eleven, Mr Trellis.

Oh not so bad.

Not so bad. Ages.

Where are you, young lady, I'm holding the fort here, clearing up the mess a bit for your poor old ma.

That's kind of you, Mr Trellis.

Where are you, are you outside?

I'm by the side of the river Thames.

Oh, good, well that explains that.

It's sort of lapping at the stones.

Ri-ight.

I'm cold, Mr Trellis.

Oh. Yes. I should say. Can you not make your way back? We had all sorts of nonsense here all day but it's pretty quiet now and you do have a well-stocked frigidaire I went to Waitrose.

I need to be here, Mr Trellis.

Well <u>do</u> you now. No questions asked.

I have something to ask you though.

I'm all ears, Susan.

My cat, Mr Trellis, how is he.

Bonner's in fine fettle, I think he misses you sometimes, he sleeps all night on your bed.

How do you know he does.

Well. He tells me. In cat-speak.

Good, okay, that's good then. There's a number on the frigidaire, next to the name Roberta.

Do you want me to look right now?

Just write it down. If anything happens, I want you to call this girl and say she can take Bonner. He likes her.

R-o-b-e-r-t-a I can do that if anything happens. What do you think will happen? Is there something I should know he wondered darkly. No? Well. Who <u>*knows*</u> *what will happen? Sweet Thames run softly and so on. Just you mentioning the Thames back there brought back the old*

What's on television.

I beg your pardon?

What's on television.

You know, same old Sunday night fare.

What are you watching.

I was watching that Zoo Game. Total crap, eh?

Tell me about it.

Yes, yes.

No. Really tell me about it.

Oh, I see. Well, before I nodded off in a stupor there was a chap got Snakes, which was quite funny actually, he lasted about five seconds, not very impressive!

No.

Then this other girl, this, she was rather a beauty but very peculiarly dressed in black velvet and what have you, suspenders, she got Vampire Bats and of course it was right up her alley.

Yes.

She just sat there grinning in her cage and she won about ten grand! She should get some new outfits. Madness eh.

How's Cassidy Plume doing.

Ah, now, this is interesting, you would know her, would you not? Very professional. What's she like face to face?

She's very rich, Mr Trellis.

Very. Well she earns her corn in The Zoo Game I can tell you, it's chaos all around her! Total mayhem! They had a grizzly on the lawn and it didn't look pleased! Do you have, other projects Susan?

No.

Nor should you, necessarily, it's not for everybody, that media type game. You've still achieved more than most in your,

And I also, very much so, wish to pass on from both myself and Rowena, my very great condolences on the,

Thank you, Mr Trellis.

Passing, what a nice man he was. First, do no harm. And now, are you going to tell me exactly what you're doing on the banks of the Thames on a Sunday night in late November?

You're not, are you?

No.

Now the key is where it always was, I'm sworn to secrecy by your ma but I think if I say gluepot we'd be on the same page?

Gluepot

Gluepot it is.

Goodbye Mr Trellis.

Bye for now. And I know I'm not your, I'm not your,

Mum

Parent but keep warm, Susan, it's winter, whatever your secret projects!

*

####### ####### ####### #######
####### ####### ####### #######

I'm not answering that, Dad.

Are you not Sukey no am I Terry Vine?

I'm thinking I should be running Dad why's that, no reason. To get to the pub in time Sukey oh yes oh now you're talking!
####### ####### ####### #######
####### ####### ####### #######

I'm not here Mrs Vine, I'm not available Mum I'm having pizza with the girls. Or no, they've all gone home now and I'm switching off the big black scoreboard it says HOME O AWAY O hey sounds like an old sea shanty. I'm jangling my keys and going. I hate that Susan very much Mum I keep thinking about her voice.

Maybe she was a girl after all Mum. Maybe she was a fibber.

Where's this pub then Sukey I don't know Dad I'm looking. I don't know what it's called. There are buildings with lights but everything's behind fences and it smells very awful here Dad I know! It's a sewage plant Sukey so let's be moving on quickly.

####### ####### ####### #######
####### ####### ####### #######

Could be the mater eh Sukey, stored the number chappy?

Don't worry Dad. I'm being hurried along here I'm on my running track I'm running towards the Crossing ah the Crossing the old Crossing. I can make out the cars now Dad in the fog, little lines of cars up there and I'm thinking of all the times it was you and me Sukey you and me there

####### ####### ####### #######
####### ####### ####### #######

It's calling me Dad, It's very very insistent, It has Its long thin finger on redial and I can't find the pub I want! The air smells better now and the track runs right by the river. You wanted to know where I was Dad and I'm here, here in my scrape. Look at yourself Sukey I know you're a right royal mess at the end of the day with your shoes such a sight and your hair like matting, and your ankles bleeding. No daughter of mine, my only daughter!

####### ####### ####### #######
####### ####### ####### #######

I am, I tried hard Dad, I gave It a fight, I gave It what for, I gave It my all.

My all's what It wants. My all's all It wants.

It was never far away, It was close, It was courteous, I neglected It badly.

####### ####### ####### #######
####### ####### ####### #######

You can see the tollbooths now Sukey you're lucky you have your coin but Daddy you don't need coins if you're walking across because nobody walks across. Somebody's running, Dad, there's somebody running on this running track behind me what a nerve is that to be running it's so late now

####### ####### ####### #######
####### ####### ####### #######

Do you think Marie is calling I think Marie is calling you but somebody's running Dad. Every time I turn round it's stock-still it's like that game we played. If it rings again then maybe

####### ####### ####

You rang?

Mum?

Who is this?

I'm going to fucking kill you before you die of fucking AIDS you freak. I can see you.

*

*

*

*

*

*

*

You see, you see, you have to stop now, you run against me miss you have to stop now, I beat you I am fast runner I am fit man

I can't I can't I'm sorry I thought you were someone else

I start to run and you turn round and you give me good looking over miss, and do you not see I am runner, I am in my running garb do you not see? Why you run away from me?

I'm, can't speak, can't speak

You have tire yourself out, why you run away from me?

Someone else, I was running too I was running

You run away from gentleman, I am gentleman I make my running every night, I am fit man but you turn around and give me good looking over and what do you see? You are not telling the truth miss, you are not, you are not dressed in running garb miss, you are dressed God knows in what, you turn round and see me and what do you see my dark face, do you think I am terrorist?

No, no,

You think I am terrorist?

No I don't, no I don't, I was scared, there was no one

What do you think I am dress in my running garb miss to scare people, no, if I want to scare you I dress in all in black or with a mask like Freddy, okay?

It's okay, it's okay

So you do not think I am Freddy

No I don't think you're Freddy I was scared

You think I am terrorist, you think you are target for me, okay I take you with me to paradise?

I don't think that, I promise

You think I want to insult you, because I am man alone, at night, running, it is not rocket science I am going to insult you miss, you think you are so pretty all I want is fuck you okay?

I don't think that, I promise

Why is it a dark man is running after me, well, he must be terrorist, okay, or he must be rapist, okay?

I don't, I don't

No, no, I am gentleman and I am athlete, I make my running every night to stay alive in this damn country

It's okay, I know, it's okay

What do you think I am English? What do you think I am?

I don't know what you are

You do not care what I am

I do care, what are you?

You do not care, you do not care if I am running right into the muddy marshes and drowning myself, do you call a policeman?

No an ambulance

Did you call a policeman now?

No, what?

Did you call on your celly when you hear me running, did you say 'Ooo help me help me there is rapist after me?'

I threw my phone in the river I don't speak like that

Shall we wait for the policeman?

There's no policeman

You think you are so pretty all I want is to catch you, you are not so fabulous you know, you have eyes which are very red colour and your hair is very dirty you know.

I know I'm very ugly I've been crying

I would not look at you twice, you know but I would be gentleman despite of that. Guess what country do I come from.

Look. I don't know, whatever I say you'll be angry

Guess what country it is not hard.

I'm sorry I just can't tell

My soul is on the runway. I am flying home to the island.

That's, good, you come from an island

There is nothing left for me here.

You'll be fine on your island maybe

You think about my island? You know where is my island?

I'm just picturing an island and it's very tiny and there's only room for a little tree-house I'm sorry I'm very childish

You think I live in a tree-house, I am monkey you think?

No I think you live in a palace

You are wrong.

I am wrong and ugly, look I'm sorry I ran away from you.

You cannot run away from me. You cannot run away from me.

I know. I know.

Because I am fast! I am Sir Roger!

What?

Sir Roger Bannister! I am four-minute-mile man! Yet, I will leave on the jumbo and I will never be coming back for they will not help me to my gold medal at London. The correct thing to do is, if you are walking on a jogging track, and an athlete is running behind you, is to move to the left side and allow me to overtake on the right side as if I am a vehicle. I am gentleman, miss, I am not terrorist, I am not rapist, I am gentleman.

I understand.

Now I run on, set new records! And goodbye.

Goodbye now.

Goodbye running man.

I'm okay, Dad. I was making new friends, like you always hope I'm doing. No one's going to hurt me. Terry Vine can't see me, he can't know where I am. He's realised I'm a girl so he can hate me again, it's fair. But I left him far behind, Dad, with Tyra Povey and Paula and Kel, and the lowlife who helped me back to my feet and the friendly old lady of Dagnall, and Eleanor and Marion and the vicar of St Jude's, and the dead men who wrote Abide With Me in their spare time, and Janet and Tone and Robson and Vamilla, and Bob Trellis, and Ed Hardhouse, and John. I've been falling all day, falling through their arms and all of them are still waving as if I could come back. But there's nowhere I've been I can imagine being again.

I'm nearly at the Crossing now and the time is half past eleven. I'd tell you the temperature Dad if I knew it, but I don't feel cold any more. I'm watching myself walking, watching my arms going forward and backward, I'm marching to the place. I feel special Dad I feel known. I feel known I feel important. Someone saw me. I don't know how she did it. She saw everything, from the First Light to the Fifth and then she told me to repeat it and I did: I will be famous. I will be rich, I will journey, I will meet, I will say and say and say and on the next day, I accepted it all. I'm in the arms of something that's never left me once, never dropped my hand, never took its eyes off my eyes. Loved me like an animal. When life was nice it just stared. When life was shit it just stared. It doesn't know the difference, it follows my scent and my name-tag, it too wants to find that pub with the Belgian beers and the roaring fire it wants to nip in front like a dog and lead me there in triumph, in through the big oak door to the light so bright you have to bow your head.

I feel loved, Dad, like it's home time, Dad, like it's quarter to four on a sunny day in June when I was young, and there's not a teacher in the world who can keep me in this building.

I'm right where the bridge begins Daddy. Not much traffic tonight. It's frozen and high and fogbound. People are where they want to be, talking about The Zoo Game.

I remember us driving home, I had new books and games and souvenirs in a bag, I was trying to read in the back of the car when the lights flashed by and you said suddenly: Shame we can't get out of the car and see the view, it's a grand view! As long as you don't look down! If we stopped our car we'd stop the traffic, wouldn't we Sukey, shall we?

We were coming back from something. Endless stream of cars at night like little jewels Sukey. Red lights ahead like? Rubies! White lights behind like? Pearls!

Beautiful great crossing at the ford of Dart. Bloodstream of pearls and rubies. Here we go, now we're actually passing over the Thames can you believe it?

We're driving southward from the far side, Dad, it only goes one way, but we did see rubies and pearls didn't we I can still see them now. The northward way is a tunnel. But another way is this path, this frozen blustery uphill corridor by steel fences. Cars go by like there's no one in them.

I'm taking the path now Dad, it's very cold and narrow, no one looks this way from the little tollbooths of men watching television. Don't turn round, little uniform! No one sees the first and last pedestrian on her way.

Who would ever walk to the height of it for the grand view of everything? Who ever would but Sukey? But there she goes up the bare frozen empty English mountain. One step, two step, sshh, sshh . . . What's the time, Mr Wolf???

I really enjoyed that day, Dad. Me too! Me three! And now we're going home. You took me round some museum or other, we saw old trains and engines you'd read about, we went for chicken and chips at a place and you let me try your beer. Gently

Does it

Oh it's disgusting. I had a coke to take the taste away, then we played

A round of I-Spy!

On the Circle line and picked the car up from the car park and now we're going home

Over Dartford Crossing

And I said what's Dartboard Crossing and you said

This is the Dartboard Crossing

I'm in the back seat, staring out. Feeling very happy and sad as we rise up over the river.

The red lights are like?

Rubies!

And the white lights are like?

Pearls!

Why do we have to go to school Dad

Ah well

Why do we have to

Oh Sukey

I'm halfway to the top now Dad, you'd be proud of your mountaineer.

When we get home I'm going to lie in my lonely bed and watch the car lights move across the wall. It's how every day ends for me. I try to sleep before you go to bed, and you and Mum are talking downstairs over whisky and the news, then the news is gone, and kitchen taps go on and off and the stairs creak, then bathroom taps, then the lights start going out.

Why do we have to go

Ah Sukey

Why can't I stay home

There's a line of light always under my door, it's a line I hold and it's going to be gone. I don't want to see that moment so my eyes are shut by then and I'm wishing myself asleep but I do always hear the click. And then I know if I open my eyes there'll be no light at all. Only soon the one last car going by, and if it does I pretend I'm in it. Me and all my school chums going out to this place we know.

My clock says it's twenty to midnight. I must be asleep before midnight. God let me be asleep before midnight. Shut my eyes.

When I wake up in the morning everything will be bright, and I'll have to collect my things, and I'll have to go to school with all the work I didn't get round to, as I was drinking beer with my daddy in the great city of London! I must be asleep before midnight, before the clocks chime everywhere.

Look at that grand view.
You can see for miles and miles.
I'm making it to the very highest point you can stand at.
It's very windy Daddy I can hardly hear myself now!

Hey North London!
South London!
Bright city
Dark estuary

Bright city
Dark estuary

Everything in my hands
Nothing in them

Look at that grand view

Look up, look down, no don't look down Sukey

Look left, look right before you cross

Look left, look –

Right. What?

There's someone. There's

There's someone there Dad, like a child, in a coat, she's outside the last railing I'm, I'm seeing things it's a bunch of rags. No it's a bunch of rags in the form of a figure, flapping at the edge of the rail but it seems to have two little hands, look I'm trying to enjoy the view here Sukey, wait wait wait wait there's a little girl

It's you Sukey

It's not Daddy she's real.

She's in your mind

No Daddy I'm sorry I love you but

You are

Hello

Hello there, you

You're very quiet I didn't see you. I mean I did, I have now

What you doing out here then? No one stopped you? Silly question. No one stopped me either. Do they want us to be up here do you think?

But you know it's dangerous where you're standing.

It's dangerous where I'm standing but at least I'm behind this fence. You could stumble and, you know, be hurt. What's your name, little one?

Name? Do you understand me at all?

You're not from here, are you, do you understand English? Speak English?

Look. Don't be scared. If you come with me, just slowly, we'll get a hot meal somewhere, cup of tea, yes? Yes?

Look what I'm showing you: this means hot meal, with the hands, this means cup of tea obviously I'm really a bit shit at this I'm afraid no DON'T LOOK DOWN, look at me!

Don't look anywhere but at me. Don't do anything but hold on.

Good, good, easy, easy . . . Where have you been walking? Your shoes look as fucked as mine. Where have you come from?

Down there? From the South?

Further that way, okay south. From, from far away?

From far away. Another place? land? country? planet? okay not planet, don't laugh!

Look at me. Look, here's my hand. You squeezed out through that fence you can squeeze back through it, come on, you're a clever girl grab my hand.

Please?

No? Well let's talk instead. We're not really dressed for this, are we? Brrr, see? Cold. Cold cold cold, Christmas Christmas Christmas! Hey Christmas is coming little one does that mean anything where you're from?

On the first day of Christmas my true love sent to me . . . what? Don't sing? Did you just make the universal sign for Don't Sing? Yes? Or the universal sign for Susie Don't Sing. You did? okay I got it.

Hey I'm on my way from over there. I was looking for a pub. Pub? Drinks? Yes? You see? SHIT WATCH OUT!

Oh my God oh my God, look, hey, keep your hands on those bars, right, don't do any more mimes, I'll do the mimes, you just watch, okay? okay easy now, easy . . . okay?

Okay. Look at me, only me, only me. You hang on there and I'll talk you through some famous sights of old London yes? just to welcome you to our country okay? while you, well . . . you listen.

Now let me think . . . yes . . . Those little sort of tollbooth huts down there, yes, see? are actually where those men live!

Yes! It's true, don't frown, those are the only homes they could find in the middle of a big motorway like this! Thing is, the little huts were built in olden times, nice little row, like beach huts, course the sea used to be right there in the age of the dinosaurs and the motorway came later, worse luck, no warning! Mm-hm.

Each man wears a uniform, not sure why that is. I'll come back to that, and each one has a little room with a little cheap TV and old photos of them younger with pretty girls who left them. They're lonely these fellows, no listen, so they get the autographs of everyone who drives through. Yes! It's funny, isn't it? Did you smile then? You don't know. I think you did, but you know, no pressure. So, that's the housing situation. Tsk. But you know it's better than this sort of ledge you live on. Now what else can we see in my world . . .

Banana Wharf. Over there, yes? Hold on tight to the bars please, if you want to hear this information. That building there, was built only the day before yesterday, incredible but true, by the English Queen, to show the people how tall and manly a building can be. Take that! she said. It's true! Then yesterday, in answer to it, you see that big round sort of dome off over there? That was built in answer to it, by the English King, to show that buildings can also be soft and round and altogether more girly. So there! he said. Even-stevens. I don't make these things up, you know. Now both the King and Queen are thinking what to do next. That's why it's gone so quiet. They just shrug, like this, look. Don't shrug, it's true! You're shrugging, hold on tight if you're going to shrug, eh.

I've got some others, when I think of them. I haven't done this job for a while. Do you want to hold my hand yet? Please I'm very frightened. You must be very brave because I'm old and look how frightened!

No? Well. Whenever: it's right here look, on the end of my arm, see? For safekeeping. What else what else what else. The stars. They're up there somewhere behind the clouds. Stars, yes, well, I'm sure you have them where you're from, so they don't really fall within my remit. I just do London really and some outlying areas, some, areas of, outright lying. I do know this about the stars, no don't look up! Okay, hold on tight if you're going to look up. Well you know the way they wink at you? Mm-hm. They're saying psst, we're not here any more. How d'you like that? They think that's funny. The planets don't wink, because they don't know. They're little boys who want us to watch them going round and round in a circle for ages. That's nice, dear. Course we live on one of those. But you don't want my speculations, do you, you want hard facts. Hold on.

Well this bridge itself is very old, of course. The Angles saw the Saxons on the one side, and the Saxons saw the Angles on the other side, and of course one afternoon they shouted out Oi you lot, we're bored, let's have a war! Yeah all right. Hold on.

Hey don't laugh, it's war I'm talking about! Anyway they didn't fancy getting wet, so first they had to build the bridge, and agree on how to do it, and design the lamps and carvings and that, and go across on little rafts with catalogues and shiny brochures with Post-it notes to remind them where their favourites were, so in the course of all that they became quite friendly and hence Anglo-Saxon England. Yep. What else.

Well you may be wondering why I turned up to watch you playing on your own up here. Well why did you come here? You got a message, didn't you? Was it a call? Or maybe a text.

Someone outside or something inside told you you had to be here, it was written, it was ordained, sorry long word, it was your future. Someone's made you believe that. Nailed you to a belief. When that happens something clicks and an alarm goes off somewhere, if I could tell you where it does I would, love, and they send someone, they, yes, they, send someone like me! Or you! to say actually nothing's written, maybe nothing's written. Because you weren't written, were you? They send someone to say Don't believe that, because look how foggy it is in front of us, and we see about the length of a breath. That's what it's really like down here, and life might be longer it might be stranger it might be better if you knew it was up to you now.

Someone wanted to get us together to hear something.

You can hear it now, can't you, it's here, it's playing. Listen.

Silence, you hear that? Almost. No, it's not an invading army it's my stomach rumbling, or yours. They're saying you and me let's eat together, no? Soon? Now?

Someone wanted to tell us there's no one who can tell us. There's no one who can tell us. Someone thought we should hear that together. He, or she, I'm not sure it matters when there's no one who can tell us, wanted us to hear this while holding hands, do you think? No? Not yet?

Something wanted to say also there might be nothing. Or there was something and it's gone. Or there'll be something but not now. But it's peaceful where it's gone. And everything that's gone is peaceful too. If you listen.

Oh that sound? What sound? Oh that's nothing, that's . . .

That's just a clock striking. Pompous old sort, making the same point twelve times, like my, my dad at the end. It's okay I heard you. I heard you. Alec. I lived, I get it. Watch me now. Hush.

Come on, come on, yes yes yes yes God your hand makes

mine seem warm, there, one step, there, two step, through we go, here we are . . . hey . . .

Hello. Welcome. Welcome you. You know what they call this? Tomorrow. Round here they do or they used to. Invaders came. Invaders came and said No no no no no. It's Today. The word you're looking for is Today. Get used to it. Also, said the invaders, we're not invaders, we've always been here! It's always been Today! So Tomorrow went underground, like Yesterday its old mucker, went into legend, crops up in songs and poems and shit, but the power-that-be won't have it. Today, mate, always was.

Look you're wearing even less than me ya mad little bastard. You young people.

Look at us. Think we had a toe in Tomorrow? A toenail?

Come here let's get properly warm here! Here here, there there, everywhere everywhere . . . warm warm warm . . .

Someone told me a story, little thing, and I've lived like it was true. Someone was all around me, like I'm around you now, like a friend you didn't know you had but he was just following the story, he had boxes to tick, his pencil was sort of quivering over us, but he's gone now, it's quiet. It's peaceful. Isn't it? The world without its stories.

Hey your hands are warming up.

You heading on down there? Shall I come with you shall I? You want to go north? I sort of don't live there so I sort of don't.

You do? Really? Okay then. You want to have new adventures alone. You want things to get worse so they can get better. Well. Bye then, nice chatting. Any time. Find yourself a different climbing frame eh. Start small. Learn some sodding English. I'm,

I'm heading back this way. Yes? Understand?

I'm old, I'm cold, I'm going home. It's been cleaned up, you know, by industrial cleaners. There's food. No? You're sure that's it? Okay little one. Okay. Right then. Good luck then. Just, if,

My name's in the book, if you ever do need, you know, some sort of guide.

Acknowledgements

An extract of the book first appeared in *Open City*.

'And Death Shall Have No Dominion' by Dylan Thomas is reprinted by permission of David Higham Associates Limited.

With thanks to Robin Robertson, Alex Bowler, Joanna Yas, and the Santa Maddalena Foundation.